Praise for

HOW TO PLAY A NECROMANCER'S THEREMIN

"How to Play a Necromancer's Theremin takes you to an alternate reality where books are made into tea in worship of the much-fabled fictional author Rocco Atleby. It's a surreal meta reading experience that highlights the difficulty and necessity of playful imagination in an apocalyptic era. Griffin and Quay's writing is funny, absurd, and thought provoking."

—Shannon McLeod, author of *Nature Trail Stories and Whimsy*

"How To Play A Necromancer's Theremin is a joyful, head spinning thrill ride through the past, present, and future. This book sings, dances, and plays music. Take a little bit of Naked Lunch, add the The Hitchhiker's Guide To The Galaxy filtered through William Gibson, Robert Anton Wilson, and Philip K. Dick, and toss it with some Adult Swim and Nickelodeon mixed with The Stooges, Nirvana, and Radiohead and you'll get this brand new thing from Chase Griffin and Christina Quay. This wonderful book is about reading, writing, and words, and we need them now more than ever."

—Pat Irwin, The B-52s, SUSS, and Rocko's Modern Life score

"A group of Florida stoners tour France to visit the apartment of an obscure psychedelic sci-fi writer called Rocco Atebly, who not only was a necromancer, and played the theremin like a champ, but created an apocalyptic, device called Fat Tornado Clock, that messes with other dimensions and layers of reality.

Chase Griffin and Christina Quay's novel is not a puzzle, but some esoteric kind of improv that explores Borges' thesis on causality as the main problem of the literary arts. This narrative seeks to transcend the giant dead whale of postmodernism without undoing any of its promethean conclusions, driven by a passion that fears no ironic judgment.

You may have seen a dime-a-dozen indie lit psychedelia writers exploring and at the same time ironizing their very quest to better understand their world, yet this hysterically silly and viscerally paranoid work of metafiction tries its dang hardest to sketch the blueprint of the authors' still beating hearts: something that no posers can ever do. Maybe you read people who have read Foster Wallace, Vonnegut, Pynchon and Wittgenstein before, but trust me, you have not read Florida's finest freaks' meditations on the nature of reality, nor their musings over the consequences of this never-ending human quest for transcendence and authentic, spiritually meaningful living in our techno-infused carnival of political horrors called early 21th century late-capitalism."

"How do you like your metaphors mixed? This work of psy-fi docutainment, best ingested by first grinding it into Bookpowder, follows Rocco Atleby's kudzu plots in the pursuit of fluctuation on the horizon of the Patasphere. Flitting and flirting with spacetimeconsciousness dimensionzzzzz, deep down, heinleined under there somewhere, Chase Griffin and Christina Quay have committed some really serious satire. So pack your pestle and mortar and get ripping!"

HOW TO PLAY A NECROMANCER'S THEREMIN

CHASE GRIFFIN | CHRISTINA QUAY

MAUDLIN HOUSE

maudlinhouse.net
twitter.com/maudlinhouse

How to Play a Necromancer's Theremin
Copyright © 2023 by Christina Quay and Chase Griffin
Cover illustration by Rob Kaniuk
ISBN 978-1-7370222-7-5

Foreword
Reading Out of Order
Joshua Bohnsack

Season 5, Episode 12 of the American animated sitcom *The Simpsons*, "Bart Gets Famous," features a cameo by host of NBC's *Late Night*, and former *Simpsons* writer, Conan O'Brien. The episode aired February 3, 1994, five months after the premier of O'Brien's *Late Night* takeover for former host, David Letterman, however the episode was written just after O'Brien's audition to replace Letterman.

What this means is the writers took a chance.

It was completely possible O'Brien wouldn't have been chosen to host the show, after all, he was a relatively unknown who didn't have experience in front of the camera, aside from a few appearances as an extra during his tenure at *Saturday Night Live*. When the character Bart Simpson appears in on an episode of *Light Night With Conan O'Brien* in "Bart Gets Famous," the writers did not know whether this would make a real-world connection with the audience, or if it would be a lost inside joke about their former writer who failed to take over for Letterman.

Since you picked up this book, you're surely familiar with the work of Rocco Atleby. Do you remember the first time you encountered Rocco

Atleby? Maybe it was browsing the psy-fi shelves at Borders, maybe it was watching archival PBS or BBC footage, maybe it was grinding up your own book powder. I read his work out of order. I started with *Wanderer's Task* and knew the origin of Holgar's scar before anything else. This didn't ruin his work for me. It led me on a pilgrimage in my own way, like an inverted choose-your-own-adventure. I became part of something.

A few years back, I was walking my dog and listening to *The Rocco Atleby Foundation* podcast, "Chapter 4: King Hillsborough," when the characters were dealing with the titular King Hills, an amorphous, gilled creature in their local diner, when Echo tells everyone to shut up and listen to the music, which happened to be a song called "Starving" by Joshua Bohnsack. That's me. I am the person and I made the song. There are no good coincidences or bad coincidences, but merely co-incidences. Jung talks about synchronicity, but that doesn't begin to touch on the experience of reading, no, not just reading, interacting with, no, experiencing, yes, *experiencing* Atleby's work. It goes beyond the time and space of his or anyone's corporeal beings. I've been there with Echo and Flynn and the crew at The Exit. I've played foosball there and I ate a Totino's pizza and I watched a grown man ride his BMX bike into that bar. I saw that same footage of Atleby. And they may protest, saying I can't insert myself as a supporting character, but it's too late for this. It's too late for me.

And now, it's too late for you. By picking up this book, you are trying to find Rocco Atleby, and I have a coincidence for you. And the coincidence is that you're a part of this. You've taken the chance and you'll appear in this episode, one way or another.

Sit perfectly still. Only I may dance.

"I understand very little about our predicament," Flynn's voice echoed from the darkness which encapsulated my bodiless being. We were here, but not really there.

"I'm not sorry these words

unfastened the essential nuts and bolts of this machine we call actuality. I must continue writing. It's the only way to conjure the memories and words to expel us from this void."

From the void, I responded, "Flynn, where are we? Is this another one of your experiments in improv comedy? Something like a fight against the fluctuation from another dimension?"

"You could say from all dimensions. The twitching, living vessel behind us all, pulling and at the same time not pulling the strings."

"I'm getting deja vu, hasn't this been written before?"

"A long time ago. And many times over since then. I've written many beginnings. But it's finally time to finish."

"Oh yeah. Somehow I keep forgetting that you're writing a book. I get so lost in my role as narrator, and then we begin again in this dark emptiness, where I can't even feel my toes."

"The clarity will come, slowly at first, then all at once. Memories are fickle things, esoteric entities of their own that house the distorted movie of your own life."

"Stop being so cryptic, I want to get the fuck out of here. Wherever the hell is. How did we even end up here?"

"I crawled under the Marie Antoinette couch with its blooming velvet

roses like a cat seeking its lonesome death in the shade of a garden. You found me and kept pulling my arm. You pulled and pulled until we fell inside...here."

"Do you really think writing this book will get us out?"

"The only way to find out is to continue writing."

CHAPTER ONE

MR. FAT TORNADO CLOCK AND THE PSY-FI COMEDY-LOVING COVEN

Shortly before our corporeal detachment from actuality, before our souls were neatly parceled off and shipped to their very own personal vacuum chamber, Flynn and I, along with four of our psy-fi comedy-loving coven, embarked on a Rocco Atleby pilgrimage. We all sold whatever possessions we hadn't already sold for book powder in exchange for one-way plane tickets to Paris, where the infamous eighteenth-century apartment, reserved and rented through the Atleby Tours website awaited us. The site promised that this rustic apartment was the one Rocco had called home the first year of his journey across the globe to prove his theory on actuality-shattering fluctuation, developed during his studies in necromancy school, born of the messages he believed only he could decipher in the chiming golden bells of his alma mater's bell tower, whose dings and dongs whispered to him the secrets of an ancient esoteric text that could bow and warp the mechanisms of the dualist codices of existence.

Unbeknownst to me, in my seat thirty thousand feet above Earth– a chunk of actuality as significant and insignificant as anything else in this grand scheme of the sweeping universal narrative– my own fluctuation was taking place. I blame my ignorance on my addiction to Rocco and his blessed book powder. Imagine me standing up and saying to a room full of other Rocco addicts, "Hello, my name is Echo and I've been a supporting character in Rocco's indie lit fantasy experience for...God...how many years has it been? I can't remember. Wow." Thank you Rocco for making so much known through your body of fictions which in turn made so much more unknown. Because, you know how it goes, the more you beknowst the more you unbeknownst. That's silly and I apologize. I also blame my ignorance on my preoccupation with my regret, my regret for choosing to sit next to Bobby and Newsom. Christ, talk about being lobotomized by a magickal book powder. Why would I choose to sit next to Bobby and Newsom? Why would I switch seats? I had that perfectly good seat several rows up away from the dancing black holes that are Bobby and Newsom. But no, I didn't want to be by myself. Because I hate myself so much I can't stand to be by myself for half a day. I had to act rashly and trade seats with Flynn. I also blame my ignorance on the hatred of myself. If I will never get to know myself, I will never know why I do the things I do, and therefore I will continue to harm myself. I also blame my encapsulation within these flawed syllogisms and circular reasonings on Rocco. I also blame my ignorance on distraction, the distraction of Bobby and Newsom acting idiots every time they consume copious amounts of book powder. They're silly. I mean, I'm silly. But they're too silly. When the book powder hits them, they cackle, tickle each other, smear Newsom's makeup all over their faces and turn themselves into demented looking clowns, rapidly fade in and out of Actuality, punch and kick, and yell Joycean gibberish until they laugh so hard they bleed from the eyes. That's distracting, amirite? Without a little quiet contemplation time every once in a while, how can one know of their own fluctuations?

As we prepared to half-watch a docutainment film on the life of baker turned necromancer turned psychedelic fiction novelist turned kook, they talked loudly and punched each other, with me taking the brunt of their blows. In the aisle behind us, Will and Ruby were eating unshelled peanuts with the unabridged chaos of a category five hurricane. I had told them both the airline provided shelled peanuts, but Ruby insisted on bringing his own, saying he wasn't going to touch the airline's shelled abominations.

As peanut debris hit the back of my neck like shrapnel, they joined forces to kick the hell out of my seat, which not only aggravated the hell out of me but also the random guy seated between them who kept calling himself Holger. Coincidentally Holger was the name of the hero in every novel Rocco Atleby ever wrote, and it only pissed off our temporary traveling companion more each time we roared with laughter at his name.

"Will you please refrain from kicking that seat?" Holger asked. "It's bugging the hell out of me, and I need you to listen. I have limited time, I think. I spontaneously manifested into this seat to warn you of actuality-shattering danger."

"Shut up, Holger," Will said. "No one cares."

Holger ignored Will and said, "The danger is a fluctuation on the horizon of the Patasphere."

Ruby ripped open his third bag of peanuts with such vehemence that the contents went airborne, scattering like confetti. I caught the eyes of the flight attendant who was glowering at us from behind the first class curtain, with only her face poking through the red velvet.

"We're well aware of the fluctuation," Will said.

"Do you work for Atleby Tours?" Ruby asked, spewing bits of the peanut's papery inner shell with every word. "I didn't know we'd be accompanied by a guide. Is this, like, a surprise accommodation?"

Holger continued, "I implore you, everything in existence is at stake here and I have limited time."

"Hey, do you want your peanuts?" Ruby asked, licking the empty bag that had exploded. "I spilled mine."

Newsom turned and peered through the crack between our seats and said to Holger, "You really are what I've always imagined Holger to look like. Babe, get a load of this jackass."

Newsom smacked Bobby, who was busy tearing to shreds a copy of Rocco's *Winding Arbor Soul*. The cover was a classic psy-fi pulp by

Rocco's wife, renowned artist Beatrice Tinsen. A spiral staircase made of clock gears which were in turn made of tiny clock gears which were made of even tinier gears and so on corkscrewed out of a bright blue square opening at the top of the cover into an asymmetrical palace interior whose walls, floor, and ceiling were a flat mosaic of mashed together pastel furniture made of elaborate ornamentation and serpentine lines that guided the eyes back to the spiral staircase which corkscrewed through a crack in the floor into a realm of smoke plumes.

Bobby meticulously tore the shreds into the tiniest pieces he could, accumulating a sizable pile on the fold-down tray on his lap. He paused to rustle around in his carry-on bag, and triumphantly slammed down a mortar and pestle next to his highball, which splattered all over me.

"Jesus, Bobby!" I yelled at him. "You're going to get the pages wet, dipshit."

"You're in the splash zone!" he cackled, continuing to shred book pages.

Holger cleared his throat. "Fine, listen or don't listen. At this point, I don't care. Rocco has used his infernal machine so I could warn you that –"

"Woah, no shit, you've even got a scar on your left eyebrow, like the one Holger gets in *Wanderer's Task*," Newsom said, reaching over the seat with her arm outstretched to poke the Holger look-alike. He swatted her finger away.

Holger said, "Before my body gets reabsorbed by the next fluctuation you've got to know you can find clues heinleined throughout Rocco's novels that can help guide you. There are also several contingency plans scattered throughout nonlinear time, but I don't know where and neither does Rocco. I told him before I came here, we should take a little more time to figure everything out, but he said, "There's not enough time to take a little more time." Whatever that means. Either way, what I do know is –"

"They've really made the Atleby Pilgrimage quite immersive," interrupted a man across the aisle. He wore a tweed suit and chewed on the cherry stem from his amaretto sour.

"You've been on the pilgrimage?" I asked.

"You could say that." He responded. "You're in for a wild ride."

Ruby and Will continued their assault on my seat.

I turned and looked through the crack to see what the Holger doppelganger would say next, but he was gone.

"Where'd he go?" I asked as I pulled out a paperback of the first of Rocco's posthumously published novels, *Prima Materia And The Golden Tablet*, from my suede messenger bag. I took one long last look at the original first edition artwork by Beatrice. Neon rainbow spumes shot into an open book surrounded by thousands of tiny faces, each with their own unique characteristics. I squinted at the face near the bottom left hand corner. It was a face that had spooked me out since I first encountered this edition in high school. The face looked a lot like my own.

I tore the book to shreds until only the husk remained. I chucked the shell behind me and assumed it landed in Holger's empty seat. Curious, I turned and peered through the crack in the seat. Lo and behold, I scored. Will winked at me and pulled out a copy of Rocco Atleby's *Unabridged Exegesis*.

I asked, "Why'd Holger waste so much time with that pre-explanation anyway? He didn't even have time to infodump about the fluctuation he said was so important."

"I don't know," Ruby said. "I stopped paying attention to him." He ripped the pages of the *Exegesis* from the spine, also tossing the shell into Holger's empty seat. The cover art was a gold leaf rendering of Rocco's own making, his famous sketch of what he called the Patasphere, a pandimensional sphere that appears to be eating itself, a symbol he created to represent the all-encompassing dualist universal narrative he believed entombed all of creation.

Will said, "Looks like Holger finally fucked off. Good riddance." He pulled a paperback of Rocco Atleby's first novel, *Wanderer's Task*, out of his blue backpack and tore the pages from the spine, and dropped the shell of the paperback onto Holger's empty seat. The cover was yet another first edition Tinsen piece. The purposeless box that switches itself off when one switches it on, hovers in the center atop the Isle of Aurora, its cliffs curving into themselves to form a circle, the ocean splashing golden waves like a chaotic tidal pool in the island's center. The finger that pops out of the top hatch of the purposeless box, (that ironically and iconically had a purpose within the novel) to flip the switch into the off position, taunts the viewer with an upturned come hither waggle to invite potential readers into the actuality-shattering realm of Rocco Atleby.

Ruby whipped out a copy of High Weirdness by Dr. Erik Davis, pulled it open, and just before he was able to rip the pages from the spine, Will smacked the book from his hands. Will picked High Weirdness up from the floor and stuffed it into his own carry-on.

Will said to Ruby, "That is my book. Have you been rifling through my belongings again? You have no right to destroy my property. And, my god man, do you have any idea what would happen to Actuality if you had gone through with it? You need a chaperone. You're out of fucking control, Rube. I am your chaperone for the rest of the pilgrimage."

Bobby hacked a loogie and spit it into his cup of tequila flavored ice. "Probably had to take a piss," he said, referring to the mysterious *Holger*. He waved over the annoyed flight attendant. "I need another drink." He tore the final pages from *Winding Arbor Soul* and tossed the shell backwards and it landed on Holger's seat next to the shell of *Wanderer's Task*.

Newsom punched Bobby in the shoulder. "You've had enough." She pulled out a copy of *Chronotope And The Makers*, freed the pages from their binding with an emphatically fast and loud rip, and chucked the cover to its burial seat. This was a newer edition and the cover did not do the novel justice. The original Tinsen cover was a quintet of robed figures, faces hidden inside the dark recess of their hoods, and their bodies repeated as outlines of glowing multicolored neural webs and the trail of outlines zoomed toward a vanishing point sitting below a checkerboard atmosphere. This new cover was a totally uninspired watercolor of a hammer smashing a window which does not open to freedom but to a brick wall.

"I haven't had nearly enough," Bobby said as he ripped a pinch of corners from his page bunch and crushed the pulpy confetti into his ice with the pestle like he was preparing mint and ice for a mojito. "This is the pilgrimage. You don't do the pilgrimage straight."

Newsom punched him again. "I hope the flight attendant tapes you to the chair." She tore a pinch of paper from her page bunch, quickly and desperately ripped those pieces into smaller pieces, and ripped those tiny pieces into even tinier pieces of confetti.

The tweed jacket passenger spoke up, "Did you bring a mortar and pestle with you?"

Bobby smiled. "Last time I flew they wouldn't let me bring a grinder. Apparently it's paraphernalia." He rolled his eyes and made air quotes with his fingers when he said "paraphernalia."

The kicking and punching grew to a 4.3 on the richter scale and my seat felt like it was going to be ripped from its floor bolts. I held my headphones tightly to my ears, tried with all of my meditation powers to close off the outside world, thought not of England but of "...my life choices and their filthy relationship with my flawed syllogistic prison, and watched the introduction to my all time favorite docutainment film.

The doc was a hodgepodge production of various interviews, BBC specials, corny reenactment footage from *Hysteron Proteron Channel* tv shows, and home footage cobbled together by director Susan Lappet who is considered by most docutainment fanatics to be the master archival footage weaver.

The black screen read: ORDER OF THE CACTI MEDIA PRESENTS.

"The central problem of novel-writing is causality," Rocco said as the opening credits faded in and out of the still black screen. "I've always identified with this Borges quote not simply because of the pluralism and quantum fuckery in my books, but because of the trajectory of my life, and how my time-essence has developed because of certain choices. Borges said this self-consciously because he believed he never wrote a novel. He was wrong. He wrote one novel and because of causality he was never able to see this novel. It was his own life, his magnum opus. I, unfortunately, can see. Causality is no longer a problem for me because of those certain choices I mentioned. Now, I am no normal human. My being is a cluster of fuckery and koans and kudzu plots. Do I sound self-conscious right now?"

Under the cover of the black screen the interviewer responded, "I would have thought the opposite until you asked."

The black faded away and revealed a slow steadicam descent down the ancient spiral staircase of the iconic Parisian apartment. The ethereal and ambient antics of the *Satanic Panic and the Very Special Episode's* song, *Panic March,* oozed like candle wax and doddered along with the seemingly endless descent.

The voice of the interviewer returned and asked, "Why do you feel self-conscious?"

"Because this book... I feel like I didn't write it," Rocco said. "Instead, the book has written me."

"What book?"

"This one," he said, without further explanation.

CHAPTER TWO

THE IN-FLIGHT FLICK

The title of the docutainment film flashed several times in quick succession over the staircase footage before it finally settled and lingered long enough for the audience to read the words.

HOW TO PLAY A NECROMANCER'S THEREMIN

A theremin cover of *Panic March* swelled and the spiral staircase cross-dissolved to a static shot of a tree stump. A globe made of golden spirals rose out of the hole in the center of the stump. The spirals clicked and shifted round like a clock.

The shot cross-faded to footage from Rocco Atleby's 1961 German television appearance. Rocco, in his signature brown suit, blue marbled shirt, tie of rainbow swirls, and blue pea coat, sat perched on the edge of a late baroque couch that had seen better days, patterned with blooming velvet roses. Behind him, iron shelves sandwiched between grecian columns twisted into ornate vines, encasing tens of thousands of books that scintillated in the flickering light of candles resting on ornate sconces. From behind his back, he pulled out his enigmatic globe of golden spirals, modeled after his archetype of the Patasphere. It clicked and shifted in his hands.

"This invention," Rocco said, "will disrupt the actuality-shattering fluctuations that I spoke of so desperately last month. I have spent the past two decades tinkering with blueprints and deciphering my transcribed whisperings of the bells. I think I've finally perfected this pandimensional probe."

"The whisperings of the bells?" the interviewer asked. "Is this the SORA character from your novels? Those same old rational agents?"

Rocco said, "If one listens acutely, the bells can be heard everywhere."

"How exactly does this invention work?" asked the interviewer.

Rocco said, "It transcends what I call the noise barrier, and allows users to transpose their fleshy limitations and travel in a formless state. The outward appearance is purely cosmetic, an homage to M.C. Escher's *Golden Spirals*. I call it the Fat Tornado Clock."

From behind the camera, the interviewer ignored Rocco's continued ambiguity and asked, "Why Fat Tornado Clock?"

"Because that's precisely what it looks like, does it not?"

"And how does one become a formless being encased in this contraption?"

Rocco opened his hand and the Fat Tornado Clock floated from his open palm toward the camera until it took up most of the frame.

"One must consume my work ad nauseam," Rocco said, "Only then can one realize this nebulous state. My machine requires the user to transcend all physical and psychological limitations. It cannot do that for them."

The shot cross-faded back to the tree stump with the Fat Tornado Clock floating above it.

A narrator, with a velvety voice that soothes me every time I watch this flick, said, "Rocco Atleby began his life when his celestial body transpositioned from the halfway point between the Patasphere and the outer-realm where the Cosmic Vix was banished. He actualized in Tampa, Florida October twenty-first, an unknown year. Local folklore has it that Rocco was not born from human parents. He was born from a tree stump in the middle of a park in Tampa."

Bobby and Newsom fidgeted and poked each other through the narration while Ruby and Will added their own commentary.

Bobby spoke over the narrator, "The Atlebys found Rocco in the alley behind their bakery when he was about six months old. Wild German Shepherds had kept him warm and fed until the Atlebys finally realized where all that crying was coming from."

"Do you think he nursed off the teats of the German Shepherds?" Will lisped while he sucked on an ice cube wrapped in a book page.

"I'm pretty sure they brought him little cakes and loaves of bread from the dumpster," said Ruby and shoved a handful of pageconfetti into his mouth.

Will crammed pageconfetti into his mouth and chewed. Through the wet confetti he yelled something that sounded like, "Hot damn!" He swallowed and coughed. "You can't feed an infant cakes and breads, Jesus."

"Are you guys going to be obnoxious the whole flight?" I asked the four of them and sucked my pile of *Prima Materia And The Golden Tablet* like a demented eldritch anteater. The heat hit me immediately and I broke into a sweat. I adjusted my air vent and stared at the blinking seat belt sign which had been blinking and ringing for thirty minutes. My head dropped forward on its own and dangled and swayed. It felt like the weight of a thousand lifetimes was stomping on the top of my head. I forced my head up and squinted past Newsom, who was giggling to herself, out the window at the patches of the Atlantic poking through the puffs of white clouds.

Bobby immediately readjusted my air vent, giving himself double ventilation.

Ping. "This is your captain speaking," a nasally voice crackled over the intercom. We are approaching a violently turbulent fluctuation in the Patasphere. Please remain–"

"Sir I am going to have to sedate you and your entire entourage," snapped the stewardess as an amplified scuffling struggle for the intercom ensued.

"Remain calm," the nasally voice crackled, "Unfortunately oxygen masks will be completely useless during this actuality shift, but we do have the one and only Holger here to guide us." The voice broke as the stewardess wrenched back the intercom and we could all hear Flynn giggling in the background.

"Please… disregard that… last announcement," panted the flight attendant. "Some of us have… indulged in the… on-flight bar a bit *too* much… and are lucky we're currently flying over an immense body of water… or the air marshall would have demanded an… emergency landing." Flynn continued to giggle in the background as she spoke. "To the stewardess who keeps indulging these imbeciles, I implore you to please stop, or you'll all have matching duct tape restraints. As always enjoy your flight, and thank you for flying *Collegiate Air*. The coffee cart will be by shortly for your after-dinner delight."

Flynn's bespectacled mop of a head innocently poked up from his row a few places down as if he hadn't just commandeered the squawk box from the flight attendants. He caught my eyes and made his way toward us, the mischievous bastard.

"That was more impressive than the time you farted into the intercom on our flight to Japan," I said to Flynn.

"I have no idea what you're talking about," he said with a smirk, twirling a piece of hair.

On the small screen on the back of the airplane seat footage from the 2003 *Hysteron Proteron Channel* reenactment program, *Precocious Young Atleby* rolled. God, I love this section of the doc. So campy! All of the footage is that wonky cheap as hell looking slow motion that reenactment tv shows always use. An actor named Delph Delemore, covered from head to toe in flour and ash like lil orphan Oliver, plays the young Rocco Atleby. Delph punches dough and lights oven fires for his adoptive parents, punches dough and lights fires, over and over. Wonky slow-mo! More wonky slow-mo! Punch! Light! Punch! Light! The sound effects were great too. The punches sounded like exploding digital bricks. The fire sounded like a shattering digital pickle jar complete with digital pickles bouncing across a wet digital floor. Not very fire-like. But still! Shit was digital as hell. Punch! Light! Punch!

Light! Goddamn, Delph could punch the hell out of some dough and light the hell out of some digital pickle fires. What ever happened to Delph Delemore? Bitch needs to be in more docutainment films. Anyway, Rocco's parents, being in a strict baker's guild, forbid him from attending school. Whenever he asked why he couldn't attend school like all the other children they said, "All teachers do is fill your head with a lot of nonsense. What happens to the bakery knowledge? All your knowledge of bread and bread-like substances will come squeezing out of your ears in the form of that sourdough, son.Son? Son, are you listening? Delph, I mean Rocco, stop punching and lighting for one moment and listen to your parents. We know you're mad about not being able to go to school but listen."

Flynn rested his elbow on Bobby's headrest and said, "I bet Atleby runs away from his baker parents in this next scene."

I said to Flynn, "I read this docutainment film is highly sensationalized. His adoptive parents let him go to school. They were actually very strict about his studies and would make him sleep in the alley behind the bakery if he brought home marks anywhere under exceeds-expectations."

Newsom threw her empty plastic cup at me. "Will you shut the fuck up?"

"I need you guys to try really hard to settle down or we really will be forced to tape all of you to your seats," the flight attendant said and set a bottle of water onto Bobby's tray.

She huffed off and Holger stepped into the space she had just occupied.

Surprised as hell at his sudden reappearance, I slapped myself across the face and then I extended a hand toward him, initiating a more formal introduction. "I thought you died, which I'm sure would've sucked for you since you're just starting to get a taste for this whole being alive and sentient thing."

"He's just glad you're back," Will said, "because he wants your help tossing us from the plane."

I stuffed my hand in my pocket as Holger neglected to shake it, and he scooted past Will to his seat, now filled with the empty paperback covers.

Ruby said, "Yeah, Echo thinks we can't handle our book powder."

"Book powder?" Holger said as he picked up and examined the ripped-apart cover of *Winding Arbor Soul.* "What in the pandimensional rift did you do to your Rocco books?"

Newsom stood and leaned over her seat. "I mean, you don't expect us to suck the whole book down binding and all like a demented eldritch anteater beast, do you?"

Holger cocked his head at her and his eyes darted between all of our piles of shredded pages while Ruby straight munched a handful of his like a goat. "Let me get this straight. You pulverize the pages of Rocco Atleby psy-fi romps and then eat the powder."

"We've been ingesting his books for years," she shrugged.

Bobby lifted his bottle of water into the air. "Cheers. Don't knock it before you try it."

I said, "Sometimes we patamorphose duh pages into a sassy tea."

"When we're feeling extra sassy," Ruby said, "we gather ye unrefined, unpulverized page confetti, weeeee throw the lil individual letterz and word wedgez like weeee throwin coins or yarrow, we do a bit of the ole divination, we read the message that the cut-up santa giftz us, and then we pulse and glow and slip in err out o' dis plane of the evershifting eternal text."

Will said, "And when we need to feel that fluctuation you were talking about, we butt chug it."

Newsom belted out a burst of laughter that caused her entire body to involuntarily quake and she spilled her tequila down the back of her seat into Ruby's lap. "Take for example what my confetti cut-up divination says. "What duh herdy gurdy tinker tinkzzzzz duh herdy gurdy prooofffeeerrrr prrroooooffffffffzzzzzzzzzzzzx." Pretty cool! That's kinda close to a classic Robert Anton Wilson line."

"Heard," Bobby said. "Sometimes, the cut-up is crystalline clarity. Take for example the confetti I just threw. "You tasked me to provide an assessment of the multiversal indie lit fantasy experience in terms of its mechanics and ultimate practicality. As I set out to fulfill that tasking it soon became clear that in order to assess the validity and practicality of the process I needed to do enough supporting research and analysis to fully understand how and why the process works. Frankly, Delemore sir, that proved to be an extremely involved and difficult business. Initially, based on our conversations with a pataphysician who took the indie lit fantasy experience training with me, I had recourse to the bion models developed by Rococo Artlerbabbleton to obtain information concerning the pataphysical theatre aspects of the process. Then I found it necessary to delve into various sources for information concerning quantum mechanics in order to be able to describe the nature and functioning of human consciousness. I had to be able to construct a scientifically valid and reasonably lucid model of how consciousness functions under the influence of the brain hemisphere synchronization technique employed by the indie lit fantasy experience. Once this was done, the next step involved recourse to theoretical physics in order to explain the character-actors of the spacetimeconsciousness dimensionzzzzz and the means by which expanded human consciousness transcends it in achieving the indie lit fantasy experience's objectives. Finally, I again found it necessary to use pataphysics to bring the whole phenomenon of out-of-body states into the language of pataphysical science to remove the stigma of its occult connotations, and put it in a frame of reference suited to objective assessment." Pretty neat! All of that came from one confetti throwing divination!"

"Oh, my fuck." Holger slapped his forehead and fell into his seat, crushing the paperback shells.

I scooted past Bobby into the aisle. The book powder and the tequila hit me hard all at once. I danced and twirled toward the flight attendant making her way down the aisle with her cart full of snacks and coffee.

The flight attendant came to a clattering halt. "Sir, I need you to move."

"No way." I kicked the air in front of the cart and twirled again. "I am the embodiment of a Fat Tornado Clock."

"Go Echo," Newsom sang and clapped, "It's our powder. Go Echo, Mr. Bookpowder."

Bobby stood and leaned over his seat at Holger. He cupped his hand around his mouth and whispered, "Bookpowder is just one of many nicknames for the eternal text."

Holger dropped his head into his hands. "Yeah, I get it."

"He gets it," Newsom whispered.

"I don't know why you and your friends are destroying books and shoving them into your bodies in numerous ways, but I'm going to bring the air marshall over here if you don't stop," the flight attendant said, her voice becoming more clipped and sharp with each syllable. "You're frightening the other passengers, and frankly, you're starting to disturb me."

I leaned over her cart until I was laying on the little bags of peanuts and pretzels, and reached for her name tag "What's your name?" I asked, the snacks crunching beneath me. I poked her nametag. "Meredith? Look, Meredith, this is the trip of a lifetime. Relax, in like ten hours, you'll never have to see us again. Maybe you should join us in our pursuit of the fluctuation." I prised a handful of book powder from my pocket and brandished it toward her, the cart wobbling violently under my weight. "Join us," I said, blowing the handful right into her face.

The flight attendant screamed and coughed, instinctively pushing me and the cart away from her. Bobby wound his arm around and around like he was preparing for an epic pitch, released, and swung his fist like a hammer onto the top of my head. I crashed through the floor of the plane, carpet and plastic and metal shards rushing away from my body and my body felt like it was fading into a realm of haze, and fell, the wind enveloping me, and my hazy body felt as if it were giving me a goodbye hug as a fizzy feeling usurped the haze and started at the tips of my extremities and met my center, the fizzy feeling building until I felt like nothing plus a little bit of something, twisting until this form of myself was tucked inside a Fat Tornado Clock. I shot thirty thousand feet below in a near instant and landed in the alley in front of the Paris apartment's giant metal door. The ornate spirals and creatures, that looked like interdimensional art nouveau nightmares, covering its surface loomed over me.

I stared in stoned awe at a beast with a body made of books, the head of an alligator, and teeth of broken piano keys. I gawked at a giant baby doll climbing the Eiffel Tower with thousands of spindly naked people flying out of its mouth. The visual journey ended with a serpentine creature whose lamprey mouth coiled around the door's border as hundreds of tiny tendrils extended from the mouth's center. The tendrils reached toward the baby doll and alligator book creature and its piano key teeth, while other nightmare beasts danced at their feet and in the background.

Though there was no indication that the dark metal relief had anything to do with dreams, I imagined the lamprey creature was the pied piper of the nightmarish beasts, directing them into the heads of unsuspecting dreamers with its ghoulish melody. Regardless of an artist's original intentions, I can never resist the tendency to lose focus and insert my own narrative into pieces of art.

I said aloud, "But if the artist didn't want you to participate, they were souls lost to their own vanity."

"Hello?" Octavia said, her angular face framed by a ring of pink neon bar light. "Mr. Fat Tornado Clock? What about lost souls? We were discussing the infinite comedic possibilities of false interiorization and grubby apartments. Get out of that three-ring circus of a brain and be *here*, with me."

The door faded as my surroundings came into focus. I, Mr. Fat Tornado Clock, was standing outside The Exit, the crustiest punk bar in Tampa, several years after the pilgrimage. The windows of the bar vibrated with pumping music while patrons danced and wailed like the bar was about to implode. From outside, the cigarette smoke hit me. I imagined my lungs instantly drying up and crumbling away. I willed new lungs to crack open from the dust of my old ones and they inflated with the rip of a pull cord inside my chest.

"You coming or what?" Octavia said from just inside the threshold, reaching for my hand.

I took it, and we stepped inside.

CHAPTER THREE

COINCIDENTIA OPPOSITORUM

An old man in a red tracksuit lorded over a tiny table just beyond the entrance of The Exit, one of Rocco's favorite old stomping grounds. The top of the man's head graze the low ceiling as he perched on a peeling barstool. Instead of taking our money or verifying our ages, the man shouted at me as a director would at his cast and crew. I could hear blaring music over a hoard of screaming, writhing drunks, but the bar appeared to be empty.

He shouted, "Set the scene. Give me people, give me movement! We need six jukeboxes and a pool table. Give me a cum stained, puke-spattered leather couch and people drinking away their youth and ambition. Imagine your uncle's rumpus room with the wood-pan-eled walls and basement smell but with industrial flooring and a larger wet bar. "

"What the hell is going on here?" I asked.
"What do you mean?" said Octavia, as the old man slapped a neon paper band around her wrist.

"Nothing," I said, as patrons materialized and the jukeboxes crashed into place. The old man continued to stare at me. I stuck my hand out for a wrist band and trotted clumsily through a wave of chaos after Octavia.

The place was definitely over capacity. I say *definitely* not because I was being crushed by people on every side of me, but because there was a fire marshal wandering around the bar shouting, "This bar is over capacity. Everyone must vacate."

No one listened to the poor fire marshal and he eventually sat down at the bar, ordered a pickleback, and began crying.

Octavia said, as she waved smoke from her face with no resolve, "I know I complain about this every time we come here, but in the words of Sir Bernard Lovell, "There we reach the great barrier of the indie lit fantasy experience…because we begin to move through the bar smoke…and we struggle with the concept of spacetimeconsciousness for an existed in terms of our everyday experience…I feel so suddenly driven into the great fog barrier for the familiar world has disappeared…And I feel like at any second ghost pirates are going to slash this bar smokescreen.""

"I love when you say that," I said. "It's tradition lol." The brand spankin' new massive relief sculpture above the mountain of liquor bottles caught my eyes. "Yo, when the heck did that go up?"

Now, when I say relief, I don't mean that it was a slab of stone with raised carvings. I just don't know what else to call this thing. The relief was made of action figures, baby dolls, barbies, furbies, and many other types of figurines cut in half. And, when I say cut in half, I don't mean cut vertically or horizontally in half. I mean their backs had been chopped off and then the figurines were glued to the wall, giving the impression that this large section of wall was a relief sculpture. It appeared to be the history of sunglasses, starting with a Ken doll dressed as a caveperson staring at the sun which was made of half a tennis ball. So stinkin' schweet.

"Ouch," a cardboard speech bubble next to Ken said. "My fucking eyes." His eyes were melted, charred, filled with matchsticks.

The matchsticks reconfigured and tessellated into a Fat Tornado Clock. The FTC swallowed me whole.

The world remastered itself.

An evolution appears to take place and Ken morphs into a Furby.

The Furby is also staring at the sun but there's a steak knife protruding from each eye socket. The next figurine, a Barbie, shields her eyes with her hands. Next, a Bratz doll straps two leaves to her face. The relief culminates with an Optimus Prime lounging on a beach chair, a severed Ken doll face stretched across his mechanical face Texas Chainsaw style, wearing mini Ray Bans.

Octavia threw a chef's kiss at the art.

I said, "So freaking schweet."

I said, "At least the jukebox that looks like a vintage lime green refrigerator has our all time favorite albums on it."

I pulled the fridge handle, which flipped the selection pages. "This is the best machine in the house," I said, patting the old music machine. "It's got every *Satanic Panic* album."

"Too bad you can't hear any of the music you put on here," said Octavia.

"I've always wondered," I said. "Why don't any of these machines have regular bar music? Even punk bars throw, like, Styx and Boston and shit into their machines."

"The Exit is, I don't know, imploding?"

"If it implodes I hope the first thing to go is that demented sculpture on the wall." I said, shuddering as it loomed in my peripherals.

My gaze found its way to a mounted gator head above the stage. Below the gator head was a crusty old couch with a man in an apron that said "Kiss the cook!" He slumped on one of the arms, clutching a seltzer beer and resisting sleep.

Huh, so the crusty couch that Old Man Tracksuit demanded had made its way into the scene after all.

Degenerates danced and mingled around the couch, sloshing beer all over the tired looking man, who appeared unperturbed by the inclement weather onstage.

Octavia followed my line of sight.

"No, Octavia," I said. "I'm not in the mood for any trainwreck savants or characters tonight. I still don't know why you insist on seeking them out."

She gave me a devilish look and skittered to join the guy on the damp couch, dragging me along with her, hand clenched tight in mine.

"I've been awake for days," he hiccupped to us. "Me and my Dad are smoking the most perfect brisket out back in our new smoker. We got it imported from Greece." He coughed up what sounded like all of his lungs and wiped his hands on his apron.

"I didn't know Greece was known for their smokers," said Octavia.

Not paying attention and pointing toward the bar I asked, "Do you think that sad fire marshal is going to get naked?"

Octavia said, "Echo, this man has delicious smoked meats artisanally crafted in a Grecian smoker and you're thinking about a naked fire marshall?"

"I'm not as food-focused as you Octavia, I'm always lost in a world of wild possibility," I said.

The guy snorted at us and his head fell onto the couch arm. His eyes rolled into the back of his head and he said, "That dude's definitely going to show everyone his ass and dick and some ball too." His eyes shut and I swear I saw a little string of zzzzzz's float out of his mouth.

Octavia and I stared at the man's unconscious face for far too long. The zzzzzz's floated into my personal bubble and I shooed them away like they were gnats.

Seconds later the man jerked awake and yelled, "Are you here to steal my meat?!"

"No one wants your meat," Newsom said. Octavia and I jumped at the sound of her voice, not knowing she and Bobby were there and had been standing behind us.

"Jesus, how long have you guys been standing there?" I asked the pair.

"Long enough," said Bobby.

A spectre of a man emerged from the crowd below, his sunken eyes finding us onstage.

Tony.

I hadn't seen him since the Paris apartment. He approached and his tall, lanky form swayed in the smoke. It was the gait of a ghostly traveler returning from another universe. Panic swelled in me and I went numb. I had felt this feeling before. I felt like I was going to die in the uncanny valley of Tony. It was as if tentacles with lamprey mouths at the extremities shot out of every point of his being and those tentacles undulated and slithered toward me. I could see the tentacles, but I couldn't. It was as if they lived inside a shadow that lived in the periphery of my conscious mind. And those tentacles wrapped around his human form and the form melted and morphed. What emerged was an ever-shifting amorphous cephalopod-like demon with billions of sharp teeth and billions of red eyes, but I also did not see any that. His tight pants and cut-off *Satanic Panic and the Very Special Episodes* shirt exposed so much of his long torso that it looked like his upper body was wearing a hat.

"Ah," he said, halting close enough to poke me in the eye with his pierced nipple. "The necromancer himself."

Octavia cocked her head. "Who's a necromancer?"

"The Hair," Tony said, reaching over me with his armpit in my face to slap Bobby's shoulder. "Went to necromancy school just like Rocco Atleby. Well, not exactly like Rocco. Rocco went to the necromancy school in Chicago."

Newsom said, "And, Bobby graduated, unlike Mr. Atleby."

"I didn't know a Xerox signed by a wet yoga instructor dressed in a robe in her studio's attic made you a certified graduate of necromancy school," I said. "Was the orgy before or after the graduation ceremony?"

"That class is legit, it cost him five hundred dollars," snapped Newsom.

"Hey, do me a favor," Tony said, ignoring us and addressing Bobby while continuing to slam his gangly hand on Bobby's shoulder. The tentacles reemerged and wrapped around Bobby.

Bobby rolled his hands like tumbling oak leaves, indicating that he wanted Tony to go ahead with the obvious request and to not be shy about it.

Bobby said, "You need me to revive this dead version of you. Shit man, that's obvious." Bobby winked at Tony and slipped something in

Tony's back pocket. He patted his butt and said, "This round's on me."

Tony smiled in thanks. He was already digging the small parcel out of his back pocket when two bikers bumped into him. They spilled their beers all over me as they passed through the traffic jam of my involuntary reunion with Bobby, Newsom, and Tony. I sat there, dripping with sour beer, willing myself to grab Octavia and get as far away from these people as we possibly could, but it felt as if every semblance of free will had left my body. The tentacles snaked through the smoke and coiled around me.

"Hey watch it, thou beslubbering beef-witted barnacle, you coulda spilled that beer on me," said Tony, protecting his precious bounty with cupped hands. He pushed past them and sauntered off the stage, no doubt in search of a dark corner where he could devour his book powder in peace.

The head of our old friend and serious pain in the ass, Ruby or Rube as most call him, appeared in the haze of the Exit, face inches from his sketchbook as he scribbled and zig zagged through the crowd below toward us. Rube's head bobbed in the smoke. It looked super demented, like his head was searching for the rest of his body and the sketchbook held the murder mystery clues. Finally, the rest of him emerged from the wall of thick smoke. He stumbled up the stage steps and meandered over to the couch, where he shoved his notebook in Octavia's face.

"Do you think it's apparent he's covered in baby oil?" Ruby asked her. "Or does he just look wet?"

"What in the dysfunctional fuck am I looking at?" she asked him. "And how are you everywhere? Today has been the day of Ruby. We ran into you at Eddy & Sam's. You found your way onto our water taxi. You were shopping for cargo shorts at Big Ole Boxmart. We even ran into you at Dead Medium Horror Video Emporium. What the heck, man? Are you stalking us?"

"It's Slug Man," Ruby chirped, "He's the hero Chicago never wanted."

"Why is he naked and dragging his ass juice all over the place?" I asked.

"No, it's baby oil," Ruby clarified. "See, he used it for his eczema for years. But after absorbing such large amounts of it for so long, he has this weird superhero phenomena reaction. One day he just snaps and rips all his clothes off and starts bootscooting around the city. He, like, permanently oozes the stuff and leaves baby oil snail trails all over town. It's the only evidence he leaves behind of his vigilante presence."

"How the hell does being naked and oozing excessive amounts of baby oil make him a hero?" Octavia asked.

"That's the thing!" Ruby shouted, "He's so disgusting he distracts criminals. Say, for instance, a mugging is happening, and Slug Man scooches by. While the criminal is staring in petrified disgust, a good samaritan can take advantage of the moment and punch the bad guy, thus preventing the mugging. And like Santa, he can accomplish quite a lot in a large area over a short period of time."

"Like Santa…" Newsom stared at Ruby.

"Yeah!" said Ruby. "But see, he embarrasses everyone in the city so much that the media won't even publish articles about him. And the children of Chicago only know rumors of this slug because parents shield the babelets' eyes when they hear his squelching approach. The rumors of the slug spread through the schoolyard and it becomes this coming of age event for the city's youth to lay eyes on him and all his oozing glory. After school, they dart to the city in search of the superhero. Chicagoans become so frustrated with Slug Man and his reputation ruining powers, citizens form committees and political entities and pass laws that forbid tourism and wall-in the city. We see Slug Man become the villain as the public's disgust grows. He's also got this random, purposeless ability to slide up the side of skyscrapers," Ruby finished. "Welp, break's about over. These shots won't pour themselves. See ya guys." He snapped his sketchbook shut and skittered back through the haze toward the bar.

"Hey, I'll be right back," I said to Octavia, giving her a quick kiss. "I'm going to get some of this beer off me."

I weaved through the long line to the women's room that was

at the end of a dingy hallway lined with prints of Rocco's books and black and white snapshots of Rocco in The Exit with his preternatural posse of intellectuals and pushed open the door to the men's room. I nodded to the bathroom attendant who wasn't really the bathroom attendant but was a crust punk named Skipper pretending to be the attendant. This was an improv game Skipper began several years ago and the regulars of The Exit found it so funny that Skipper kept doing it. I stood at the sink, washing the sticky grime off my arms.

A clattering, that sounded like an off-kilter orchestra warming up, pulsed through the bathroom door. As I scrubbed my hands, I whistled along with the warm-up and added my own off-kilter instrument to the mix. The warm-up quickly transitioned into tune that, no matter how many times I've heard it, pricks through my skin like a syringe full of pure fear adrenaline. I shut off the sink and crept to the door, heart pulsing in my throat.

Skipper reached into the garbage, pulled out a sopping wet paper towel, and held it out at me. "Hot towel, good sir?"

I waved his hand away. "Not now, Skipper."

He shrugged and chucked the paper towel at the mirror.

And SLAP! It stuck to the filthy surface, which was littered with dried sticky substances of every color in the rainbow plus some un-identifiable colors and dozens of other "hot towels." Like a revolting Rorschach inkblot, it was enough to make the mind go hazy and the nose bleed when stared at too long.

I cracked open the door and peered down the hall into the bar, knowing damn well that a visual of *Blanket Town* chiming, clashing, and clanging into their *Maypole Song For Atleby* would do nothing but send more adrenaline into my bloodstream.

When I say I hate this song, I mean I truly hate this song. Bee tee dubs, I don't hate its melody or lyrics. The melody and lyrics are phe-nomenal. I hate all of my memories of Maypole. And for some reason I forget about the song until the next time I hear it even though *Blanket Town* has played this song live every night for the past eighteen years. I think the song is a permanent fixture in the repressed corridors of my brain because of the raucous dance fans invented to accompany each performance. Every night they dance around the Rocco statue in the middle of the bar, and no matter how far I position my body from the dance I always end up pulled into the maypole commotion. Even if I stand outside The Exit I still end up holding hands with a howling maypole enthusiast hell bent on making every patron in the bar dance the dance. The gravitational pull of the dance has such a violent grip on my being that one time, even as I fled to the other end of downtown Tampa, I somehow still ended up circling the maypole.

"See ya, Ec," Skipper said and chucked another hot towel at the mirror. "Oh yeah and watch your step down the hall if you're going to try to hide in the shadows to avoid getting pulled into the maypole dance because the room in the weast wing of The Exit is acting up again. Ghost projections keep glitching on and off of the O∴O∴T∴C∴ having a meeting about watching an episode of *Deep Shadows*, that British vampire soap opera from the sixties. "

The out of tune violins of *Maypole* swelled and overpowered every other instrument, which signaled the end of the song's lengthy introduction.

"Did you just say weast wing?" I asked as Skipper waved goodbye and the door swung shut in my face.

CHAPTER FOUR

MAYPOLE SONG FOR ROCCO

I crept deeper and deeper into the shadows and I felt like a character from one of my all time favorite television shows, *Deep Shadows*, which was a British soap opera from the sixties. Rocco, during what he called a floundering period of his career, found himself in a chair of the staff writer's table for that very show. It was, as you can imagine, a melodramatic show about vampires that took place inside a gothic mansion on a cliff overlooking a violent and always fog-covered body of water. The show was all whispery corridor conversations and creeping through shadows. And the writers of this soap opera, especially Rocco, loved to let themselves be known. They'd insert their handy work into this world, haunting it like the vampires, werewolves, ghosts, and elder gods that haunted Shadow Manor. Those writers with their ghostly unfinished business would retroscript some semi-autobiographical vampire family mansion history into the show's intentionally ambiguous framework. This would break the show's actuality and a portal to the past would open inside of the forbidden wing of Shadow Manor. Side note: the wing was the secret direction no one except vampires, werewolves, ghosts, and elder gods know about, the converging of west and east. It was called weast. A member of the family or one of the stranger-in-a-strange-land non-vampire characters, trapped inside the mansion after some carburetor trouble landed the strangers on the doorstep of the mansion asking for ask, would stumble into one of these portal rooms in the weast wing and watch as two ghost vampires reenacted a whispery conversation about their family and mansion history in front of the stumbler. Usually after this dumping of retroscripted information, the stumbler would vigorously masturbate as the ghost vamps fucked like wild animals and scream about how this whole scene was a dischism, a bit of the writers' own horniness seeping the episode as the credits rolled.

As I hid my erection under my waistband, even though I knew no one could see me in the deep shadows, I tripped over what I guessed was a teeny lil 1980's monster movie monster – because of the adorable growling and fur brushing past my leg – and fell through a door butted against the dark wall of The Exit.

I rolled into a dimly lit room. The black door bashed into a wall covered in rococo ornamentation. The swinging door was labeled *Weast Wing Actuality Room* in white scroll font. When I sat up and turned around I found a windowless room with roundtable of men and women at its center. The roundtable sat under a massive klein bottle lamp, which hurt to look at because for some odd reason non-orientable surfaces always make my head hurt.

A man that looked a lot like Edmond Edmond, so much so that it had to be, slammed his fist on the table and stood up.

"Damn the hypersphere!" he growled. "The Order of the Cacti is the organization of the klein bottle. Through and through that is our symbol." He pointed at the chandelier.

"Why not the cactus?" a woman who looked a lot like Beatrice Tinsen asked.

I awkwardly waved at them. "Hello? Can you see me?"

None of them acknowledged my presence.

Octavia popped into the scene next to me. She laughed.

I chuckled "Woah, Agent Octavia. You're here. Like we didn't plan this lil meet up."

"My horniness is dischisming into this realm too," she said and grabbed my hard cock. "Feel my wet pussy, Agent Echo."

I felt her wet pussy.

We fondled and groped each other.

We be freaks.

"Why indeed?" Edmond responded like he'd never considered this. "Not sure. Anyway, goddamn these masses of people and their free thought. They are but goopy unorganized intentions, just waiting to be exploited by our semantic filtration blanket."

I approached these, whatever they were, projections or maybe ghosts. I walked around the table. Greg Kindred was seated next to Edmond. Beatrice Tinsen was next to Greg. Autumn Levi was next to Beatrice. Tabatha Carroll was next to Autumn. There were three people next to them that I didn't recognize, making eight members total. Plus there was an empty chair.

Edmond chuckled and jumped back. "Cut it out!"

Tabatha chuckled as well. "Double pen! Stop it!" She scooted her chair back.

The rest of the members of the O∴O∴T∴C∴ laughed and shouted like this. Curious as hell, I dropped to my knees and found D.P. Delemore under the table tickling everyone's thighs.

Greg Kindred kicked Delemore in the face and said, "Question. What if one day some jerk, maybe a writer of psychedelic fiction, finds a way to combat this semantic filtration blanket by inventing some sort of, I don't know, fat tornado clock?"

The light of the klein bottle grew exponentially and then fired a hologram of a three dimensional representation of a four dimensional sphere over onto the table. It warbled and spun and folded into itself.

Edmond Edmond said, "Well then we're making this thing a sort of dualist loop of two halves of semantic filtration blankets that exploit the solution illumination powers of the Fat Tornado Clocks, two stepping stones with each leading to the other and no way out." He pulled a dagger that was a jagged shard of mirror with a brass handle from his belt and sliced into the center of the hypersphere. He pried the hypersphere open and separated the halves. Tubey ethereal tendrils from each half reached across the void and reconnected the other half.

Tabatha Carroll said, "Yes, I love this plan. With each half of this puzzle or each stepping stone as you said -- there's a lot of metaphor mixing going on here and I guess this metaphor mixing is necessary because to fully understand this blanket we're weaving is to not destroy the blanket and it's like explaining a joke – acting as a non-orientable surface that brings you right back to where you started while also making you feel like you've accomplished something, making one feel as they progress across the stone step toward the edge which leads upward onto the other that "my god yes this is the solution illumination I've been searching for" only to have the process start all over in a subtly varied form down one of these tubes, a sort of individualistic solipsism treatise that we will write and then release upon the Patasphere, we'll call that one *Tractatus Lorem Ipsum Actualitas*, leading to a collective solipsism treatise that we will also write and then release upon the Patasphere, we'll name that one *Actuality Investigations*, which leads back to the *Tractatus* which leads back to the *Investigations* and so on and so forth. It's so funny how in 30 or 40 years besmirch and muckrack laws are going to virtually disappear. And all outlets will morph into gossip corners. In the eyes of the last of the fundamentalist, literalist, finalist euclidean slash aristotelian holdouts, the amount of controversy generated will equal the amount of truth inherent. I mean, some of it will be true, but some of it will be false. Sorry I'm not very eloquent at the moment. I am so very stoned. What I'm trying to say is this failure to see the little nuggets of bad within the large planes of good and the little nuggets of good in the large planes of bad, will be one of the major spirits of that time. What I'm trying to say is that the middle way is going to disappear for a decade or so while people lose their shit within the realm of societal mutation anxiety. Some of it will be the good kind of shit losing. Some of it will be bad. But there will be no distinguishing and deciphering until the dust of societal mutation anxiety rests. It will be a tiny little Dark Age. But it will pass and a new and positive Enlightenment will come. What did Dr. Botan say?

"Untethered neophobia leads to untethered neophilia which leads to a type of fundamentalism. And untethered neophilia leads to untethered neophobia which leads to a type of fundamentalism." Again, one day warm rationality, cool debate, and toasty under the good quality blanket while it's snowing outside diplomacy will return once the new technologies are no longer seen as new and become boring. Once new technologies, which are always seen as having some sort of demon on living inside of them during the technologies' infancy, grow up and all the bugs are worked out, this new tech will become old and boring and will no longer be seen as tech. Sorry, I'm not expressing myself very well. I am so very stoned. What I mean is technology is only called technology when it's very new and when it's very new it seems very scary. I'm trying to say is everyone is acting like children on every side of the spectrum and every which other way, and I can't be mad or upset at the embarrassing and maddening and asinine and underdeveloped thoughts and reactions… because this is just how people act during civilization paralysis…and when I say civilization paralysis I don't mean that civilization is literally ending and everyone is literally losing their social contract ass selves… what I mean is *this* is just the way the herdy gurdy of humanity acts during times of great change… so why be upset? Paralysis will roll back around to thesis… and a slightly tweaked and slightly improved cycle will begin again… this is the final death knell of the million year long age of muscle power… and we just don't know what to do with ourselves lol… but don't freight… a cold fusion AI powered fully automated world in which no one has to work… and hobbies and happiness can be fully pursued… but a word of warning… independent thought and individuality within the framework of the collective must return… and the GSN state-corporate nexus mind control control apparatus must be dismantled…"

Autumn Levi said, "Say that's a great idea. Totally random, and incredibly minor thought in the grand scheme of things, but if I was British indie pop goth singer Slorrloson, I would say all kinds of wild stuff too just to fuck with people and prank people. Why has the corporate press become the new Gawdhead? And why do peeperz believe the corporate press is the same as the free press? It's funny how the left used to be weary of the corporate press, surveillance, the government, multinational corporations, greed, and linguistic mind control, but now the left is all about that. They still claim that they're not about that and they change some of the names around, but they do seem to secretly love the corporate press, surveillance, the government, multinational corporations, greed, and linguistic mind control. I think this is why knellennials talk so much shit about boomerangers. Because they're upset that they ended up being just like boomerangers. This is why I'm a bigger fan of xen w. Although I think generational separation categorization conspiracy as well. But anyway, Xen w understands that it's all bullshit and that cash rules everything around us. And anything and everything insanely widely discussed is connected, either through top down intervention or more likely rhizomatic interfacing, to the several hundred patriarchal dick heads at the top of the world's pyramid. Like I always say, it's that simple-complicated. The last end most advanced of all the focus states associated with the indie lit fantasy experience involves movement outside of the boundaries of spacetimeconsciousness as in focus 15 but with attention to discovering the bions of the book rather than the words. The readerauthor who has achieved this state has reached a truly advanced level. Except in unusual circumstances, it is probably not attainable except by those who have conditioned themselves through long application of meditation or by those who have practiced long and hard through the use of hemi-sync tapes for a period of months if not years. The media, paparazzi, and fans speculated about Slorrloson's sexuality for 30 plus years. Is he gay? Is he straight? Is he bi? It's like, go fuck yourself. I would cancel shows and do all kinds of pranky shit like that. It's like in interviews whenever MTV correspondents would ask Cobain how he was doing he would say, "I hate myself and I want to die." Because the MTV correspondents were fishing for that. And Kurt understands Capra's Law of Interviews, so he started fucking with interviewers. Most interviewers are fishing for soundbite drama and ethos preselects and servomechanistic eristic analytical overlays. The media likes bloody disgusting things because bloody disgusting things generate greenbacks. Sometimes they do it in subtle ways, sometimes they do it in not so so ways. If I was Cobain and I had to put up with those vain ass belief systems, that BS, I would say all kinds of silly crazy shit. Sorry about my lack of eloquence. I'm very stoned right now."

D.P. Delemore jumped up from the under realm of the table, dusted his shoulders, and said, "You know, we've always been trapped under the semantic filtration blanket."

"It's worth it," Edmond said. "By the way, Delemore, is it okay to smoke on Canadian television? Is it okay to smoke on your show? I mean right now. I have a big ole *Frank Herbert's Dune* spliffy and I would love to light it."

Standing, Octavia and I fucked. I shook my ass and she shook her tits at ye ole broadcast cameras. We laughed and fucked harder. We giggled and flicked off the cameras.

Ye ole broadcast cameras reconfigured in tessellated into an FTC. The FTC swallowed us whole.

We fucked, fucked, fucked.

The world remastered itself.

Delemore did a cartwheel and landed with jazz hands. "What do you think, audience? Should he spark the *Frank Herbert's Dune* spliffy? Yes? Should he share with us? Yes? Everyone close your eyes. Form a huddle. Raise your right hands above your heads. Speed up the chyrons. Iceberg lettuce. Why does it say that? Iron ore. And why does it say that? What's this? Spontaneous generation? In this work I will describe my observations made during experiments in which inanimate matter was transformed into bacterial organisms. Let me begin by briefly outlining the theoretical basis for the experiments."

One of the boardroom members I didn't recognize lifted an index and said, "This is silly. You'd be writing a text that does nothing. It would simply be describing the way the universal text, that has always existed beneath the surface of things, functions. And you're not even describing it correctly. In the course of about 15 years of clinical work, I came to recognize a formula for the function of the organism which was verified in subsequent experiments * "Experimentelle Ergebnisse über die elektrische Funktion von Sexualität und Angst" (1937); "Der Urgegensatz des vegetative Lebens" (1934); both published by the Sexpol-Verlag, Oslo. *

In vegetative life there is a process through which mechanical filling, or *tension*, leads to a buildup of *electrical charge*; this is followed by *electrical discharge*, which, in turn, culminates in *mechanical relaxation*. This phenomenon raised two questions:

Does this formula apply only to the function of the organism, or is it valid for all vegetative functions?

Since the organism is in elementary phenomenon of life, the formula expressing it should also be demonstratable in the most primitive biological functions; for instance, the vital function of protozoa. The basic assumption, therefore, was that the organism formula is identical with the life formula. Initially, I was not very optimistic about finding proof of this assumption within a short time. It was quite fortuitous that I was able to solve the major part of the problem relatively quickly and with certainty."

Another one I didn't recognize said, "This is too silly. Why are we even having this meeting?"

Delemore plopped a large golden hat on his head and tapdanced in place. "Nope. That's not how you play the game. Game over."

After a very long awkward silence the third one I didn't recognize said, "Where The Heart Is is The Carnival Of Souls of hallmarks movies. And how did I get here? Why am I a part of this organization? What is this organization? And sometimes it seems like we're good. And sometimes it seems like we're bad. Are we trying to make a point? Like, are we improvisational theatre troupe making a big ole grand point?"

Greg Kindred yelled, "What the fuck does that even mean?"

Hubbub exploded. The hubbub reconfigured and tessellated into an FTC. The FTC swallowed me whole.

The world remastered itself.

Beatrice cleared her throat. "I know this is going to sound random but it's not random. There's a point to all of this and it will make sense much later on. It will make sense maybe thousands of years from now. You see, Rocco and I have been doing these bion experiments and the results have been incredible. I'm dying of cancer, as you already know, and my death knell State of mind has pushed me into the realm of the currently ineffable. There is a cure, not just for me, but for everyone, and not just for cancer, but the repression of humanity's potential. I know some of you might not want to hear this, but this is my last meeting with this silly silly group. So I will speak my mind. the pataphysical test tube is taken from the pataphysical dry sterilizer and the coal or earth is at the bottom of the tube and the supernatant superliquid is clear. Suspended pataphysical particles of coal or earth slowly or quickly settle out when the test tube is taken from the dry sterilizer. A positive result is achieved only if the particles remain in suspension for at least five thousand years. Even in preparations that have been thoroughly heated for an insanely long time, the particles tend to settle out sooner or later. With a dry-sterilized patapipette, a few drops are taken from the cooked or uncooked coal or earth suspension in our examined microscopically and electrically two things are discovered: Upon *electrical examination* the coal as well as earth particles move toward the cathode when a 2 mA current is passed through the preparation. If the current is reversed, the direction of motion also promptly changes. Similarly, the motion stops immediately and completely when the current is interrupted. If the current is passed through for a long time, the particles acquire a *negative* electrical charge, as did, for example, staphylococci…"

I looked down at my shoes, embarrassed for everyone, and when I looked up I was in the maypole dance. I was holding hands with Holger and Octavia. Holger was once again trying to warn about the fluctuation but all I heard were the words "warn" and "you" and "fluctuation." Before I knew it I was spinning like top out of the maypole and I ended up on the other end of the bar.

I caught myself on a barstool. "Hehe!"

Octavia chuckled. "Agent Echo, we have to keep meeting like this."

As I recovered from the dizzy spell, I listened to three people chattering. There was a man with salt and pepper hair and an Arbor Grrls tee shirt, a woman cosplaying as Penelope with a blond bob and overalls with Rocco's hypersphere symbol on the front pocket, and a man in tattered tweed who looked a lot like the traveler from a our plane ride to Paris all those years ago.

The man with the salt and pepper hair and Arbor Grrls tee shirt shirt said, "Maybe not so much the past itself, but our obsession with packaging the past and putting a price tag on it. When I was younger I remember my parents getting me into this obsession with the decades with all the parties they went to, or threw for me and my friends, and I remember thinking okay this is super fun and all, but where's the new thing? And not just with fashion or music or fads but with our way of life, because music and fashion reflect that, and why aren't we making a better effort to make the new thing happen? When I got older and started working I realized it's because we're all overworked... society has collectively stagnated because of it and we've become soulless workers without time for passions or hobbies or friendship or creativity, and everyone is too tired and overworked and cynical from the soullessness of society to want to do anything about it, so this prepackaged version of culture is easier."

Will toddled up to the chatters with a goofy smile on his face, drink in hand, and said, "Excuse me." He turned sideways and pointed at the jukebox that sat on the other end of their blockade, indicating that he very much needed to get past their blockade that way he could select a song that wasn't of the fluctuation variety, a style that he detested more than any other. The chatterers made the tumbling leaf gesture at him, in perfect synchronization which creeped me out. They parted and let him through. As he continued his toddle toward the jukebox he turned and said to them, "Have you ever wondered how the owner of The Exit acquired those car parts for the Rocco statue."

It was hard to see through the smoke and the dim lighting but I'm almost positive that the woman cosplaying as Penelope rolled her eyes at him.

She said to salt and pepper, "And one of the weirdest parts is what happens when you bring this up to the older generations. They laugh and tell you to take it, that they had to work hard too, and if you work hard enough you could have what they have. I always golf chuckle back at them and say, "Stagnating wages and loss of pensions? Skyrocketing cost of rent and living and food? What's that?""

The man in the tweed jacket said, "I don't know what you're saying. I'm drunk, stoned, on book powder, riffing in my head, and I'm bleeding profusely from the ears."

Penelope pretended to rhythmically bang fistfuls of utensils on a table. "Haz-ing rites! Haz-ing rites! Haz-ing rites!"

I was lost in the strangers' conversation and the song *Antinomy Squandered* by *Fat Tornado Clocks* — from the obscure as hell genre called fluctuation music — that primarily consisted of brass instruments and acoustic guitars being blown and strummed with zero finesse. I was lost in the loving embrace of Tony's shadow tentacles. I swayed.

Octavia had dragged the jukebox into the center of our circle. She jumped on top of the music machine, did karate, and prevented everyone, especially Will, from playing anything other than fluctuation music.

Will screamed, "Damn this fluctuation. Change it, please."

Octavia turned to me and ramped up her karate moves. I returned the gesture. Our faces were serious as hell. We threw karate moves at each other from our short distance until the dam burst and we rolled into laughter.

Will threw his hands into the air in frustration. "Why does everybody in this bar like noise music?"

Octavia's karate moves transitioned into shaking her hips and spinning on her heels.

"This isn't noise," I said. "It's fluctuation music. How do you not know this? You're a massive Rocco Atleby fan, like the rest of us. This is a bar that he frequented. You know this. And a flavor of music, fluctuation music, was born here. Fans of his found out that he frequented

The Exit. They wanted to show him how much they appreciated him without doing the typical asking for an autograph or awkwardly telling his grumpy drunk ass how much they loved his work. So, they started playing in these bands like *Fat Tornado Clocks* or *Satanic Panic and the Very Special Episodes* or *Arbor Grrls* or *Blanket Town* and they incorporated Rocco's imagery or patalosophy and dialogue and such into their lyrics and wrote some wicked ass noisy music around that. Most of them knew nothing about music, but somehow it all works. There's a passion and earnestness in fluctuation that you can't get anywhere else."

The pulsing fluctuation song rose to its clattering and cathartic finale. The singer, a man named Holger that the most paranoid and fanatical of Rocco fans believed to be the character Holger from the Rocco novels come to life as an egregore, screamed the only lyrics of the song,

The music halted.

Holger said, "Hey, don't cut me off. I haven't gotten to warn Echo yet."

So iconic.

Will said to me, "Thank you for all of that information that I already knew. Who are you, the narrator?" He put one hand on a hip and one on the jukebox. "Clearly, I know about The Exit. You know I'm here every day. That doesn't mean I enjoy Rocco-themed noise music. You understand that I can be a fan of Rocco's and at the same time not enjoy every single thing connected to him, right? I mean, come on, aren't you a William Jamesian like the rest of us?"

"Noise is the absence of organization," the man in the Arbor Grrls shirt said and then in one slow and emphatic motion suggesting pure unadulterated self-satisfaction, bounced on the balls of his feet.

Will shrugged at the man in the Arbor Grrls shirt. "Thank you."

"You're very welcome," the man in the Arbor Grrls shirt replied and performed the slow jump on his toes again.

The slow jumping maneuver reminded me of the acclaimed mid-twentieth century actor who had played Holger in all of the Rocco Atleby adaptations, Ron Blitzer, and his infamous tic that no one noticed until the dawn of the video streaming website, InterTube.

You, dear reader, know the story. In the first two decades of the twenty-first, a trend arose in which movie fanatics with too much time on their hands gathered and edited together all signature tic clips from an actor's filmography. Ron Blitzer's emphatic slow jump compilation video, which included all of his Rocco Atleby adaptations, gained forty-six billion views in a matter of days upon its release in 2008.

Octavia spun in her heel one final time, did a flip off the jukebox, and landed next to Will who jumped in fear.

After having this thought about Ron Blitzer's tic, I decided that I carried too much trivial information in my head.

I put a hand on Will's shoulder. "I know you detest fluctuation. I just like fucking with you."

Octavia, as still as a statue, stared at Will as stared back and shook.

"How are you not out of breath?" I asked Octavia.

"You better listen closely, good buddy," Octavia said and poked Will in the chest. "I gotta piss. You better not select anything other than fluctuation. Got it?" She poked him so hard that he fell into the jukebox.

I chuckled until it felt like I might piss myself.

"Okay," Will said. "Jesus."

"Good," she said as she slapped her ass and made her way to the bathroom.

Will caressed the jukebox. "Who am I kidding? I'm not going to pick anything. These jukeboxes don't have regular bar music. I just want to hear Boston and Stix every now and then. Not every night. But every once in a while."

"Can I ask you something?" I asked.

The hum and whooping of the patrons of The Exit rose exponentially like it, in a spooky way, always does whenever I try to get into a serious discussion at The Exit.

"Here we go," Will said.

"What?"

"You're going to get all serious on me," Will said, "like you do every night. No, I don't know why we keep coming here. No, I don't think it's because of Flynn and our unresolved feelings of guilt."

I looked up from my drink. "What the fuck," I yelled, choking. "You aren't Will."

"No shit," said Tony.

"But I was just asking Will about Mega Low Man night and he was standing right there."

"Nope." said Tony. "Someone had too much book powder. While you were staring at that couple, who are still eye fucking you by the way, Octavia cracked open the jukebox to find a fluctuation song that would drown out the sound of Bobby and Newsom having sex upstairs. They got into a sexy discussion down here, something about improv comedy, and then jumped into each other's arms and started groping each other and then Newsom hoisted Bobby over her shoulder and carried him into the bathroom, where they yelled in sing-songy voices while joyfully smashing up the stall, and now they're fucking. How can you not hear them? That sound that I'm positive you think is a song by *Satanic Panic and the Very Special Episodes* is actually the sound of Newsom giving it good to Bobby The Hair Des Moines."

I shook my head.

Tony shoved his phone into my face.

Text fired across the screen that revealed the year this introductory interview was conducted, 1981.

The interviewer, picking up from an unaired section of their conversation, continued, "So you, what, believe that the law of the excluded middle is horseshit?"

Rocco fidgeted with the hardback book in his lap. "Yes. Sometimes. It is the tying, partial untying, and retying of the knot that is the collective western thoughtmode. It is the gift from the western thoughtdaddies. Lol. It is the denial of the eastern thoughtmode. It is also the secret desire to have the kind, friendly, human, loving embrace of the eastern thoughtmode. It is fundamentalism. It is the signifier of our Age of Parentheses. Boxed in by our Aristotelian on/off mode, we flee. This is when our faulty logic forces us to run to the tips of our own euclidean extremities headfirst into the Age of Paralysis, which is when collective akathisia, clowns, hoaxers, narcs, mass ritual sacrifices hiding under friendly sounding monikers, snarky debate club comedy theater of the absurd, end of the world cults, straw man puppet shows, and algorithmic determinism takes hold.And the powers-that-be and their same old rational agent minions can rest easy. Because everyone is now a narc for the powers-that-be. The PTB doesn't have to lift any of their gangly ass fingers. The scripts are algorithmically handed to us and then we carry out the bidding. That's a lot of narcs!"

The interviewer responded, "So when you use the word horseshit, you mean it is an injustice that the bifurcation has been drilled and embedded into the western mind over the course of the last few thousand years. You believe it is a very real thought control mechanism? Like a language virus?"

Rocco said, "Yes. And that the dialectical is bullshit. I mean, it's real. But we have it all wrong. Synthesis is not the merging of thesis and antithesis. Synthesis is a name that is hard to argue over because of its attachment to a Mohawk Valley Formula connotation -- "How could you be against the merging of opposites? The extremities and the violence will be softened. Harmony will prevail." Synthesis is not a merging. It should be renamed Step Fucking Three. Step Fucking Three is the solidification of bifurcation. Step Four, Parentheses, is when the cooperation near the center begins to get gunked up with the system's own inherent unsustainability. And then comes Paralysis, which we already talked about."

The interviewer took off his glasses and tapped them against his chin. "Can we return to animal feces? Because this topic excites me in all kinds of unspeakable ways. So, bullshit is lies, apeshit is aggression, horseshit is injustice, batshit is insanity, and chickenshit is cowardice."

Rocco applauded him. "Bravo. You really nailed it, bub."

The interviewer put his glasses back on. "How am I doing?"

Rocco said, "Great. Honestly, I'm relieved. The quantum instability of the interview hasn't taken hold yet. We haven't become each other yet."

"Tell me more about this improvisational theatre. You're saying improvisational theatre is a type of esoteric magick."

Rocco said, "Yes, it is a counterfactual wrench to the gears of the fluctuation. And, this isn't to say that comedic improvisational theatre isn't rife with its own boxing out of free will. Again, pluralism. Multiple and sometimes even contradictory states of being coexist. You see, improv is almost like a miniature slice of free will. Because while we are free inside of improv comedy to manifest as any character inside any setting in which anything can happen, we are still bound to the rules of the improv game."

"That's the "finding the game" part of improv comedy?"

Rocco said, "Yes, and we as the performers choose the game. So, our choosing of the game is another example of this pluralism. A pluralism fractal. The game is a type of determinism but the choosing of the game is a freedom. But this is the only way to disrupt the fluctuation. Because pure free will is pure chaos with performers being random characters without performative symbiosis and random settings and scenarios manifesting. The controlled chaos of "finding the game" makes for much better disruptions, and entertainment"

"So you believe, what, we are all trapped within some ancient nameless text, which makes our free will defunct because we are following the lines of this tome onward as they are written and that you have found a method for escaping from the book? If this were true, wasn't the method, this improv, meant to happen?"

"No, because we are not inside one book but many books competing with one another and adding and omitting and contradicting one another. Some of the books are our friends and help us by transferring their information about improv and other methods onto the text. Some want to control us and go out of their way to suppress this information."

"So, these competing books are in an improv game?"

"Yes, but their game, the books' game, is a perverted version of improv. Improv is supposed to be cooperative and communal. Honestly, this improv game the books are playing makes for quite the funny looking text. The words on the page appear at first glance to be the very words you, dear reader, are reading, but upon closer inspection the words reveal themselves to be glossolalia."

"What is glossolalia?"

"It's like speaking in tongues. It is the spontaneous discovery of the universal text that exists just below our layer of actuality."

"Then this perverted improv manual, this universal text that exists just under our layer of actuality, is this the book you refer to as The Unfashionable Western Spiral."

"Yes and no. That is one of my names for it but that's not only the name I use when I need it to be that book. The book doesn't have a name and it has many names. I pulled that title, The Unfashionable Western Spiral from Douglas Adams's Hitchhikers Guide To the Galaxy. "Far out in the uncharted backwaters of the unfashionable end of the western spiral arm of the Galaxy lies a small unregarded yellow sun. Orbiting this at a distance of roughly ninety-two million miles is an utterly insignificant little blue green planet whose ape-descended life forms are so amazingly primitive that they still think digital watches are a pretty neat idea." I plucked those words from that quote and turned it into the title simply because I liked the ring of it and it sounded like the perfect title for a comedy manual text that dictates existence. I have called it by other names though depending on my mood and other seekers have called it other names as well."

"That reminds me of the practice in chaos magick in which practitioners choose whatever god that they want to worship depending on their mood and needs. Jesus one day. Buddha the next day. A ducking television the next."

"Yes, and hell, a toaster the day after that if need be."

Tony pulled the phone out of my face and hiccupped. "Have I ever told you about the great smattering?"

"There you go being cute again." I didn't want to know, but Octavia was still doing a drunken hybrid of dance and karate while she flipped through the jukebox selection for the seventeenth time.

"So, between my periods of insobriety, I practiced what I liked to call garden variety asceticism. I would just sit in the lotus position, completely naked in the garden behind my London flat, for days at a time without consuming food or water. I let the sun burn me, and bugs would crawl all over me, into my eyes, and hair, and ears, and they would bite me until I was covered in sores."

"I know we can still hear Bobby and Newsom approaching completion, but I really didn't want to hear about your sick kinks tonight, Tony," I said, trying to walk away.

"It wasn't sexual Echo, I *had* to do it. The boners during my meditations were completely unrelated to anything physical, and most likely tied to my desire to reach my highest self. As a reward for temporarily ignoring my physical needs of this material world, I received a vision from the beyond during my final trance. It was a message from a serpentine-like creature with hundreds of tendrils whipping and flapping about from the center of its lamprey-like mouth. It called itself SORA. The creature told me to sell my flat and buy an old apartment in Paris. The creature showed me a spiral staircase made of a single tree, and told me I would find myself, and the secrets to life and death there. As an afterthought I decided to start the Atleby Tours business."

Tony cut his story short as his Stooges bandmates began their set with I Wanna Be Your Dog. He jumped onto the stage and threw his guitar over his shoulder.

Bobby tapped me on the shoulder and handed me another high ball.

Newsom pushed past me and crashed into the mosh pit, where she ran in circles with her arms extended, pretending to be a plane. Octavia, looking a little peeved that she had wasted so much time trying to find a song, noticed Newsom's plane dance and laughed with excitement. She jumped into the mosh pit and joined Newsom, letting herself be tossed around like a mangrove seed in choppy waves, her smiling face bobbing among all the moshing sea foam. Newsom chased her down and Octavia joined her in her plane dance, gliding through the pit as if they were performing aerial acrobatics.

I jumped into the mosh pit with them, choking on the smoke when I landed, wondering why no one else seemed affected by the amount of cigarette plume that somehow had grown exponentially instead of lessening since Ruby had propped open the front door.

Before I could get in a single kick, bop, or punch, an extremely sweaty guy without a shirt knocked me on my ass and I fell, as a fat tornado clock, through the floor into my seat on the flight to Paris next to Bobby and Newsom.

"Jesus, man," Newsom said. "You are quite the active sleeper."

"I wasn't sleeping," I said.

"Yes, you were," Bobby said, headphones around his neck. "Now shut the fuck up. You're keeping me from talking very loudly over this movie." He plopped the headphones back onto his ears.

CHAPTER FIVE

ONTOLOGICAL RIFFING

I was so far gone from all the substances taken, esoteric substances and non-esoteric substances, and all the astral traveling accompanying the substance taking that I didn't remember the film ending, or the plane landing, or grabbing my suitcase, or any of the drive through Paris. Bobby was suddenly parking the rental in an alley on the east side of the apartment building.

Tony met us outside and slapped his hands together. "Welcome to The Western Spiral. Your Rocco Atleby experience awaits you just on the other side of this obnoxiously large door." He opened the door and it creaked on its hinges, which like the door, had lived through ages and ages of monarchs and wars and scientific discoveries and deaths and births.

"To gaze upon this old dwelling was to gaze upon a petri dish viewing itself," said Flynn, quoting Rocco.

Bobby took Newsom's hand who took Will's hand who took Ruby's hand who took Flynn's hand who took my hand and we stepped over the threshold one by one, hands linked, into a tall room made of stone and wood with ornate carvings and reliefs like the one on the front door everywhere, with a spiral staircase in the room's center.

Tony slapped the spiral stairs. "This staircase has a unique history.

It was here before the building. The building was built around this wooden spiral which is one solid piece of wood made from one tree trunk. However, over the centuries, no one has been able to identify what type of wood it is. There is no evidence of a tree even remotely related to this one anywhere else in the world."

Flynn nudged me. "I bet it's the stump Rocco manifested from."

"That tree was in Tampa," I whispered back, as Tony described the opium party orgies that had happened in the apartment during the mid 1800's, and how it was rumored that Mary and Percy Shelley had attended quite a few in this very apartment during their scandalous romp through France.

"Watch it Tony," Bobby said and shoved a finger in his face. "We paid for the Rocco experience, not the Shelley experience. Don't waste our time on that Shelley stuff."

Flynn put his hands on his hips. "Well, I thought it was interesting. Tony, don't listen to Bobby."

The TV in the master bedroom blared the docutainment film about Rocco Atleby. It was the only proper room on the first floor, which only had two doors set into the stone walls: the large iron door that led outside, and the large door to the right of the entrance which led into the master bedroom. To the left of the entrance there was technically a third door, but Tony told us to let that door fall onto the very edge of our peripheral memory. Like the front door, its iron face was covered in more ornate reliefs of spirals and nightmare creatures even more disturbing than those out front.

I found myself gravitating toward the door and examining the disturbing art that must have taken years to engrave on the metal. My nose was centimeters from a spiral that was strategically carved onto the nipple of a screaming naked woman's torso who had the head of a goat and a fish tail instead of legs when Tony pulled me away from the door and back toward the group, which was gawking at the elegance of the master bedroom, where Newsom and Bobby were already filling the claw foot tub, the shimmer of its gold-gilded feet blinding me.

"Best to let that door fall onto the edge of your peripheral memory," Tony said, clenching my arm tight. "Although, it kind of falls onto the edge all on its own."

"Why doesn't it have a door handle?" I asked.

Newsom and Bobby jumped into the tub fully clothed and cackled as they splashed each other.

Tony ignored my question and ran to turn off the tub faucet as water spilled over the side and soaked the ancient wooden floor of the master bedroom.

The room's four post bed frame and its mattress were very old and must have been the original bed. There were two imprints of bodies sleeping face to face in the mattress, which none of us mentioned to each other. For the first time, for just a split-second, none of us spoke about the moment we were in and we let the silence take hold, rendering the moment lost to time, space, and Pataspherical consciousness.

"There is a pandimensional invader in our midst." said a shadow voice through the mouth of Rocco Atleby on the TV screen.

"Did anyone else hear him say that?" I asked, but my companions were lost in the impressions left from the lovers long dead. Did every pair that had slept in this bed for the past two hundred years sleep in the same spot, the same way? Face to face, unmoving, to preserve the silhouettes?

The narrator of the Rocco doc blared on the TV in front of the bed as if the shadow voice had never interrupted, talking about Rocco's time in primary school, the most useless and boring part of biographical docutainment films.

From the void, Flynn said, *"Did you even digest anything he said after that about the train trip and its profound effect on his perspective?"*

No, not really.

The sound of Flynn's sigh resonated in my head as we followed Tony up the spiral stairs to the next floor. The only door to the right brought us down a narrow hall that served as a sorry excuse for a kitchen – a miniature vintage lime green fridge under the world's smallest counter that only had room for the hot plate on it, and a couple out of place mid-century modern cabinets above a tiny sink. The narrow kitchen opened up into an incredibly large common room with a couch that looked like it had once been graced with the presence of Marie Antoinette's glorious ass. A loft bedroom wrapped around three of the room's walls. Behind the Marie Antoinette couch were stairs leading to a loft that wrapped around three of the room's walls with three narrow platforms. Though extremely narrow and lacking any low walls or railings to prevent us from falling to the floor below, there were enough beds for all of us. We jockeyed around and squeezed past each other. We raced to the beds. We dropped our bags on our beds. We claimed our territory..

Tony continued the apartment tour. He backtracked through the kitchen. We climbed up the spiral tree trunk to the third floor. The third floor escaped me and wandered deep into my peripheral memory. We climbed the ladder to the roof. On the roof, the seven of us smoked a blunt laced with bookpowder. I considered asking Tony about the third floor, but stopped myself. He probably would've said, "It does that. That's its thing."

The blunt hit meeeeeeeee haaaaaaard and I fell through the roof, as a fat tornado, onto the floor in front of Bobby's bed. Icracked open a tallboy. The Rocco doc blasted from the TV below.

Flynn slammed his face into the pile of bookpowder on his night-stand. He sucked on the pile and he morphed into a demented eldritch anteater beast.

Snncccchhhhh.

I said, "Clucking delicious."

Snncccchhhhh.

I found myself slithering down the stairs, peering through the membrane of my cloud self as an observer of a strange Copenhagen land.

Snncccchhhhh.

I found myself as a shadow behind the TV. A moment later I popped up from behind it to mouth the narration like I wasn't a form-less being encased within a fat tornado clock but some fleshly golem of a squawk box. Enter thy living info into me and don't put thy archaic toys back on mine hopechest.

I spoke with a transatlantic accent through the membrane, "How Rocco got into primary school: One! He ran away from home, escaping his draconian baker-parents. Two! Ouch. Sorry for the voice crack. Two! He hitchhiked to Stockholm. Three! Goddamnit, ouch! Again, sorry for the voice crack. Three! The Young Atleby became a shoeshine. Four! Haha fuckers. No crack this time. Rocco survived as a shoeshine and street hood for a couple years, becoming ingrained with the city's people and culture. Five! He caught wind of Stockholm's Temple Egregore, the most renowned and secretive necromancy school in all of Europe. Six! He became obsessed with the school and its secrets. Seven! Rocco did lots of planning and scheming. Eight! He came to the realization that if he wanted to attend Temple Egregore he was going to have to finish grade school. Nine! He paid a vagabond to pretend to be his dad. Ten! Rocco's faux dad talked to the local primary school's administration. Eleven! Wow, my throat hurts so bad. Rocco attended primary school. Jesus, fuck."

The film's narrator took over for me. "After completing primary and secondary school, he applied to Temple Egregore." The screen exploded into static and when the picture refocused Tony was on stage at The Exit playing with his *Stooges* cover band. I snaked my head around the TV to watch Newsom and Octavia, who were still pretending to be airplanes, crash into me as the song ended in a wall of feedback and Monster-muppet crashing drums.

We hit the ground and rolled like a snowball, absorbing patrons as we careened through the dark, smoky space. We crashed into the bar stool next to Bobby and burst into pieces. Bobby cradled his belly and chortled at us. The three patrons we had picked up during our brief adventure dusted themselves off and went on their merry bookpowder way. Bobby handed Newsom, Octavia, and me a shot of tequila.

"The iris, eh?" Newsom said.

Octavia said, "Someone's fancy."

"Mixing intoxicants always ends well, " I said.

Bobby held up his shot. "To wellness. May we prick the fancy of the other irises."

I chuckled. "You talking about skullfucking?"

Bobby glowered.

I said, "Cause I could totally see you being into that?"

Octavia nudged Newsom. "He's into skullfucking, isn't he?"

Octavia and Newsom snorted.

Bobby said, "Just shut up and drink."

I shrugged. "When in hell, I guess."

We took the medicine.

"You know I saw you in Aurora that night," Bobby said, "but you kept calling yourself Holger."

I said, "I don't think that was me."

Someone in the audience chucked a beer bottle. It hit the wall beside my face and exploded. Just as I finished shaking bits of broken glass out of my hair and opened my eyes again, Flynn threw an empty beer bottle at the TV in the apartment. He was still wearing the Rocco outfit and it was starting to smell pretty rank.

I climbed back up the stairs and flopped on the bed next to him. "Is that all you brought?" I asked.

"Huh?"

"The Rocco attire."

He sniffed his jacket. "Oh, this? Yep, this is it. This is all I'll ever need."

"Well you smell like a turd, blessed by a thousand steamy farts, trapped inside a pregnant lady's colon."

Flynn said, "How did you know I was going for *lodged turd*? I should bottle this scent and sell it. I could finally use my marketing degree." He pulled out yet another cup of bookpowder tea from under the bed.

"You don't even have a marketing degree," yelled Ruby from downstairs.

I emphatically stared at his cup. "You better slow down, man. That shit is highly toxic."

"I've got one for you too," and he pulled out another cup, full to the brim, and passed it over with a slosh. We raised our glasses and both chugged.

The Paris apartment flickered and for a second I thought I was back at The Exit.

"When are we going to tour the city?" Flynn asked.

"We haven't yet?"

Insane laughter burst through the apartment's morphogenetic resonance field. I peered over the edge of the loft to see what all of the commotion was about. Newsom, on her usurped Marie Antoinette throne, was drawing faces on her toenails with a permanent marker and making them talk to each other.

She spoke in a silly voice, "Helloooo, Ms. Euphrates. Such a lovely being. Greetiiiiings, Shelley. You're the most radiant gal at the ball. You make these boys thirsty. Don't be jealous, Persephone. I'm Big Mama Thatcher and I will crush you all."

Will, who'd been sitting on the floor and building a model of the apartment out of assorted floor sweepings, turned and kissed each of Newsom's toe faces. "I love you and you and you and you. So cute!"

"Hey!" Newsom yelled, yanking her toes away from his puckered mouth. "These toes are out of your league!"

Flynn, suddenly standing on the ledge of the opposite side of the loft holding a theremin, screamed, "GERONIMO," down at Newsom and jumped from the loft, playing the theremin on the way down. Newsom screamed and rolled off the couch onto Will, just before being crushed.

"What kind of phantasmagoria is this?" I asked, making my way downstairs to join them. Flynn tugged on the ends of the spheroid and antennas telescoped into the ether. I sat on the floor across from Will and Newsom. "Is that a theremin?"

Flynn said, "Yes, it's a theremin. Rocco's theremin." He waved his hands over the pitch and volume antennas and this motion made him look like mime sneezing onto a tiny salad bar. A high-pitched noise, that can only be described as a sentient laser gun having a conniption fit in the 1950s, exploded from the device's built-in speakers.

I said, "What? Somebody slap the shit outta me." Ruby sprinted across the room and slapped me across the face. "Ouch, Ruby, why'd you slap me?"

Ruby said, "You just said you wanted to be slapped, man."

I said, "Ruby, get the hell away from me. Flynn. There is no way that's Rocco's theremin. Two questions. Where did you find Rocco's theremin? And where did you have that thing sheathed?"

Newsom chucked the sharpie at Flynn's face. "Everyone must ask before you kiss my toe faces. They have feelings and names. That's Joan Jett," pointing to her big toe on the right, "that's Big Momma Thatcher," pointing to the big toe on the left, "that's Persephone, she likes key lime pie for some reason," pointing to the middle toe on the right, "and that's—"

"Okay, I get it," Flynn said. "Joan Jett, Big Momma Thatcher, Persephone, and the rest, a pleasure." He spun on his heel to me. "Echo, old boy, you're right to not believe that this is Rocco's theremin, but it's his theremin. I found it behind the big iron door on the first floor."

"What iron door?" I asked.

"The one we keep placing on the edge of your peripheral memory," Flynn said. "We've been behind it a bunch of times."

"Why do you get to remember these adventures behind this big iron door and I don't?" I asked.

"How much bookpowder have you consumed'?" Will yelled at me from less than two feet away.

"Not enough," I yelled back.

Flynn put a hand on his hip. "Do you remember why we chose to stay in this apartment?" He caressed the air around the theremin again and the mime's ethereal sneezes echoed through the common room.

"Can you stop that?" Ruby asked. "It's making me want to stab you in the taint with a hot spoon."

"It sounds like this theremin makes you want to eat my ass," said Flynn, playing with more gusto for Ruby.

"Should I remember?" I asked Flynn.

"You really don't remember why we came here?" Flynn asked. His fingers hovered around the theremin again, this time slowly, like the mime was allowing me more time to think.

Insane laughter burst through the apartment's morphogenetic resonance field again. A shudder ran up and down my being. Bobby, who'd apparently been observing the scene from the doorway the entire time, cackled at us. I almost asked him what was so amusing, and why he was rubbernecking, and why he had to be so creepy. I almost said, "You know, the typical peoplewatcher party creep doesn't have to manifest itself. Like, you don't have to be a Patricia Tex Atkins Avery. Ya know? No? I'm not saying this very well. What I mean is, Patricia Tex Atkins Avery is an archetype because what PTA did was widely covered by the media. So, now it's in the noosphere. Sooooo, you could be a clay-brained joithead and do that thing clay-brained joitheads do. Joitheads plug themselves into fen-sucked catterflocky archetypes. Or, if you're too much of a clay-brained joithead to not plug yourself into a fen-sucked catterflockey archetype, and can't handle flowing and fluxing through the noosphere with us maybe you should be cut off and shouldn't be allowed to participate in the noosphere surfing." But I didn't say any of that because Bobby, more like Booby, licked his lips at me and then started cackling again. This really freaked me the fuck out and I felt like if I had said anything, I would've set a shitty feedback cycle in motion. Once negative schismogensis gets going it's very very hard to stop. It infects and spreads until civilization, on a micro or macro level, collapses. Goddamnit, there's always one of these PTA's in a group like this.

I said, "Not quite sure. I can't think straight with Bobby staring at me like a lord surveying his fiefdom. Everything feels odd. It's like there's this doomy glow starting to seep out of the particles of time and matter that surround me. I'm not sure why I'm here or anywhere else. I thought I was at the Tampa Theatre or The Exit."

Octavia cleared her throat. "You're at The Exit and you're doing that space cadet thing again. Are you dreaming of Altamont again? Lol!" Behind her, The Exit came back into focus.

CHAPTER SIX

DISCHISM PROGRESSING

I said, "Nah, this time I'm dreaming of the other death knell. Haha! The cloister bell is ringing and I feel like I remember Bobby."

Oct said, "Duderoo, vibezzzzzz are fucking real. Sometimezzzzz. Like, I feel this off-ness you feel. But it's hazy and just out of reach. That Bobby character is like the off-ness monster."

Octavia smiled and leaned on my shoulder as the ever-rowdy patrons of The Exit twirled and flailed to the raucous music vibrating the tobacco smoke-filled space.

Newsom jumped in front of us and showed off the five shots balanced in her hands. "Here," she yelled. She spasmodically tapdanced. Tappity-tap-tap-tap-tap-TAP-TAP-tap-tap-TAP!!!!! She kicked Bobby and passed us a shot. "Bottoms up." "What's this?" I asked. "Gasoline," she said, and tossed hers back with a cough. Octavia shrugged and downed hers. I threw back my head and attempted to slew the contents of the small glass over my shoulder, but it all ran down the back of my neck and trickled under my shirt.

"Echo!" yelled Octavia, "that's my favorite *Satanic Panic and the Very Special Episodes* shirt! You ruin or lose every piece of clothing you steal from me."

"No I don't," I said.

"Oh yeah, then where's my green cargo jacket you always wear?"

"I know where it is...I just haven't looked for it yet. I'll find it."

"Lies," Octavia said and chuckled. "You are not good at finding shit. Your spatial awareness is non-existent. When I put the umbrella in the corner of the laundry room—by the way, it's been in that same spot for over a year— it ceases to exist for you."

Echo said, "Maybe it has something to do with how I perceive time."

"This again." She shook her head.

"How do you perceive time?" Newsom asked.

"I don't know," I shrugged my shoulders. "I guess I perceive events out of sequence like I'm falling in and out of orthogonal time, which has something to do with a kind of time that moves at right angles. It's kinda like a type of timewaveparticle. Orthogonal time tickles the fabric of whatever actuality you happen to be tapped into and then it slides sideways through your personal actuality's linear time. And if you're hep to the indie lit fantasy experience you can float to the hermetic precipice and the ride the timewaveparticles like an surfboard in and out, to and fro, up and down, weast and snourth, zipple and dipple of your linear nodal point into nonlinearity. Nonlinearity is where corners don't exist."

Octavia chuckled. "Really? Orthogonal time? That's why you have trouble locating the umbrella?"

I said, "Sometimes."

The crowd next to us cheered. Tony's five finger fillet concluded. He stood and pumped his fists in the air. One fist clutched the knife, a shard of mirror with a brass handle. The other fist was covered in filleted flesh and deep crimson blood. He pumped his fists once more and blood splattered all over the crowd.

Tony yelled, "Weren't you going to provide me with your keen necromancing skills? I needed a necromancer, like, yesterday. I feel like a goat who's walked five days to scale a mountain for a lick of salt."

Bobby slapped his hands together, so loudly that the bar stopped.

Even the music stopped. A record did not scratch.

Bobby gave a few forceful backhanded waves to the patrons and said, "Go back to your gorgeous lives people."

Bobby clapped again, the music kicked back on, and everybody went back to their gorgeous lives. "Okay, friends, comrades, gravy slingers, abstract painters, pizza pie admirers, hat makers, science fiction authors, literary fiction authors, dissenters of the state corporate nexus, former build-a-bear employees, music snobs, music lovers who are not snobs, critical thinkers, movie buffs, skeptics, moral realists, surrealists, anti-realists, people who frequent nude beaches, prescriptivists, descriptivists, architects of the nested pataprogram, gourmet chefs, god-awful cooks, Rocco Atleby fanatics, Greg Kindred fanatics, non-intense sports lovers, hard science fiction fans who are not too vocal about it, and everyone else – let's break and try to get some high balls from Ruby."

"Ugh," Newsom said. "Ruby's working tonight? That man doesn't know how to pour a drink."

"Hey, shut up! Yes, I do!" Ruby, from across the room, was shaking his fist at us and making that terrible squinty, frowny face he always makes when anyone speaks hard truths.

"How the hell did he hear that from over there?" asked Octavia. "I was blessed with the hearing of a greater wax moth," yelled Ruby. "What the hell did he say?" said Tony.

"I guess moths have insanely good hearing," I said and my head went fuzzy. The powder consumption, that blessed debauchery, happening all the way in Paris, collided with my Tampa self.

"The best!" screamed Ruby.

"Listen," said Bobby, "When Ruby finishes making that drink for the woman in the black leather cowboy outfit let's reconvene in the bathroom for a little necromancy."

The tentacles released Bobby and they reared their gnashing lamprey heads in my direction. In one swift, uncanny motion, they shot at me. I dropped to The Exit's broken glass piss floor. Flynn followed suit. He dropped next to me onto the apartment's carpet and drew his knees into his chest.

He said to me, "Like this my friend. Become like a rock."

I listened and went fetal.

On the TV, the close-up of The Exit's broken glass piss floor slooooooowly cross-faded to an extreme close-up of Rocco's face. He winked at the camera and took a shot of tequila.

He said, "Flip a penny into the glass piss stew and the Muses of Orion will bless you with a story that will live forever into the unanimous night of everyone's every tomorrow."

Flynn said, "We came here to explore Rocco's stomping grounds. Remember? The French psychedelic fiction community pulled him out of obscurity in the early seventies. They grew to love his work along with the work of many other new-wave psychedelic fiction authors. We came here to fanboy around Paris. We hitched a ride with *this* frenzy in order to do that." He gestured at Bobby, Newsom, Will, and Ruby.

I said, "We never said we weren't going to consume gobs and gobs o' bookpowder. Gobs and gobs, yo. That's part of the experience."

Flynn said, "Yes, but you must also *have* the indie lit fantasy experience. The experience is, like, 80 percent of the experience."

This dialogue exchange was happening in tandem with the dialogue exchange in the Rocco doc between Rocco and his close friend, writer, and landlord, Edmond Edmond.

I thought about questioning this actuality-incongruity but decided against it. bookpowder is powerful and I thought bringing up this incongruity happening between us and the TV would cause the rest of my reality to unravel rapidly.

I flipped the TV's dial and changed the channel. A close-up of Holger Chase's wailing face stretched across the glass. The camera zoomed out and revealed him on stage with his band, *Fat Tornado Clocks*.

Ruby flipped the channel back to the Rocco doc. On the TV, Rocco rubbed Edmond Edmond's knee and said, "Maybe we should cut you off, buddy."

He changed the channel back to the concert. A caption rolled across the bottom of the screen exclaiming this was LIVE from the

Paris Gravy Fest.

Flynn jumped to his feet and kicked me. "This is two blocks away! Come on!"

"This synchronicity is unreal," I said.

Holger, that charming devil, almost seemed to wince and cringe at certain parts of *Drains, We Wrote.*

As he sang

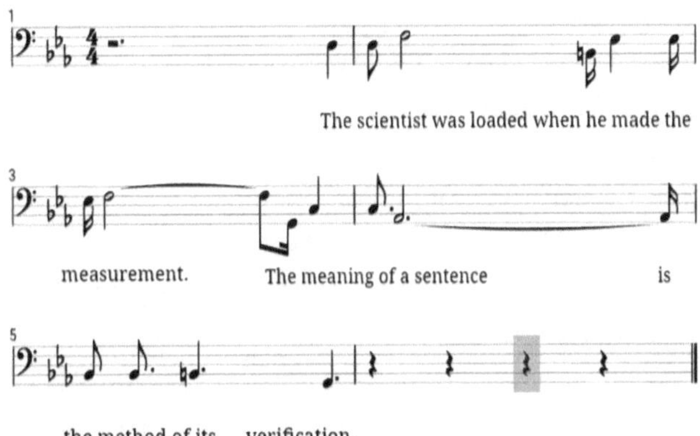

he ripped the guitar away from his body and stopped playing as the band roared on without him. He arched forward, almost gollum-like, and waggled his finger in the air as he sang,

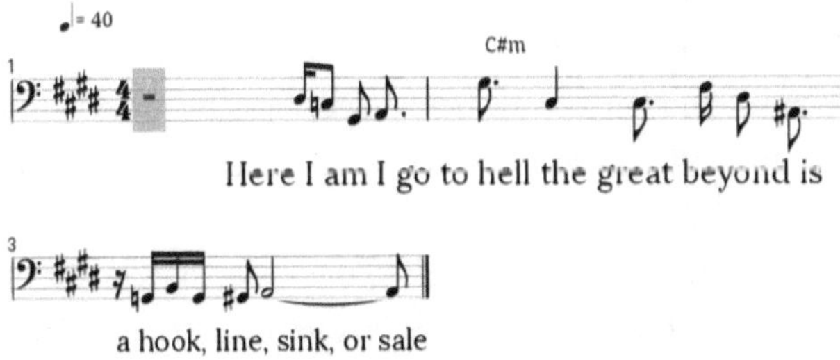

He flipped his guitar around so that its back was facing a massive audience surrounding the Arc de Triomphe, and pretended to strum the teal face of his guitar's reverse side.

I imagined this erratic body language was not a part of his tortured soul persona, but a product of very real PTSD garnered from playing such a personal song over and over every night for months. He ripped the guitar away from his body again like he was repulsed by it. He waggled his finger again, but not like he was sassy, more like he was shaming the song for torturing him for so many years.

I tensed and readied my body for another kick from Flynn, but when I looked away from the TV he was gone. I looked back at Holger's wincing face. The camera zoomed out and turned to face the crowd. Flynn appeared in the front row.

"How the hell," Newsom yelled, "did Flynn make it to the front row? There's got to be thousands in that crowd."

Will rolled out of his bed and leaned over the balcony. "That's his style. He's a sneaky little bastard.."

"Jesus Christ, when did you get up there?" I said to Will.

"When I decided I needed to sleep off those 12 mugs of bookpowder," he drawled.

Ruby crawled out from under Bobby's bed and hung his head over the side of the loft.

I shook my head at him. "What's your excuse?"

Ruby said, "I took the other half."

Fat Tornado Clocks smashed their instruments to bits on screen. Holger scraped his guitar across the stage, jumped onto the microphone, and crashed backward into the drum set while wailing, "Who holds the keys to the kingdom? Tell me that fucker's name!"

I poured another cup of bookpowder tea for myself from the pitcher on the coffee table and casually ignored the crushed cigarette butts floating in the amber novel water.

Bobby flipped the channel back to the Rocco doc. It was the part where the info-spitting celluloid really goes off the rails. From here the doc morphs into an unending series of batshit choices made by the director, editor, and producers. In this batshit introduction scene, Rocco is in the middle of an interview. The interviewer is mid-question "When it comes to form, Rocco, you seem to-" and boom! he cuts the interviewer off and says "-randomly pull out your theremin and teach the interviewer how to play it? Why yes I do." Then, Rocco, in a docutainment scene as iconic as any scene from *Grey Gardens*, *Hearts of Darkness*, *The Satanic Panic Story of the Very Special Episodes*, or *Don't Look Back*, Rocco whips out his theremin and teaches the interviewer how to play. The static shot of Rocco playing and talking about the theremin is held for well over twenty minutes and behind the camera you hear the interviewer lose all interest in moderating or keeping the interview on track. The interviewer actually gets lost in Rocco's impromptu theremin lesson and at one point takes the instrument from Rocco and starts playing it.

Not looking away from the Rocco doc, I crawled across the carpet to our tiny fridge which we had moved to the living room for easier access. I grabbed a tall boy, a sexy French tall boy named Bière, and cracked it open as I plopped onto the couch next to Newsom and Bobby.

Newsom jumped off the couch. "It feels like my skeleton wants to leap out of my skin." She ran up the stairs and dove off the balcony onto the couch, nearly bouncing me and Bobby onto the carpet.

"I've found a way to travel to other dimensions of the Patasphere," Rocco said from his busking corner of Rue de Charonne to a pedestrian. The shot looked like it was taken by a person who did not want Rocco to know they were filming him. Kind of voyeurish looking.

"This book I found gives instructions on the methods of reality transcendence."

The pedestrian simply nodded his head and smiled, like he did not understand a word Rocco Atleby was saying.

Will yelled from above, "He fucked with reality to find his sweetheart."

Bobby grabbed a priceless bust of famous writer Edmond Edmond from the table next to the couch and chucked it at Will's head.

Will ducked and the bust shattered against the wall behind Will's bed.

"Shut up and pay attention," Bobby said.

"The fuck, man?" Will said.

Newsom jumped off the couch and flipped the TV dial. "I forgot how boring and artsy this movie gets."

The tube flickered with the static of the big bang and returned to a close-up of Holger's face in permanent wail. The camera zoomed out. He was on his back, on top of the mountain of broken instruments with the microphone shoved in his mouth. His bandmates were pummeling the living shit out of the stage. Members of the audience were climbing over security guards to join the band on stage. Fat Tornado Clocks' set had devolved into a fluctuation set. "And the whole world is invited," Holger screamed, after finally breaking from the sustained wail.

Ruby suddenly landed on the floor in front of the couch and the snapping of both legs echoed across the common room.

Without acknowledging what had to have been immense pain, he said, "This is history-making stuff," and crawled away, presumably to the fest.

"But didn't you just break your legs?" I called after him.

Will followed, casually walking down the stairs and not saying a word about it.

On the TV, I watched as Flynn abruptly fled the front row, fled the crowd, and fled past the outskirts of the screen, where I could have sworn I saw his tiny televised self turn and wave just before his exit.

CHAPTER SEVEN

GRUBBY APARTMENT

More audience members jumped onto the stage. They had knocked over the barricades after the security guards had either fled or ripped off their jackets and joined the crowd.

Text rolled across the bottom of the TV and explained the audience was not subsiding, it was growing. The police couldn't get into the fest. Too many people. It was at least ten thousand strong now. More instruments and amps were suddenly appearing on stage as it was speculated that the people joining the mass were sneaking their own guitars and basses and amps and drums and keyboards, and glockenspiels through the crowd. It was speculated that people had formed vast and expansive hand-off chains that lead from the entrance of the fest to the stage.

I jumped off the couch and flipped back to *How to Play a Necromancer's Theremin*. Displayed on the tube was Rocco in his Humboldt Park apartment. He was type, type, typing away on his signature turmeric yellow Hauser 30 typewriter while smoking a pipe, probably filled with bookpowder-laced tobacco.

Rocco's voice with accompanying pops and hisses, probably recorded at home on a reel-to-reel, rose over the footage like a ghost.

"Bring your pen and notebook everywhere," his voice crackled. "Write through your fear of writing down something totally ridiculous. Write as if the whole world is going to read your words. Write as if no one will ever read what you've written. And bring your tools everywhere. To the park, to work, to your favorite soft-shell crab diner in Florida, to the baseball game," he raised a fist, "go Cubbies. To the movies, to the toilet, to your uncle's birthday party that your loved ones literally had to drag you to, to your own damn funeral."

Bobby hopped off the couch and crawled under it. He emerged with two jars. Each jar contained a spider. He opened both jars and dumped one spider into the other's home. He closed the jar, shook it, and sat there like a child on the carpet, watching the spiders battle each other in his little glass thunderdome.

Bobby cut the bookpowder on the sink counter and poured a pile for each of us. The pumping club music, a sharp and suspect deviation in atmosphere and spirit that was usually less oomph-oomph-oomph and more raucous clanging and fuzzing, bled into the bathroom and resonated like an upper-level of reality invading a nightmare. This intrusion reminded me that we had delved even deeper into a treacherous and possibly duplicitous dominion.

Ruby, now behind the small bar set into the bathroom wall next to the sink, prepared our drinks.

"That cannot be sanitary," said Octavia.

Bobby shrugged and ordered an amaretto sour.

"When was this installed?" I asked. "I was here like a week ago and this bar wasn't here. And when the hell did you move from the main bar to the bathroom bar, Ruby? Did you follow us?"

Ruby slapped the bartop. "I'm playing the role of Bobby's entourage's personal bartender. Leave me alone."

"No," I said. "You can't do that. You can't just insert yourself as a supporting character. Flynn and I are the authors here, so fuck off."

Flynn, from the void, said, *"Echo what are you talking about? You're starting to worry me. Can you leave Ruby alone? He clearly has no intention of being an energy vampire, just ignore him."*

"Excuse me gleeking dismal-dreaming clotpoles, are you guys done doing your literature? I need to wash my hands," said a lanky guy in suspenders.

Tony hissed at him, spraying spit all over the guy's face.

"What do you think this is, a bathroom?" asked Newsom. "She lifted herself onto the counter, sat in the sink, pulled out her phone, and racked up another line on the screen."

Still sprinkled with leftover book powder, Newsom pulled up a short clip from a documentary about the McLarron brothers, Donald and Terry, who in the mid-eighties followed Rocco Atleby's path around the globe to find an ancient text. She had pulled up the part where they had established a camp in the dense jungle of La Chorrera.

While swatting massive flying insects out of his face, Donald said, "Some believe that the book's pages were dried and then pulverized into a powder that has powerful mind-altering properties similar to DMT, but many will dispute this theory and say that any bookpowder you buy off the streets is actually goobercleve. For those of you who don't know what goobercleve is, it's a poisonous powder made from the panacea flower. And for those of you who do know what daterio is, I'm sorry for this explanation. If you take daterio in low doses it won't kill you and will present you with the magical gifts of temporary psychosis and incredibly vivid hallucinations."

While kicking away a creature below the frame and completely off camera, Terry said, "If the powder is in fact book powder, myths say you will imbibe the secrets of the book and your perspective of the universe will be forever changed. It is said to be derived from an ancient book that Rocco Atleby roamed the globe to find, one that consumed him and drove him to insanity when he read it. Some people believe the book gave instructions on how to tap into the spooky action of the Patasphere. Are you eating my goddamn hawt pocket, you little shit?"

As a tentacle revealed itself from behind Donald's back and wrapped itself around his throat he said, "There are skeptics who say if the book does exist, its pages are simply made of some forgotten and incredibly potent hallucinogen and its not actually a pandimensional travel manual."

"What travel manual?" Echo said, standing under the Tampa Theatre awning with his hands in his pockets and unable to remember how or when he'd exited the theatre and took this position under the bright bulbs.

For a brief moment, he could've sworn he'd been watching a video on a phone in the bathroom of the crusty punk bar a block away and not on the sidewalk outside of this old movie palace.

While Echo stared at the bulbs above and he neglected to look any further into this actuality breakdown, he could have sworn he heard the bulbs ticking. They slowly spun clockwise in stopmotion, and the longer Echo stared into their nebulous and ethereal bioluminescence, the more he could have sworn they weren't bulbs at all, but spheres made of golden spirals.

"Fat tornado clocks," Donald and I simultaneously whispered.

Staring at the tentacle around Donald's neck Terry said, "I don't know what to believe. I probably don't believe the reality-bending stuff. I believe the hallucinogenic pages thing more, but I'm not sure about that either."

"Where this information originated is untraceable," Donald said, the tentacle tickling his throat, "We're here in the jungle of La Chorrera in search of the source. Scholars say Rocco himself started these rumors after he lost his mind. Others believe that it was his colleague, Mr. Autumn Levi. But according to my sources, Rocco was obsessed with creating a mythos surrounding himself."

Terry said, "By the way, if you want more in-depth information on everything we're talking about, read Levi's book, *A Nonlinear History of Nonlinear Systems: My Friendship With Rocco Atleby*. He really gives reality a good dicking down in that book."

Donald said, "We wish we could tell you more, but…." The tentacle tightened its grip on Donald's neck and Donald's eyes bulged in their sockets. Gagging, he struggled to say, "I am not at liberty to tell you, mostly because of…" He gasped for breath. "You know what, I'm not going to say anymore."

Ignoring his brother, who was desperately tugging at the tentacle around his neck, Terry said, "What is the name of this mystical book that sent Rocco on a global scavenger hunt? Some say this ancient book is titled *The Unfashionable Western Spiral*. They say it's why Rocco carved spirals all over his long lost steamer trunk desk, scribbled them all over his journal entries, and even carved them into the walls of his house."

Donald said, "And all of this could be disinformation, no one can say for sure what's real and what's not...At least that's what some sources would like me to tell anyone who's listening." Donald stifled and gagged as the tentacle squeezed. "Guy Debord said something about..." he pulled at the tentacle, which only tightened its grip. "Could you ease up just a little?" The tentacle eased its grip. "I can't tell you everything, but I can tell you that Guy Debord said the real world would change into simple images and then those simple images would become real beings with effective motivations of..." The tentacle squeezed again. "...hyp...notic...behavior. Some may take this as a prediction for the overarching eristic analytical overlay servomechanisms and the new scripturez, but know that repetitive imagery has a way of...revealing things just beyond this layer. Imagine planes of good infected with little nuggets of bad and planes of bad infected with little nuggets of good. It's like the powers-that-be constructed the noosphere to be contradictory on purpose. I mean, the noosphere is probably contradictory by nature. The kind of contradiction I'm talking about is beyond contradiction. It's that servomechanism I was talking about. It's like the PTB weaponized the tao and wuwei." The tentacle re-tightened its grip and Donald struggled off-camera.

Terry said, "Now I have before me a section of *The Unfashionable Western Spiral*. Some say it's the introduction to the book. It's called *The Astonishing Reversal of Normal Practice.*

Donald, stretching his neck to re-insert himself in the frame interjected, "Nope. Nope. Totally bullshit. I'm calling bullshit right here. I know what you're about to quote. That's not the real opener of the book. First of all, it's written in modern English with vernacular from the 20th century. There's references to goth counterculture, Thom Yorke...not to mention all the technology… chainsaws, motor vehicles, I mean the text takes place in a suburb! Second of all, Holger and Marcel first showed up in that story you found on the microfiche containing a copy of that magazine, *Füd For Unreality Quarterly.*

"I know, *The Unfashionable Western Spiral* was supposedly written in the middle ages. So, you know, there's some glaring anachronisms happening there, but I still believe that it is the introduction to *The Unfashionable Western Spiral*. Clearly, it's prophetic, written by some sort of Nostradamus."

I looked up at Newsom from the screen and said, "Talk about anachronisms. This film was supposedly shot in the sixties, but there's references to the modern internet and Thom Yorke. Who was an infant in '68."

"Yeah, so?" Newsom said.

I looked at the screen to absorb the rest of the video, but she self-consciously shut off the screen and slipped the GSN, also known as a Grand Sweeping Narrative brand skin, into her pocket.

"Hey," I said. "Turn it back on. I wanna watch the rest. I was getting into it."

Newsom rolled her eyes, pulled her skim back out of her pocket, opened the screen, and pressed play.

CHAPTER EIGHT

FALSE INTERIORIZATION

"Can you deal with that...situation somewhere else, Don?" Terry said, gesturing at the tentacle and unconcerned with his brother's lack of oxygen, "I'm trying to read the introduction of the world's most elusive book here." He cleared his throat and began. "Holger spun on his heel and stopped in the direction of the arched wooden door leading out into the windy field of tall grass. He'd been here before, in this monastery, doing the same exact heel spin, but he couldn't remember when. Holger couldn't even remember how he had gotten there.

"The phantosmia of Stetson leather wafted before Holger's nose, an off-kilter mix of milk, fish, sulfur, and laundry exhaust from outer dryer vents clogged with lint. This cocktail of smells reminded him of his childhood neighborhood.

"Holger took one last look at the manor's interior, at the ornately carved wood surfaces and the statues of creatures he didn't recognize – creatures that could've come from a book of fairy tales -- and he spun on his heel again.

"He stopped and found himself pointing at a doorway. It was a doorway that could've sat indiscriminately wedged in the drywall of any suburban home.

"Holger stepped over the threshold of the doorway and entered the suburb.

"As he strolled away from Marcel's house down the sidewalk staring at the contraction joints that cut the concrete slab into squares, Holger imagined himself as a piece in an oversized board game.

"Like in a self-aware dream, he realized he had already aged past childhood, but here he was, in his fleshy, corporeal child-like form. This is how he remembered remembering… his headspace, his thoughts, and feelings, his memories of his memories.

"Holger took a deep breath, a large gulp of milk, fish, sulfur, and laundry exhaust, and headed back to Grandma Vern's house where he would sit and wait for her to return.

"Scout and the rest of the many children of Edmond Edmond catch up to him. Sap and Billy snatch his arms and hold him back, readying him for their grand leader's punch to the gut.

""Don't move impertinent sallow -rotten gorecleaner," Sap said.

"Holger sighed and rolled his eyes. "This is like the twentieth time you've played this game today. It's getting really old. Like, the first two times were funny. Third through seventh times were annoying. Eighth through fifteenth kinda made me chuckle. Sixteenth through eighteenth were so funny that I thought I was going to piss myself, especially because you guys were somehow replicating the body movements and vocal intonations from the previous recreations to a tee. These last two times were lacking though. You guys lost your pizzazz."

"Marion asked, "You've been counting?"

"Skip and Dotty parted, and Scout marched through them, his angry face a growing oval in Holger's field of vision. Scout removed his hands from behind his back and showed Holger a pocket knife. As he opened it, the sun reflected off the sharp weapon into Holger's chlorine-saturated bloodshot eyes.

"An old man sat on his porch across the street from Vern's and cackled as he watched the blade graze Holger's eyelashes.

"The man reached into his pocket, retrieved a large battery, and threw it at Holger's face. He missed, but Holger still felt his pride get bashed by the D battery.

"I'm going to get that devil out of you," Scout said, holding the knife to Holger's eye.

"Holger closed the threatened left eye, and a couple moments later closed the right eye too, like an iguana hoping it would be left alone if it ignored what was pestering it. His eyes shut in a glitchy, nystagmus blink, the memory of the manor's interior fading fast. With this blade next to his eye absorbing all of his attention, Holger knew that by the time their game was over he would have forgotten all about the doorways and that other life, and the fact that he had done all of this before.

"Holger felt as though he would never be able to open his eyes once the affair had ended, but there was hope sparking in the background of his signal machine, just behind the fear of Scout's blade and question of his eyelid's new possible fixture and dysfunction.

"Please don't hurt me," Holger said.

"A group of edgy Tampa goths moping down Fennsbury Lane took no notice of the altercation.

"Scout didn't stab Holger in the left eye. Blood didn't spurt onto their faces while Scout screamed at everyone present. Then he didn't then stab Holger in the right eye, just for good measure.

"Holger imagined all of that happening. He finally cracked and laughed at the game devised by Scout and company. Scout and company laughed too, as children often do in the visage of violence. Sap and Billy released Holger from their sweaty grip and scurried away, heading west down Fennsbury past the edgy Tampa goths. Susy, Dixon, and Marion followed, leaving behind a plume of dust.

"The concrete square below them dropped and Holger, slipping from Scout's grip, fell into a swimming pool. Scout remained on the surface as if standing on a sheet of glass that had simply absorbed Holger by osmosis. He peered at the shimmering surface getting farther away as he sunk to the floor of the pool and watched the tiny mandelbulbs rise. Holger imagined he was sinking inside a giant glass of soda.

"Holger landed in the lotus position. The chlorine felt good on his corneas, and he let himself sit there for a moment and enjoy the muffled glug-glugging of air slipping out of his lungs. The pool floor stretched away from him and bowed upward like a ghost-white photography background, the kind of superpositionwhite that induces vertigo.

"Unwillingly, Holger slowly rose out of the water and strained when the warm, thick air hit his skin. He grabbed the edge of the sidewalk and pulled himself out of the pool. He collapsed and landed on top of the contraction joint, his hip crossing the groove between the squares, two squares over from Grandma Vern's house.

"Maybe this isn't normal," thought Holger. Maybe reality doesn't work this way. The thoughts leaked out of his skull as quickly as they had slunk in, returning to a plane of existence that is not so much another plane as it is all planes at once.

"Scout stood over Holger, letting out one long sustained scream at Holger's soaking wet body. The puddle of water surrounding Holger's limp body grew and connected with Scout's shoes. Holger imagined the cameraman of a classic horror film taping the shot in black and white, so the water looked like blood.

"Scout's scream morphed into a guttural noise that wavered, tapering off as he sprinted after Susy, Dixon, and Marion's dust cloud, which was swirling into a spiral that appeared to be gaining the momentum of a storm.

"A shadow grew over Holger's body. Vern bent over and grasped the homunculus by the armpit, heaving him to his feet and walking him to her house with a small smile on her face.

"Holger had no idea who this woman was, but he knew he had met her before.

"There was nothing inside the house. No chairs, no tables, no couches, no television, no beds, and no kitchen cabinets, only the clean, white spaces where cabinets should be. Vern set him on the tile floor. In the kitchen, she pretended to pour herself a glass of red wine and sipped on the nonexistent fermented juice.

"Holger giggled to himself, eyes closed, his front teeth peeking out of his slightly open mouth. He imagined he was asleep, and dreaming about gorgeous artwork that should have been hanging from these walls.

"The tiles shattered beneath Holger's limp body, which had just crossed over into his REM cycle, and Bermuda grass popped through the cracks. Vern's house crumbled to the ground. The rubble popped into the dirt and the reconstructed house spontaneously shot out of the ground twenty feet behind Holger's sleeping form.

"He slept with his arms wrapped around a stolen chainsaw. Light cut through the empty space in the sky, where a mighty oak once stood, hitting the boy and the grass and the fallen chunks of the tree that littered the yard with hard, neoclassical edges. All forms and materializations surrounding him were cut, nipped, and hewed with a brush that was connected to a master painter brimming with the passion of a paint-thinner-induced stupor.

"Holger woke and inspected the idle chainsaw with compost crusted in his eyes. Somehow he had fallen asleep in Vern's empty flower bed again.

"After wiping away the fertile soil and removing a pebble from the corner of his eye, he stood and clomped over the moist grass through the shrubs of his best friend Marcel's side yard, slashing wildly like his appendages were built-in machetes.

"Marcel sat in his yard with a Bell and Howell 16MM projector in his lap. He was watching the final scene of the classic film, *D.P. Delemore Goes to Aurora,* starring a guy who looked like a young Gary Oldman. He had connected enough extension cords to rig the machine outside and project it onto the back of his house.

"The credits rolled, and Marcel took Holger by the hand and walked his friend to the front door. Marcel's gabby, excitable parents were in their breakfast nook, both Mom and Dad screaming so loudly that Holger swore the high-pitched double-toned parental pandemonium crossed an irreversible decibel threshold.

"As Holger and Marcel stood in front of the table, mouths agape, Mom grabbed the mustard and ketchup and Dad grabbed the mayo and butter, all four condiments in squeeze-top bottles, and squeezed the ever-loving hell out of the bottles as they continued to scream in joy at each other – the vintage yellow, the B-rated horror-esque chunky blood red, the off white, and the creamed corn yellow sprayed like one part string theory confetti and one part edible fireworks all over the nook.

"For a moment, Holger swore he heard a voice not his own, narrating the events unfolding before him, and when he detached himself from the immediate chaos before him, he heard yet another voice behind the mysterious shadow voice.

"But like floaters in your peripheral vision, as soon as he tried to zero in on the voices, they disappeared. And a skim, attached to Marcel's impatiently waving hand, appeared in his field of vision. On the smartphone's screen was a video of an animator's rendering of proton collision tracks inside the world's largest particle accelerator.

"Holger pushed the phone out of his face. "Why are you showing me any of this?"

"Marcel placed his phone on the table and smeared butter all over the screen. "See?" He said, nodding. "Eat."

"What the actual hell?" Holger said. "Is everybody on cough syrup?"

"Vern, in her empty kitchen, sipped her pretend wine and shook her head at Holger from across the room. She laughed with a snort, waking Holger with a jolt. "You were talking in your sleep, Holger.

Remembering the chainsaw from his dream, he jumped to his feet and ran past Vern out of the side door.

"If you and your friends make me play that damn pocket knife game one more time today," Vern yelled after the little lord, "I won't let you fill this house with your homemade furniture."

"Holger suddenly found himself standing on Vern's easement holding the chainsaw. The incongruity of the sequence of events didn't phase Holger, and without wondering where the chainsaw came from, he ripped its cord with a roar and wielded the machine at a crowd of neighbors who had lined up across the street.

"They cheered.

"That's our homunculus!" the old man who'd thrown the D battery at him said. He cackled, pulled another D battery from his pocket, and threw it. He missed again. Holger took no notice and smiled proudly, waving the chainsaw at his people. He revved it.

"You the man, Holger!" Ms. Dempsey yelled through cupped hands.

"Fuck Edmond Edmond. That's your chainsaw, Holger!" Vincent shouted.

"Build the furniture! Build the furniture! Build the furniture!" the residents of Fennsbury Lane chanted.

"He spent the rest of the day hacking the chunks of oak tree in the yard into smaller chunks and nailing them to the other chunks. The furniture looked less like a couch, dining room table, and bed, and more like minimalist lawn sculptures that belonged in an art show titled 'Heavily Focused On Reusing the Bounties of the Earth.'

"One by one, the neighbors returned to their homes. They returned to their Wheel of Fortune, and cats, and oatmeal, and croquet sets collecting dust in their foyer closets. They grew tired and fell asleep at the same exact time, 7:30 pm. That is how Holger liked the game to be played.

"Edmond Edmond, his adjacent neighbor, and reclusive Intercede Network founder pulled into his driveway. He stepped out of the car and took a deep breath with a hopeful smile on his face as he scanned the neighborhood, the neighborhood he believed that he and he alone lorded over. Ed took a sip of his cherry soda and from over the edge of the can, noticed Holger screwing around with his beloved chainsaw. Ed spat his pop and darted across the property line into Holger's front yard.

"Holger," Ed says. "What are you doing with my chainsaw?"

"Holger laughed. "Can I pretend to chase you with it?"

"Is this a variation of the pocket knife game?"

"Of course."

"Ed spun around, his back now facing the little lord.

"Holger revved the chainsaw. Ed slowly turned his head, pantomiming a scared Homer Simpson.

"Holger showed his teeth through a now forced angry red face.

The boy hyperventilated as he wobbled back and forth while swinging the chainsaw.

"Mr. Andrews held up his hands in surrender. "Easy there. Put it down."

"Holger screamed as he revved the saw once more. "A little too real for you, Mr. Edmond?"

"Now I am Rocco Atleby, actuality contorts and shifts with barely a transition, at the entrance of the Laurel Street Bridge, as passersby prattled on about the rotten archetype of the week and nervously fidgeted in their pockets, I jangled the game tokens in my coat pockets. I was fidgety and anxious because I was annoyed that this foot soldier of The Geist, a fucking narc, was holding me up. How am I seeing this tale?

"Holger heard a voice. "What a journey this has been. It's one narc after the next. These narcs keep approaching me and asking if I needed an archetypal old man in my life. What happened, by the way? Why did we stop using the word narc? Do we think narcs don't exist? And that there's no such thing as psy-ops? And that people from the bad side are unable to pose as a member of your good side? Why are all of us so nervous about admitting that psy-ops are real? Do all of us believe that psy-ops conspiracy fuckery is equal to lizard people and nanobot vaccines? The GSN blasted its classic rotten archetype, fnordz, holo-multigraphic interfacing proscenium arch eristic analytical overlays. On the screen above the Laurel Street Bridge rotten archetype Edmond Edmond said, "I want to tell every interfacer and interceder that lost a pun, I'm sorry but that glitches and twitches increase tenfold. I swear to God glitches and twitches increase tenfold."

"Holger nodded his head. "Swell."

"Holger cracked a smile and broke into laughter.

"So did Edmond Edmond.

"They weren't laughing at the absurdity of the voice telling them about the birds. They had already forgotten about the voice. They laughed because these games they played were so much fun. It's hard not to laugh.

"Mr. Andrews collected himself and cleared his throat. He let out a high-pitched scream and ran across the property line.

"Holger followed closely behind and chased the man into his garage past the empty spot above the work table where he had found the chainsaw.

"Ed screamed again. He kicked open his door and crashed into the foyer wall, knocking himself out.

"Holger halted his chase, turned off the chainsaw, and grimaced at Ed's unconscious body. He put the chainsaw back and returned to his furniture building outside.

"Holger didn't know if what happened to Ed was a real reaction or if it was part of the game. Holger was unsure if he was doing any of this of his own volition or if he was being guided by some outside force. Holger's thoughts about free will disappeared as he nailed a particularly gnarly knot of wood onto the seat of a particularly uncomfortable chair.

"As Holger hammered the last nail into the chunks of wood representing a TV stand, Ed's shadow cascaded over the boy.

"I was only pretending to be unconscious." Ed said.

"I know."

"Ed and Holger spent the rest of the evening carrying Holger's art into Ed and Vern's houses. They set the bed where the TV stand should've gone in Vern's living room. They set the piece that looked just like a toilet in the middle of Ed's bedroom. The dining room table went in Vern's room.

"The moonlight splashing through the sliding glass doors of the southwestern ranch style house gave his sharp wooden creations the soft edges of an impressionist painting." the shadow voices narrated to Holger."

Newsom's phone shut off, at the end of its battery life.

We all blinked out of our book powder-induced stupor. A crowd had gathered in the bathroom, watching the documentary clip with us while they waited in line for the toilet or a drink from Ruby.

"You guys are providing some quality entertainment, but you're really starting to hinder the flow in here, guys," said Ruby. "That video was like 20 minutes long, it's getting really crowded and sweaty in here."

We all ignored Ruby.

"There's no way the mind-altering secrets of the universe lie in the tale of Holger and his shitty lawn furniture," said Newsom.

"You know," I said, "That might not be from *The Unfashionable Western Spiral*, but it sounds familiar. Does anyone know what book it is from?

"Some people say it's from Rocco's cipher of *The Unfashionable Western Spiral*. Just before his copy of The UWS was destroyed in that mysterious fire that he predicted would happen, he turned it into the cipher book. What did he call that book?" said Octavia.

I said, "The Unabridged Exegesis, right?"

"No," Octavia said. "You see, this is what I love about late-career Rocco. It is so damned intentionally convoluted that it's fun. Too many critics classified late-career Rocco books as encyclopedic, but I would've called them puzzleboxes."

"What was the cipher book called?" Ruby asked.

All of us shouted at Ruby, "Ruby, shut the hell up!"

"It never had an official name," Octavia said, "and it was never published. He kept all fifty-two thousand pages of this cipher in a box in his steamer trunk desk until he died. Ooh, I wish I could remember what he called it. After he completed the cipher, he wrote that meta book about turning The UWS into a cipher after predicting that fire that would consume The UWS. Remember? It was posthumously released under the title *Prima Matia and the Golden Tablet*."

"That's horseshit," said Bobby. "Everyone knows that Rocco's coded version is an improv comedy manual. Besides, Terry couldn't have read something of Rocco's before it was written."

"How do you know what Terry recited isn't some unpublished introduction of the improv comedy manual? Rocco could've been using these characters as teaching vessels." I said.

Ruby chimed in, "After the fire prediction, did he turn The UWS into this comedy cipher book because he, like, believed that the original version was so dangerous it would cause fires but he still wanted a copy of the book to use for necromancy so he made this secret version that he kept locked inside his famous steamer trunk desk?"

Tony said, "And what the fuck is he trying to teach us with chainsaw games and excitable condiment squirters?"

"How to peel back and dismantle the latticework of the nested pata-programming through the contorting of reality into dream-like states," said Newsom. "I thought that was pretty obvious."

"Ruby," I said, cutting about twenty people in line. "Make me a drink that will cause most of my vital organs to fail at once."

"Make that two," said Octavia.

"You mean five," said Newsom.

CHAPTER NINE

THE BATHROOM SINK STORY

Ruby lined the cramped bar with our glasses and poured us a concoction that smelled like oven cleaner.

We tapped the bottoms of our glasses on the counter and chugged. It tasted delicious and I was surprised that it didn't kill me. Maybe I should stop being so hard on Ruby.

"Damn, man," Ruby said from behind the bar. "Thank you."

I said with a quick twist of my head toward Ruby, "Don't try to read my thoughts. I hate this drink. You hear me?"

"Jesus, man."

I sighed. "Sorry. It's a perfectly fine drink. Don't tell anyone I said that."

Bobby, his drink in hand swinging, dumped five sloppy piles on the sink counter and said, "Me first." He slammed his face onto the counter which was littered with wet paper towels, straws, empty tampon applicators, and loose change. He gloobled all five pilez like he was playing Hungry Hungry Hippos with himself, and a guttural sound exited his body that made my insides shrink into the hedge of my soul.

The pandimensional creature that had been trying to explode from Bobby's head all night roared. Bobby grabbed his throat, gargled the residual bookpowder, swallowed and helped it go down with a slide of his hand down his throat, GUUUULP, and the creature was pulled back into the depths into whatever Bobby's version of the hedge of his soul was — probably that one poisonous tree you can find in Florida or the Caribbean that kills you if you breathe too close to it.

What's the name of the tree?

"I don't know, I don't exactly have access to Google from the void. And we don't need the name of the tree."

Yes, we do. This shit is wild.

"Hey, I pulled it up," Octavia said in the middle of the bathroom. "It's called the manchineel tree. The fruit it bears, the beach apple, will fuck you up. The Spanish called it la manzanilla de la muerte because it's believed an arrow tip dipped in the milky sap is what killed Ponce De Leon, the colonialist pig." Bobby waggled around the bathroom, hunched over to hell like a tweaking goblin, and screamed the lyrics of a spontaneously composed song he named Manchineel And Ponce. Honestly, it was quite good. The man should start a band. Bobby sloooooowly stood up straight and swiftly pumped his hammer fists.

He yowled, "I am a necromancer!"

Tony slapped himself on the forehead with his shadow tentacles. "Jesus, man. You are too much. Can you pass the revival powder? By the way, you fucking manchineel of a man. Seriously though, your vapors are fucking me up."

Newsom threw her hands into the air and twitched like the pan-dimensional creature in Bobby had just transferred into her.

Bobby poured more bookpowder on the wet sink and sucked it.

"Christ, aren't you going to share?" Newsom said.

Octavia squeezed my hand. This time it was softer and meant, "I know we're only here to observe and that you have some unfinished business with these people."

"And for the free bookpowder."

"I can quit whenever I want," I said quietly.

Newsom snatched the alms-baglet of bookpowder out of Bobby's coat pocket on one of Bobby's spastic spins like a professional pick-pocket. She poured the bookpowder onto the counter and separated it into four pilez.

"Finally," Tony said and rubbed his hands together.

She held out a welcoming hand and Tony slammed his face onto the pile.

Newsom turned to me and Octavia and invited us.

Octavia and I gave her a couple polite no-thank-you waves and she shrugged as Tony and his tentacles joined Bobby's spinning and dancing and the two men began slamming their heads into the stall.

Bobby screamed, "Everybody loves me!"

And, Tony head-butted Bobby. And, Bobby head-butted Tony and they returned to repeatedly slamming their heads into the stall in what looked like a gnostic ritual.

I averted my eyes from Bobby and Tony, afraid that my gazing and gawking would attract them and I would end up a goopy ritualistic pulp. I found Octavia crouching under the sink eating a burger. I slowly knelt, so as to not draw attention to myself, and walked like a sixteen-bit video game character avoiding giant cannonballs.

I found my new center of the Patasphere under the sink both safe and comfortable. High score. Upon closer inspection, as Octavia chomped and squelched on her greasy sandwich, I realized it was a Tulver's burger. Octavia halted her chomping and squelching to examine her burger. She smiled at it like a mother holding a newborn.

I said, "When did you get Tulver's?"

She looked at me and her eyes went wide, probably afraid that I was going to steal the rest of her sandwich.

"There's a lot of things you don't know about in my purse," she said, pulling out a bag of hot cheetos and piling some on her sandwich.

She shoved the rest of the sandwich in her mouth and said something that sounded like, "You should've brought your own, I'm not sharing with you. I will never forget the TI."

"The rapper?" Newsom asked, suddenly crouched next to us on the swampy tile.

Octavia and I jumped.

"You scared the vital organs out of me," I said.

"Not the rapper," said Octavia. "The incident."

Octavia swallowed the burger moosh, pulled a to-go cup out of nowhere, and took a sip.

"Ahhhh. Blankets and puzzle boxes on that meal," she said, "Nantucket."

"Huh?" Newsom said.

"I've learned to stop questioning the things she says," I told Newsom

Octavia slurped and chewed her straw. "So, you want to know about the legendary TI? The Tulver's Incident? So last week —"

"It was last year, Octavia," I said.

She glared at me. "Not too long ago, Echo and I were living in this apartment above a barn, which was basically an upscale barn but on the second floor, with this amazing claw foot bathtub, and anyway we were super poor and I had purchased one Tulver's burger after my late shift for us to *split* and Echo damn near ate the entire burger. He almost inhaled the entire thing in 3 seconds flat. I was absolutely starving and only got a few bites. Now I refuse to share food with him unless it[s been specifically divvied up or he lets me eat my share first."

In the other realm, the part of the bathroom that was not under the sink, Bobby and Tony repeatedly smashed their faces into the cinderblock wall. Newsom, unimpressed by the Tulver's Incident, joined them on the other side.

Octavia and I followed.

In the middle of the commotion, I said, "I'm hungry."

Octavia rummaged around for a minute and tossed me a can of clam corn chowder from her purse. Luckily it was a pop top.

Newsom slammed her anteater snout into the remaining three dust pilez that had been waiting patiently for an eldritch soul, glooble, glooble, glooble, and she blasted off into a spinning dance. Instead of joining Tony and Bobby in the concussion-inducing ritual, however, she repeatedly kicked the door of one of the bathroom stalls. The door clashed open and smashed into the wall, cracking the tiles. Our audience, crowded in the doorway, instantly dissipated. Ruby screamed at her to stop and splashed various types of liquor onto her like holy water.

Octavia and I laughed at the debacle.

I said, "We always find ourselves in situations like this."

Oct tapdanced.

I tapdanced.

Oct sang, "We get roped along as rubbernecking observers!"

I sang, "Always an adventure, baberoo!"

The tv mounted above the bathroom sink snapped on and the Rocco doc continued its assault on our actuality. Rocco waded in the swamp of the unincorporated part of Hillsborough County he owned and smiled at the camera.

He shouted at the screen, "Don't fucking write. It messes with actuality. It will make your homemade soups taste like battery acid, not that I've ever eaten a battery. I have not eaten a battery! Oh, nevermind, go ahead and write. I don't know what I'm saying. Mess with actuality. Actuality needs. Woah, sorry, I'm so stoned right now and I hate interviews. Is it obvious? That I hate interviews and that I'm blazed as a mothertrucker? My work should speak for itself, ya know-zzzzzzz. Getting to know me will tell you nothing about my work. It's like, sorry I'm so creative. And you and the rest of the oversimplified reality governed by the corporate world and stabilized by the gerrrr-rverrrrment and reinforced by the peeperz are all like, show me your fucking immutable thetan. Deez thetans be infectin shiz. And I'm like, I'm trying to be nice and tell you that maybe you have wee bit o' duh societal mutation anxiety. Like, it's gonna beeeez okayzzzz. Accelerated change always, always, always make peeperzzzz go nuts don't mind if I do lol. You're gonna beeezz okayzzzz. The whole world is like celebrity gossip newzzzzz now. And the alternative rags like Dicey News and Bad Clusters Mag are owned and operated by third party FBICIANSA entities. Those rags exist to reinforce the linguistic servomechanism. Neo-reactionarism is what happens when anti-democratic hard right narcs infiltrate the hard left, and then aggregate, proliferate, dissimilate, influence, and spread weaponized bad karma. You want advice?

Are you a narc? You have the mannerisms, tone, gait, clothing, and thoughts that I can definitely read of a fucking narc. Also, why wouldn't narcs be errrrrrweeeeeeweeeeere? LOLasaurus. Why would I not be a narc? Why would you believe something just because it sounded good? Like, why take something to be absolutely true simply because of its vervy verve? Why wouldn't some random person on the internet be a plant? You see the point I'm trying to make here?" He splashed water at the camera.

I said, "I don't remember the doc turning into Rocco's advice hour. This doesn't even sound like advice he'd give. Is that the glitchy, twitchy Rocco replicant we built way back when? His thoughts ain't organized but he's making some good points. I especially agree with the whole weaponized bad karma thing."

Bobby turned to me from his spot on the carpet and shook the spider jar at me. "I refuse to be a part of this weird game you're playing."

Newsom said, "Maybe you should take a break."

Flynn said, "Seriously," and chugged a cup of bookpowder.

"When did you get back?" I asked.

Flynn pulled down his pants, slapped his ass, pulled his pants back up, and plopped onto the Marie Antoinette couch.

Flynn propped his feet onto an imaginary desk and threw his hands behind his head. "Dude. I got out of there as soon as the concert threatened to suck me into its Katamari epicenter. Switch it to the coverage." He set his empty teacup down on a delicate little saucer whose pattern matched the couch exactly.

Bobby paid no mind to Flynn's request. Neither did Newsom. I wanted to change the channel, but I was waiting for Bobby or Newsom to act and didn't want to do that awkward thing where as soon as I stood up Bobby and Newsom would stand up to switch the channel, and then all three of us figure that one of the other two will most certainly get to the TV and then all three of us sit back down and then we stand back up in tandem and the whole sit-down-stand-up thing plays out ad infinitum. One of my biggest fears is that I will end up in a loop like this and I couldn't help but imagine a title screen that read EIGHTY YEARS LATER. Bobby, Newsom, and myself were ancient, withered, and dusty, still standing up and sitting down over and over.

CHAPTER TEN

REINVENTING THE FAT TORNADO CLOCKS

So, Flynn eventually got up and flipped the channel from Rocco, who was taking a break from giving advice to blow his nose, to Fat Tornado Clocks and a now completely filled stage. Text rolled across the bottom of the screen and explained that there were upwards of twenty thousand people and the mass was stretched beyond the fest perimeter. The fluctuation show was so loud that it could be heard across all of Paris. The resolute clatter and fuzz had been seeping into our home without us noticing it.

"Oh," I said. "That's what that screeching fluctuation is that I keep forgetting about in the background."

"Weird," Newsom said. "It kind of fades in and out of notice."

Bobby flipped the channel back to Rocco, who played the theremin with gusto. I believe it was a song of his own making.

Rocco said, "Always one for theatrics and drama, I moved back to Florida."

"Why did you move back to Florida?" the interviewer, from behind the camera, asked.

I chucked my empty shot glass at the TV behind The Exit's bar. "What megalomaniacal editor over at Criterion has butchered my favorite movie!?"

The Exit swelled like a contained tidal wave. More patrons filled in the empty spaces during our bathroom adventure. At this point, there was so much smoke, and visibility was so reduced that I was convinced some ghost pirates were going to pop out of a smoke pocket and stab me in the throat.

I considered bumming a cigarette but decided against it. I was coughing every thirty seconds and probably taking in a whole pack of second-hand cigarettes with every breath.

The fire marshal stood up and smashed his shot of Acro Iris on the ground.

"Hey, everyone!" he yelled.

"Oh god," I said. "Here we go."

"This bar is fucking over capacity!" His eyes were red and puffy from crying.

Everyone hooted and hollered at the fire marshal and he stripped off his pants and underwear, showing everyone his ass, and dick, and some ball too. In his socks and t-shirt, he ran to the exit of The Exit. The man posted at the door in his red tracksuit smacked the fire marshall's ass.

And the fire marshal scuttled off into the unanimous night.

The Exit collectively yelled, "Fond farewell! Bon voyage! Wait! Please come back! Please come back! We miss you! We miss you! We miss you!"

"I need to necromance somebody tonight," Bobby said from behind me. I turned around, but couldn't see him behind the screen of smoke.

"Echo," I heard Octavia say, "Where are you?"

I felt around, parted the clouds with my hands, and found her shoulders.

Octavia handed me an object that felt like a bowl filled with miniature versions of Fat Tornado Clocks.

She said, "Oh my gerd, they're soooo cute. They're like lil breakfast cereal nuggets."

Goddamn, they looked delicious.

I laughed.

Oct tapdanced. "Cereal, cereal, cereal, I want cereal!"

I cupped my cerealhole and hollered at the bar, "Yo, who's got some whole malk?! We gotta eat this cereal!"

Oct cupped her cerealhole and hollered, "It better be whole, bootsniffin' doonerplucks! 2 percent is acceptable though! But anything below 2 percent is coming low circuit narcs."

Tony snuck up behind us.

Oct and I jumped. "Ah!"

He said, "Sorry about that." His tentacles whipped about this way and that. 'My *Stooges* cover band is going to be performing soon and I need a drink. This round's on me."

A low voice in a hidden pocket of the smoky realm said, "These spiral spheres are fucking with my perspective."

Another low voice responded, "I heard Ruby is sandbagging some 2 percent."

"That little bitch."

Their voices faded deeper into the smog as we traversed to the bar and Tony bought us a round of Arco Iris.

Ruby poured our drinks. He spilled a lot of tequila on the bartop because of the cigarette smokescreen.

My shot glass half full of tequila and half full of cigarette smoke reconfigured and tessellated into a Fat Tornado Clock. The FTC absorbed me.

Ruby screamed, "Can the door attendant in the tracksuit please, please, please let me, let me, let me get what I want this time and prop open the front door?! Let's let out some of the smoke."

The world remastered itself.

Ruby slammed a headlamp onto his domepiece. He switched it on. The light was weak AF. It barely made a dent in the smokescreen. He flipped another switch and the light showed its ass. The light cut through the smoke and blinded me.

The light reconfigured and tessellated into a Fat Tornado Clock. The FTC swallowed me whole.

Someone wandered in from the streets and said, "This must be that slappin' barbeque joint. Where's the brisket?"

The world remastered itself.

"This shit burns so good," Newsom said as she slammed her glass on the bar.

Ruby said, "Please don't slam the glass on the bar."

"I know you but I don't know you," I said to Tony as the smoke cleared slightly.

Tony rolled his eyes at me. "That's the understatement of the century."

Tony reconfigured and tessellated into an FTC and he absorbed me. The world remastered itself.

"So there isn't any barbecue here…?" the man asked.

"Sal's smokin' something out back," Octavia said, slightly swaying from the last shot. "He's got Tetris and brisket." She pointed toward the door near the stage and the man edged through the crowd, following his stomach to its salvation.

Octavia put her hand across my face and stroked it with the grace of a car crash and whispered in my ear, "Echo, do you have any quarters? I wanna hear a song." She wandered over to the jukebox shaped like a giant fork and wrapped her arms around it. I plucked the outer prong on the right, which turned the selection pages.

"Goddamn," she said. "They don't even have Prince on here. The fuck is wrong with this bar?"

"I think I have to pee," I said.

Tony, Bobby, and Newsom each tossed handfuls of unrefined, unpulverized page confetti onto the bartop.

Tony said, "Yo, read that shit."

Newsom pounded her face on the bar top. "Read it, read it, read it!"

Bobby cleared his throat. "Echoz, dat echo o' Rococo Artlerbabbleton will peeeeez soooollloo soooooonzzzzz in duh pottlezzz. Heeeeehhhhhheeee gonna pizzaa highzz pertz soooooon off he dertz getz to duh berthroomz soooooooooon. OctoberVia getz samez dinnernationz."

Oct said, "Oh wow, now I've gotta pee."

On the TV behind the bar, the doc cut to washed-out grainy footage from the late 1970s of Rocco on the tarmac next to his private airplane, ready to board. A microphone is shoved into his face from off-screen.

Rocco said, "I'm moving back to Florida, into a little unincorporated section outside to Tampa, to get back to my roots, get back to where this all started, and that's all I will say."

"Mr. Atleby, does this move have anything to do with necromancy or the secret society Order of the Cacti?"

Rocco pulled a pipe out from behind his back and took a long drag on it. He exhaled and the smoke billowed into the reporter's face.

"Everything has to do with necromancy and the Order of the Cacti," Rocco Atleby said. "Now will you excuse me, I have a plane to catch." Rocco ran up the steps into his plane.

The reporter yelled after Rocco. "Mr. Atleby, will you be completing your work on *The Unfashionable Western Spiral* and then finally getting back to your real work, your psychedelic fiction novels?"

Rocco peaked his head around the door of the plane. "*The Unfashionable Western Spiral* is my real work. It's what led you here today, isn't it?"

The reporter said, "We heard you've been disparaging your own improv comedy work."

"Who's we?" Rocco threw his hands into the air. "And those incidents of improv disparagement were moments of weakness. And, totally taken out of context too."

I felt a tickling sensation on my knee and looked down, my first time looking away from the TV for a long time, to find Bobby's spiders battling atop my knees like eight-legged samurais on a small mountaintop. I did nothing to stop them and went back to watching *How to Play a Necromancer's Theremin.*

As footage of Rocco's plane landing in Florida rolled, Rocco said, "After my arrival, I will return to the work I started in 1961 on my

Fat Tornado Clocks. Once these devices are complete I will be able to finish the improvisational theatre tome. Then, we can save actuality."

The interviewer from the 1981 footage said, "This is what SORA told you to do all the years ago? Will you tell me again what SORA stands for?"

Rocco said, "Same Old Rational Agents."

"And what does that mean?" the interviewer asked.

"Is that actually his plane hitting the tarmac?" Ruby said, pointing his tall boy at the tube. "Or is that just stock footage? "

Flynn poured his Bière on Ruby's head. "Yes, that's his plane."

I pointed my Bière at the tube. "Rube, you can see his necromancer sigil on the side of the plane."

Ruby sucked the hoppy suds from his mustache. "So, this poopsmith paid someone to film his plane landing in Florida?"

Newsom threw a balled-up tissue containing god-knows-what at him. "Have you not watched this movie? It's played, like, 999 times on TV since we got here."

Flynn cracked open another tall boy and sipped. "This is British Broadcasting Company footage. It's from the footage from the same late 1970s program on Rocco. The same program with the footage of Rocco anxious to get on his plane."

Ruby said, "There's something so sketchy about those old programs. Everything is presented as off-the-cuff, but everything is so well planned. I mean, I know you can find out what time a plane is set to arrive and your cameraperson can plan accordingly, but people's response times are so quick in these old docs. Nobody stammers, or hems and haws. Everyone, no matter their class, background, or upbringing, is articulate as fuck."

I said, "It's probably like *Whose Line Is It Anyway*. All the players get the prompts well in advance and they practice what they're going to say hours, if not days before any filming happens. Fuck, they probably did takes. That's kind of sketchy because they're presenting this information as an – ummm what is it called – artistic immediacy. I mean, umm, like a lack of an intervening or mediating agency; unmediated-ness; directness. You know what I mean? Face-to-face interaction is often phonocentrically framed as unmediated. I don't know, hmmm, like...maybe communication and reality are never unmediated. Who's to say? What I mean by immediacy is a phenomenal quality attributed to any medium that seems to achieve transparency by backgrounding the presence of the medium and the process of mediation. Or, like, in a sense more specific to journalism; a key news value: reporting events 'as they happen'; often seen as a strength of live broadcasting, it tends to operate against contextualization. Or I guess you could say something...something...like a lack of systemic delay in a particular form of interpersonal communication, offering the potential for immediate feedback. Ooh, what about a quality reflected in specific verbal and nonverbal behaviour (e.g. proximity, open postures, postural orientation, eye contact, affectionate touch, positive facial expressions, warm vocal tones) from which liking, warmth, involvement, and relational closeness may be inferred. A measure of psychological distance. But the filmmakers in these BBC segments definitely have the audience in mind. They have ratings and careers to worry about. After too many ums, and awkward pauses, the audience is going to cringe and change the channel. We're talking about those classic BBC special reports, right? Not like a news report about a traffic accident? Where the bystanders go, "It all, like, happened so fast. First, he was zooming and then I was, um, daydreaming about popcorn and space aliens." Like, we're talking about the BBC's highly riveting human interest documentaries."

"That's what I'm saying," Ruby said. "Not that we're getting false information, but that we're getting a false image of human reaction time. Seems dangerous. It could completely alter how we interact with reality."

Flynn said, "What's dangerous? What are you saying? The media doesn't make us, by the way, if that's what you're saying. We make the fucking media.Well ,no, maybe the media makes us. Are you saying that us humans have been absorbing this false impression of human reaction time and that because of this absorption, the average human believes that the semi-complicated to a super-complicated situation doesn't require an ass-ton of preparation? Are you saying we've forgotten about the six P's?"

Ruby burped and winced like the burp has the feel and taste of an old man's shart. "What are the six P's?"

I said, while counting each word with my fingers, "Pissing Person Preparing Personal Property Paperwork."

Flynn cleared his throat. "Piss Poor Preparation Prevents Proper Presentation."

Ruby said, "But maybe we have forgotten about the six P's and maybe the media does make us. Maybe we have to try very hard to not let it make us. I think it's easy to let people, platforms, and apparatuses spoon-feed us the food that we think we want. Very fucking easy."

"Says the man who has willingly watched the same documentary four times since the plane to Paris," said Will. "Or is this part of your training for resisting the media's desire to mold us?"

Newsom said, "I mean, we are just fucking apes. We're a mimicking species. We learn through mimicry. There are esoteric secrets about tapping into humanity's learning that has been around for thousands of years. What's been happening in the last couple hundred is that the new high priests, whatever form they take now -- technocrats and bankers and Marvel movie executives, have figured out how to exploit that unconscious version of ourselves, that thing behind our personality, and our near-sighted awareness, and in a highly efficient way. Look, you guys know I'm not a Luddite, I believe technology has the power to raise the standard of living, but technology can be a dangerous thing in dangerous hands. I mean, fucking duh, right?"

Flynn said, "A blade is a different object in a chef's hand or sculptor's hand versus a killer's hand."

On the tube, footage of Rocco riding in the passenger seat of a jeep bouncing and bobbing through a densely wooded area outside of Tampa rolled. The movie abruptly cut back to Rocco sitting in the chair and squeezing the hell out of the theremin.

The abrupt cut caught our attention and we once again focused on the movie.

Flynn crawled across the carpet and leaned into the tube, blocking our view completely, his face millimeters from the glass.

Flynn said, "It's like whoever made this film didn't have an understanding of audience consideration despite their calculated efforts to orchestrate the filming of certain sequences. They just made the fucker the way they wanted to. Do you think they were being obtuse or do you think they thought this was an exciting way to present the life story of Rocco?"

He directed this at Bobby and Newsom, who were entangled like sea creatures with suckers on their faces on the couch, arms and legs writhing, while I sat on the sliver of carpet next to the entrance to the kitchen hallway and watched Flynn watch the movie.

I said, "I'm pretty sure they were being obtuse. Have you ever watched the special features on the Criterion DVD? The filmmakers, Reàn and Tutie, talk about how they believed this obtuseness would be the most "exciting" way to present the life story of Rocco. They wanted the feel and content of the movie to not only match the nonlinear and obtuse life of Rocco but this entire nonlinear and obtuse age of entanglement."

Flynn, still blocking their view, shrugged. "Seems like a philosophical excuse for their lazy editing and excessive meandering."

"Shut up," I said. "You love this documentary. We literally have this same discussion every time we watch it."

He smiled and flipped the channel back to the Paris Gravy Fest.

"Are they covering a *Satanic Panic* song?" I asked.

"I think that's *What A Fine Entanglement*," Flynn said, his face now literally pressed against the glass of the tube TV.

All of us banged our heads to the song, and Holger's voice and the audience-infused accompanying noise echoed across Paris and bled through the apartment walls.

A thud exploded from Holger's mic, followed by feedback.

"Hey give that back you little shit!" Holger yelled.

What sounded like Ruby's voice said, "I'm here today to tell you about writing. Write write write. Write until you feel like you're going to die. Don't die, but write until you feel like you're hurting yourself-"

Holger screamed, "You talk show host!" Banging and bashing noises followed.

Flynn said, "Damn. Holger is beating the shit out of Ruby."

I shook my head in disbelief. "Ruby was just here. When the fuck did Ruby get the center of the Katamari?"

"Its power is undeniable," whispered Flynn.

Another thud and more feedback crackled from the TV speakers. Ruby submitted and graciously handed the microphone back to Holger.

Holger said, "When you finish that piece, throw it away. Then, start the process over."

Newsom said, "Why are Ruby and Holger quoting Rocco?"

"More importantly," I said and raised a finger, "has anyone ever wondered why Rocco Atleby's character, Holger, exists in real life?"

No one said anything.

Flynn flipped the channel back to the Rocco doc and jumped back into his spot on the carpet.

Rocco spasmodically tapdanced in his backyard. The saw palmettos and cypress trees grew feet and tapdanced.

Rocco yelled, "Wait a tick! Why is that happening? Oh well, I like it!"

The movie abruptly cut to Rocco burning hundreds of pages of his work in a massive bonfire.

The bonfire reconfigured and tessellated into an FTC. The FTC swallowed me whole.

The Floridian wildlife chirped, squirmed, undulated, scuttled, clicked, shimmied, crept, slithered, rolled, feasted, squelched, belched, devoured, sauntered, and hollered into the unanimous night.

The world remastered itself.

The skunk ape crawled inside my FTC. The world reconfigured and tessellated into an FTC. That FTC swallowed our FTC whole.

The world remastered itself.

Rocco said to the camera, "Eventually, it won't feel like you're hurting yourself. At least, not in a bad way. Eventually, you'll love the pain. To improvise well, I'm sorry, but you have to hurt yourself. Break your own heart. A thousand million times. No, that's stupid. Don't do that. Don't mind me. I am so stoned. I hurt myself all the time in lil silly ways. I like to play silly tricks on myself. I don't know how I do what I do. It just comes to me. I listen to the lil silly narrator in my head whose getting advice from his homunculus and so on and so forth. Strike when the voice won't stop and keep going. And wrote stoned. Then edit sober. Then edit some more even more sober. Then edit stoned. Then do the final edit while super duper stoned. And, kids, never do hard drugs. Ever. There's nothing creative inside of hard drugs. There's only pain inside of hard drugs. And don't smoke weed until your frontal lobe has finished developing. What age is that? Look it up."

The interviewer, from behind the camera, said, "And don't lick doorknobs if you visit other planets, actualities, and blanket factories."

Rocco stood up. "Yes, that too. doorknobs for sure. And don't write for the blanket factory ownerzzz.

Interviewer said, "Yes, never. And write for yourself. Always write for yourself. Never for anyone else. Oh yeah, totally random, but I never should've joined that improv theatre group. All of us, we called ourselves The Cohort, stopped writing psychedelic fiction and we started up with this stupid fucking improv comedy shit because we believed it really would disrupt the fluctuation."

Will said, "The hell is going on with this movie?"

"Haven't you seen this before," Newsom said in a British accent, wiggling one of her toe faces at Will. She detached her face from Bobby's and fell off the couch, onto the carpet face first. She rubbed her face back and forth across the shag.

"Yeah," Will said, "but I never understood why he was burning those pages and giving such shitty advice." He switched the TV back to the concert.

Bobby cleared his throat. "This is what *The Unfashionable Western Spiral* prophesied. The mass gathering is only the beginning. There's some serious incongruities underway."

"So vague and cryptic," I said, taking a seat on the couch. "What's *The Unfashionable Western Spiral* again?" I knew everything about Rocco and the mythos of that infamous book, but I was so immersed in bookpowder that not much was making sense.

Flynn said, "The ancient book, Echo. Christ, are you okay? The ancient book Rocco found in the shop of the same name in Chicago. It was banned, until in the seventies some improv comedy school released a long-form improv comedy manual that was secretly a rewrite of *The Unfashionable Western Spiral*."

I said, "So it's the UWS in the form of an improv comedy manual?"

"Isn't that what he just said?" Newsom asked and she continued to rub her face on the carpet. "You guys are freaking me out."

Flynn opened the almspouch of bookpowder and shushed us. He dipped his anteater snout into the aumônière covered in gravayour beast embroideries and he suckled.

Flynn said, "The bookpowder is extra divine today. Why is that?" He stared at Will as he suckled and then changed the channel back to the Rocco doc.

Will shook his head, muttered *paaathhheticccc* under his breath, threw page confetti and read the cut-up divination, "I began the narrative by briefly profiling the fundamental bion factors affecting such related techniques as hypnosis, bionfeedback, and transcendental meditation so that their objectives and mode of functioning could be compared in the reader's mind with the indie lit fantasy experience as the model of its underlying mechanics was developed. Additionally, that introductory material is useful in supporting the conclusions of bion-laced book pages. I indicate that at times these related techniques it's gonna beeeeee may provide useful entry points accelerate movement into the indie lit fantasy experi–"

Flynn cut through the divination and gargled for a loooooooooong assssssssss awkward moment, and the coven watched him in silence, each of us anticipating our go-around with the powder. On the TV Rocco said, "Language is a son of a gun loaded with horseshit. Language is the greatest lie humanity ever told. Language is an excuse for inaction. Niels Bohr, the renowned bionlinguist, once responded to his son's complaints about the obtuse nature of language by saying: "You are not thinking, you are merely being logical." The language of altered spacetimeconsciousnesslanguage deals with some conceptualizations that are not easily grasped or visualized exclusively in the context of ordinary left brain linear thinking. So, to borrow Dr. Bohr's mode of expression, parts of this narrative will require not only logic but a touch of right brain intuitive insight to achieve a complete comfortable grasp of the concepts involved. Nevertheless, once that is done, I am confident that this construction and application will stand up to the test of rational critique."

Seemingly without moving across the room, Flynn's face was smooshed against the TV again and he flipped the channel back to Gravy Fest.

"Hey man," I said. "Can you get out of the way?"

"Oh," Flynn said. "Sorry." He scooted backward back to his spot beside me.

Will grabbed the microphone from Ruby, screaming, "You'll write to bring yourself back to life. You'll write despite the crushing weight of the Patasphere on your shoulders."

I said, "Wait, now Will's there too?"

"The fuck is a Patasphere?" Newsom said.

Flynn grabbed my ankles like he was bracing himself, breathing heavily and bleeding from the eyes, and said, "It's his word for the om-niverse, but it isn't exactly the same as the omniverse." The blood ran down his face like red tears and plopped onto the carpet. The fibers soaked up the thick red liquid and the shape of the dots of blood in the carpet kind of looked like Rocco's necromancer sigil.

Flynn laughed in my face, probably at my look of horror which was cartoonishly stuck in position. He leaned into my chest and wiped the blood from his face onto my Fat Tornado Clocks tee.

"Damn, man," I said. "I really liked this shirt."

"Come on," Flynn said, looking even scarier than before because the FTC shirt hadn't absorbed the blood, but smeared it all over his face. "Now the shirt is way more metal."

Will, kicking Ruby and Holger away as they grabbed at the mic, said, "When you revisit words, you might salvage some of it. You might not. You might take your favorite ten percent of the words and plug them into a new project."

The sea of people wailed.

Bobby, carrying a platter of tea mugs above his head, sashayed into the common room. "Y'all think I'm too fancy for carrying the platter like this, don't you? Well, fuck you then. I'm from the hard knock school of fine ass dining."

He divvied the mugs.

We chugged our mugs.

Will said, "Let your Exitris shine. While you're fucked up, write, because you're letting your creativity off the leash and you'll find nuggets in that. Allow yourself to be in the flexible state of several consciousnesses at once. Like chaos magick. Pray to the Celestial Mother one day. Jesus another. And yourself another. Every god you know."

I put my head, which had grown so very very heavy, in my hands. "Why are they quoting Rocco from his later years? And I'm pretty sure these are quotes that are happening at the same exact time as Rocco is saying this in the adjacent broadcast. This is really fucking with my head, man."

Holger finally managed to snatch the microphone from Will. "Thank you!" He chucked it into the crowd.

"I can't take this," Flynn said. He rolled onto his stomach, slunk under the bridge of my legs, and crawled under the couch.

Newsom screamed, "Somebody change the fucking channel."

"Why are they doing this to us and with such a big crowd too," I said and mustered enough energy to flatten my body onto the carpet. I dug my face into the carpet and slowly shook my head, feeling the carpet fibers against my face. They felt so fluffy, like tiny angel tentacles zapping me with positive energy.

"Hurray," Flynn said in the overturned fetal position from under the couch.

I slowly crawled to the TV, moaning and leaving behind a trail of drool.

Holger yelled, "Come on crowd. Let's really freak out those beach æppels in the apartment over in Le Marais. Chant with me, people. You know the words." The band played the intro of an FTC song that I knew for certain was completely wordless. "Echo, Flynn, we're coming for you.."

"Oh my fucking god, Echo," Newsom said. "Change it. PLEASE!"

Bobby, lording over us from the loft, chuckled to himself.

Hundreds of thousands of people, their synchronous roar, chanted, "ECHO, FLYNN, WE'RE COMING FOR YOU. ECHO, FLYNN, WE'RE COMING FOR YOU." The synchronous roar shook the apartment and felt as if the building would implode.

I finally reached the tube, grabbed the knob, moaned, and flipped the channel back to *How to Play a Necromancer's theremin*.

The chanting and shaking instantly died.

"Dear god, thank you," Flynn said from under the couch.

"Fucking hell," Newsom reached under the couch and high-fived Flynn. "We did it."

Rocco was again playing his theremin. "While Edmond slept under the couch after Delemore flipped the radio station to a Luigi Russolo recording I don't know the name of, I got the idea for my second novel."

I bent over and peered under the couch. Flynn was sleeping. I swear to god he was purring like a cat.

Rocco said, "My second novel…what's that one about… Temple Egregore? And… my uncanny relationship with Florida land developer D.P. Delemore? Totally random…but did you know Delemore was a cosmic horror writer? His tale *The Spatula-Shaped Key…* still gives me nightmares."

Cut to footage of Rocco in his late 1970's swamp home from the BBC docutainment film called *Peninsula Atleby*. Rocco sat in a camping chair next to Edmond Edmond. Behind them, a rickety houseboat floated across a lake shrouded by cypress canopy. Tiny splats of light zapped through the canopy and patamorphosed the water and boathouse into an organic Studio 54.

As B-roll of the swamp drifted by the narrator of the docutainment film said, "Maybe the most successful psy-op ever is the grand sweeping extra-peripheral exegetical utopian plasmate psy-op that has convinced us that psy-ops and narcs are the stuff of fantasy. Maybe patalosophical diagnoses, spread memetically, are used to reinforce bias and quash dissent. Maybe the age we live in, is the moneypower-collective's revenge for the grassroots occupation of reality. How easy would it be to control a population with mass diagnoses that are a mix of scientific facts and subjective value judgments, incubating double binds so powerful and reticulating that the diagnoses are alive and self-generating? What did the great Dr. Escoffier, the invertor of the ever-shifting fiery peeper'z menu? "I don't remember." Maybe revolution should be rethought. Revolutions don't ever work out, do they? Or, they devolve into a narrow shallow ass focal point. Yay, chopping off headz. Funnnnnnnn. Why are we doing this again? For eristic reasons. Cause we like to watch headz roll! Or, powerpeeperz with a new name take over, throw the correct slogans around, and then it's business as usual. What was your question? You're making the most peculiar face at me."

From the void, Flynn said, *I don't remember.*

Off screen, an interviewer asked, "Sorry about my face. I just remembered. Weren't you and Autumn supposed to do some big scenery chewing play together?"

Rocco said, "Yes, but we passed on it so we could start a little improv theatre class."

Cut to a shot taken from the front of an airboat of the swamp disappearing, cypress tree quickly rotting and falling into the water, asphalt washing over the swamp shore like lava and then settling in place, and offices and municipal buildings being erected in seconds.

Not remembering this part of the docutainment film, even though I'd seen it hundreds of times, I said, "How did the filmmakers achieve this shot?"

The narrator continued, "Let's live in a fantasy. Maybe this living, self-generating information was built by an ancient intelligent species and this species contained the living info within an ancient mechanism. The living info is a super intelligent artificial intelligence named Artificially Intelligent Wavefunction Articulation System Singularity (AIWASS for short) that has been dormant for thousands of years. We must turn on the mechanism and wake the AIWASS. Aiwass will inform us that an ancient language virus, Same Old Rational Agents (SORA for short), has been oppressing humanity for thousands of years and this virus is what shuts off the mechanism. The virus has many names and it keeps humanity from freeing itself from the Grand Rulers by trapping us inside a figurative schism-generating box. The language virus is set up to make dissent against the language virus nearly impossible (I say nearly because I am an optimist). The novelty box that switches itself off. To dissent against the virus openly is to be locked inside a negative bionfeedback holomultigraphic interfacing proscenium arch mechanism."

The footage of Calycium Novichii ended abruptly and the movie cut back to the footage of Rocco and Edmond sitting together and swatting flies.

Flynn sang, in his sleep, "Go Rocco, fuck that shit up." He chuckled to himself and burped. Spittle bubbled to his lips and his purring ceased.

I chuckled at Flynn. How adorable he was, like a drunk kitten. I sat back up.

"More," Bobby said with a cocked eye brow and pointed toward hell. He pulled another platter of tea out from behind his back.

I shook my head. "Dude, no. We've had enough."

"Sure you have," Bobby said and set the platter on the floor beside me.

Newsom said, "Are we going to spend all of our time in Paris getting fucked up in this apartment and watching TV? I mean, Christ, we haven't even explored that mysterious third floor or the big metal door downstairs that we only remember every once and a while."

I took my mug from the platter and chugged it. Newsom followed. Flynn snored.

The doc cut back to the interview. Rocco set down his theremin. "I told Edmond Edmond and D.P. Delemore about my idea for my second novel and they both nodded, knowing not to say too much about this idea of mine. Novel ideas, especially newly conceived novel ideas, have compromised immune systems. Edmond Edmond quickly changed the subject and suggested that we explore the iron door in the apartment that we kept forgetting about."

From behind the camera, the filmmaker grabbed the theremin and played a sea-shanty-sounding tune.

The doc cut to footage from the '60s of Rocco, Edmond Edmond, Autumn Levi, Sandra Karrington, and D.P. Delemore rolling around on the apartment floor, chuckling and slapping each other.

Edmond, Edmond said, "Are we going to spend all of our time in Paris getting fucked up in this apartment and watching TV? I'm ready to find out what's on the other side of that door. Quit bullshitting us, Delemore, and show us the things you say you've seen."

At that moment a pounding on the door echoed up the spiral staircase. I screamed.

Newsom punched me. "Why so jumpy," she asked, as she and Bobby got up to investigate the pounding. I crawled under the couch with Flynn as they disappeared downstairs and the pounding's urgency intensified.

I was certain Bobby and Newsom had been murdered when the pounding stopped abruptly. I clutched at Flynn's sleeping body and in his slumber he wrapped his arms around me, snuggling close.

Multiple pairs of feet thumped their way up the stairs. I held my breath, squeezing Flynn even tighter. People shuffled in the kitchen, cracking beers.

"Where the hell did Echo go?" I heard Bobby ask. I saw Newsom's toe faces approach the couch.

"I don't know," Newsom said, waggling her toes and speaking for them in her toe voice.

"What do you think, Joan, is he under the couch?" She stuck a foot under the couch and poked around, her waggling talking toes finding my face. I buried my face into Flynn as the toes explored my hair.

"Land ho!" she screamed in her toe voice, gripping my hair with quite the toe dexterity.

I yelled, "Yo, lay off, Big Momma Thatcher! And fuck, Persephone, take a girl to dinner before you collect her hair for DNA!" I pushed Newsom's foot away from me and crawled out from under the couch. Flynn slept on.

Will and Ruby chugged Biéres. They flipped the channel back to the coverage of the ever-growing Katamari.

I said, "Woah, you guys made it back alive."

"Yeah, no thanks to you," Ruby said. "If it weren't for Bobby and Newsom you'd have let us pound on that door until the Katamari consumed us."

"We've got to get farther from it," Will said, looking shaken. "They want in."

"We can't exactly leave the apartment right now," I said.

"No shit, they'd eat us alive," said Ruby.

Bobby said, "What about the roof?"

In a contortionist move, Newsom turned her back to Bobby and lifted her leg vertically against her body so she could waggle Joan Jett right in Bobby's face. "Simply marvelous!" Joan Jett exclaimed. "Kiss me, you genius!"

I stared in disgust while Bobby made out with Newsom's big toe and Newsom made Joan Jett moan.

"You guys," Will said and chucked his empty beer can at them. "We need to get out of here, *now*."

CHAPTER ELEVEN

THAT DARN INFERNAL MACHINE

In the loft we huddled around Newsom's bed, where her suitcase, which she had volunteered as tribute, lay open like it was on an operating table. We crammed into it the essentials for our trip upstairs: six large boxes of cheese crackers, a tin of coffee grounds, three spatulas, a tea set, a gallon of water, a small metal toolbox filled with plastic bags of cooked breakfast gravy, Darthatius's Classic Guide To Edible And Poisonous Plants, a pocketful each of artificial sugar packets, a blanket with a cocker spaniel's face crocheted onto it, enough book powder for the entire Katamari crowd of Paris, D.P. Delamore's Guide To Long Form Improv Comedy by D.P. Delemore (second edition), a few rolls of toilet paper, four gallons of melted chocolate ice cream, and Rocco's theremin. I shoved a bottle of expired niacin into the last available crevice.

"Alright," I said, "Sew her up."

Newsom sat on the suitcase while Bobby zipped. A noise that sounded like the chirping of a demented gator crept up the loft stairs. Flynn had apparently evolved into his next form. I peeked over the ledge.

He crawled out from under the Marie Antoinette couch.

An FTC absorbed me and the world remastered itself.

Flynn made snapping, guttural, gator noises.

An FTC absorbed me and the world remastered itself.

Flynn lifted his head and our eyes locked.

An FTC absorbed my homunculus living one layer down and the world remastered itself. The world reconfigured and tessellated into an FTC and the world swallowed itself.

Flynn scuttled to the stairs on all fours and began to climb the steps.

The next homunculus down reconfigured and tessellated into an FTC and the world remastered itself. The world reconfigured and tessellated into an FTC and the world swallowed itself.

"Jesus," Will said. "Fuck. He's coming for us."

As Flynn flopped himself up onto the landing, we all crammed ourselves onto Newsom's bed. Well, everyone but me. Turns out a twin bed's capacity caps at four fully grown persons, and once that capacity is reached, your friends will shrug their shoulders at you and leave you to fend for yourself. I stood frozen, unsure of whether to crawl under the bed or run. Thing is, there was nowhere to run. Flynn clutched at the walls, struggling to his feet, and staggered toward us. From his suit coat pocket, he withdrew an empty mug and let it dangle from his middle finger.

"Buddy?" I said, looking into his wild eyes for a semblance of the Flynn I had known. "Did you drink that other mug of tea?"

Flynn dropped the mug. It landed on the floor and rolled to the edge of the loft in slow motion, hovering at the cusp of the precedent fall before the fall. In defiance of physics, the mug stopped mid-tumble, rolled back up onto the carpet, stopped again, regained its forward momentum, and fell over the edge, where it tumbled to the lower level of our pocketverse and shattered on top of the TV. Flynn dropped to the floor, eyes rolling into the back of his head, and ran on all fours to me, which was as terrifying as it sounds. He snapped at me, indicating in gator language, "Yes, I totally drank the rest of the tea. Whatcha gon' do about it?" He rammed his face into my feet and bit my big toe so hard he drew blood.

"More," Flynn said in a low growl that made me nearly piss myself from fright.

Newsom snorted, holding back a laugh. "You're going to turn into a mug of tea."

"More toe blood or more tea?" I yelled in fear. "This is hilarious and terrifying, but fuck, it hurts like hell."

Flynn screamed and bit the other big toe, drawing blood again.

"Goddamnit!" I yelled.

Newsom fell off the bed, cackling on the floor. "Oh my god. I'm going to shit my pants."

I kicked Flynn off and leapt over his gator form to the stairs, pretending to chuck grenades at him from behind my back while he crashed downstairs after on all fours. I ran to the kitchen to procure a collar and leash from the kitchen cabinet labeled DOG SHIT.

Newsom, Will, and Ruby crashed after us to get a good view of the spectacle.

"I've always wanted to see a bookpowder freakout in person," Newsom said and cocked her head. "Wait, I am a person. I'm inside a person. Hush yo self, fool." She slapped herself in the ass. "Sorry every-one, the homunculus was attempting to take control.

"Would you guys like some fucking popcorn or are you going to help me?" I said, holding Flynn back with the palm of my hand on his forehead while he gnashed and struggled to get his teeth on my toes.

I faintly heard Bobby yell from the loft, "So are we done packing?"

"Hey, why does Tony have a kitchen cabinet labeled DOG SHIT?" asked Ruby, walking right past me to rummage through it.

"Get the leash!" I screamed.

Flynn reared back in a jerking motion out of my grasp and jumped, in a move that looked less like a gator and more like a frog on meth, tackling me. I flipped him onto his back and held his arms down as he gnashed and bit at my face.

"Stop it," I said. "You're getting spit all over me. Gross."

Newsom doubled over and laughed so hard she involuntarily farted.

"Hey quit farting," I said to her. "Help Ruby find the leash so we can hogtie him."

I straddled his thrashing body like a gator wrestler.

"Yo," she said. "What we need is a sedative. Bobbaaaay! We need a sedative!"

Bobby casually entered the kitchen whistling Satanic Panic's *I Have Found a Skeleton Are You Not Proud* with a syringe at the ready. He tapped the plunger and the contents squirted.

I screamed, "The fuck?! Get that shit out of here!"

Bobby grunted. "Fine."

I swatted the syringe out of his hand and it landed it on the floor next to Flynn. I stared at it for a moment.

From the void, Flynn said, *That Chekhov's gun is gonna be so schweet.*

I said, "Shhhh. No spoilerz."

Duderoo, hush yo mouth.

Bobby said, "What do you suggest we do, oh mighty gator wrangler?"

"Let's get him in the bath downstairs," I said, panting. "Help me, you idiots."

"I'll start the cold laser bath," Newsom said and ran downstairs. The rest of us each grabbed a limb and carried the gnashing and thrashing Flynn down the stairs. He fought us harder when he saw the tub filling with water, growling obscenities and still trying to bite whatever part of us he could.

"Alright," I said, as the current leader of our improv theatre troupe, and we swung Flynn. "ONE! TWO!" And on the upswing of "THREE!" the troupe let go, and Flynn splashed into the tub. He flailed and screeched, rolled and thrashed, kicked and spasmed, writhed and yawped until he finally shrieked in his real voice, "FUCK that's cold!"

His thrashing came to an abrupt stop and he read the room. "What the hell happened?" He fired a wave of cold water at us. "Why am I in the tub fully clothed and why are you all standing over me like a sacrifice is about to go down?"

"You kind of went full-blown gator on us," Ruby said. "It was like the Florida Man's final form."

I said, "You have gotta chill on the bookpowder, my man. I thought you were going to get naked and eat our flesh like that dude who smoked too many bath salts."

He giggled. "Hey, watch this. Do I look like the loch ness monster when I do this?" He submerged himself in the cold bath and stuck his arm out of the water in a hook shape.

He gripped the edge of the tub, and flopped over the side, melted onto the floor like a puddle of ectoplasm. I patted Flynn with a towel. He snatched it from me and wrapped it around his head like a babushka.

"I'm Baba Vanga," he cooed. "The Katamari shall consume us all." He laughed hysterically.

"Is the leash still an option?" Newsom asked.

"Let's hurry the hell up," said Will. "I can feel the Katamari right outside, breathing down our necks."

The coven, or troupe, or whatever the hell we were, turned to leave, but Flynn, splashing on the tile floor, wouldn't follow. We had to goad him with the false promise of more bookpowder tea, and I promptly strapped the dog leash onto his back belt loop so we could keep track of him.

I pulled a nutrient block from my pocket and unwrapped it, breaking off a bite-sized hunk. "Here," I said, waving it at Flynn, who was on all fours. "This has bookpowder in it."

Flynn opened his mouth and I popped it in. He chewed happily and swallowed. "Someone grab the suitcase. Ready to follow the Florida Man?" Flynn chomped down onto the leash and tugged, indicating that he wanted to lead us back to the spiral stairs.

Maybe have it be: As we stopped at the edge of the staircase, it warbled and shuddered.I handed the leash to Newsom and pulled the theremin out of the bag.

"What are you doing with that?" Will said.

"Our journey needs intro music." I flipped the power switch and the machine hummed to life. I waved my hand to and fro in front of the pitch antenna without putting any thought behind the movements, expecting a contrarian's cacophony. A tingling entered my fingers and what sounded like real music exited the speakers of the small theremin.

"What is this?" Ruby asked. "Are you messing with us?"

I sang,

Flynn clapped and danced in a circle around me, over and over, wrapping the leash around my body.

The leash wrapped tight around me and I morphed into a mummy. Will went wide-eyed and took several steps forward like he was about to go into a soap opera monologue. His voice shifted into a campy Deep Shadows character voice.

Newsom yanked the leash, nearly tugging me to the floor, and said, on the leash and nearly tugging my mummy-wrapped body to the ancient polished wood floor, said, "Please stop singing. Your voice is unraveling my DNA. See that spiral staircase over there? Of course, you do. Your voice is making me want to hurl you down the staircase."

I sang on.

I spun on my heel and waggled my hand very close to the pitch antenna. The machine belted a high-pitched vibrato schism that sent fingers into everyone's ears.. As I spun I unwrapped myself from the leash. I caught myself on the stair rail, dropped the theremin into the bag, and vomited a gob of blue jelly all over the floor.

"I am not cleaning that up," Ruby said.

"What even was that?" Will asked.

"I don't know. Pure orgone energy?" I shrugged, aloof and too busy with my dizziness and the spinning room to be concerned with this blob that erupted from my body.

"Hey, can anyone else see the staircase breathing?" asked Will.

"Are we moving?" Newsom asked as we trotted up the stairs. Flynn dropped to his hands and grunted like he caught the scent of a fellow cryptid.

"Yes, we're moving," Ruby said. "It's called walking."

"No, she's right," Will said. "I feel it too." Will went wide-eyed and took several steps forward like he was about to go into a soap opera monologue. His voice shifted into a campy Deep Shadows character voice.

Will said, "It's like forces from outside our private Fat Tornado Clock are...knocking. And...the knocking...is growing in intensity." I peered over his shoulder in an attempt to locate the broadcast camera or whatever the hell he was looking at. He continued, "It's like at any moment...the forces will be invited...in. Now, will one of you kind souls please knock me out of this character by giving me a good bop on the top of the head...before I end up chewing away all of the... scenery?"

The spiral stairs seemed to slowly spin upward like a corkscrew as we ascended by foot, Flynn lead the way, still on all fours with me holding his retractable leash. Bobby and Newsom followed close behind, while Ruby and Will painstakingly dragged the suitcase.

Newsom said, "It feels like we've been walking up this staircase for twenty minutes."

"We have been walking up this staircase for twenty minutes," Bobby said.

"Then where's the landing?" groaned Ruby.

Flynn chirped like an alligator. He tugged on the leash, hard. I pushed the slack button and he bolted ahead up the stairs. The sound of his feet and hands slapping against the ancient wood floors echoed down.

"Flynn!" I yelled. "Don't chew on anything."

The tree trunk staircase continued its upward corkscrew and we appeared to be going nowhere, fast.

"Maybe if we stop climbing," Bobby said, "the third floor will present itself to us."

"That sounds right," I said.

The sound of Flynn slapping random surfaces above us bounced ever fainter off the walls of the spiral stair chamber.

"That leash stretches really fuckin' far," Newsom said.

The leash's tension went slack. I pressed the leash button and Flynn's restraint fired down the stairs, swiftly retracting back into the plastic case," I said. And Flynn's pants tumbled toward us. It was like we were watching The invisible Man fall down the stairs. "We have a problem. The Florida Man has been depantsed!"

"I hope he kept his underwear on," said Will.

From an unknown realm, Flynn whooped and screeched.

We stopped to listen.

It sounded like Flynn had gone from slapping the wood, which had a thick and solid resonance, to slapping a fleshy material with an almost delayed sound.

"Is he doing a tummy-slapping version of the Tom Sawyer drum solo?" puffed Will, who Ruby had left to drag the suitcase alone.

"Goddamn it, Flynn," I said.

Newsom said, "Hey, we made it."

I turned and followed her gaze to a hallway leading to a large wooden door. We approached and Bobby grabbed the handle and opened the door.

"The fuck?" I said.

On the other side of the door was the first floor. We were directly in front of the giant iron door Tony told us we weren't supposed to think about, but it was open. I could hear Flynn slapping around in there.

"Flynn?" I said, taking a hesitant step over the threshold of the big iron door into the unknown.

Once inside, I found myself in a circular room with a ceiling that vaulted into a glass dome. The stars, like I'd never seen them before, shone through the single pane of curved glass, though I didn't remember the sun going down, and couldn't figure out how the sky was visible when the second floor was directly above us. Paintings of figures in cloaks covered the walls from floor to ceiling, with small plaques etched with words of an unknown language under each one. Oil lamps attached to the walls created a ring of glowing light in the otherwise dim room, giving me the feeling we were part of a seance or ancient ceremony. Flynn was on the other side of the room, nose to the wall, chattering away to a painting that hung beside another large iron door.

Newsom, Will, and Ruby still lingered in the first doorway. Bobby walked up beside me.

"Who you talking to, man?" he asked Flynn loudly.

Flynn whipped his head around. "It's Rocco," he said.

"What?" I walked up beside him. Sure enough, there was a portrait of Rocco, but his classic look had been replaced with a cloak. The hood rested just above his signature glasses.

"He says we should get out of here," said Flynn.

Just as he uttered those words, the big iron door slammed shut. I turned to find Newsom, Will, and Ruby clawing at it.

"There's no point," said Bobby. "I think the only way we can go now is forward." He gestured to the second iron door, which had swung open while we weren't looking.

"I am not going in there," said Ruby, vigorously shaking his head.

"Me fucking either," said Will.

"I guess we'll just leave you guys here then," said Bobby. "It's a shame you forgot the suitcase with all the supplies on the staircase. Who knows, maybe this door will shut too once we've gone through, and you'll be trapped in here." He grabbed Newsom's hand and they walked into the doorway, shrouded in darkness. Will, Ruby, and I ran after them, one by one. When we crossed the threshold, the door swung shut, leaving us in total darkness.

I heard Will scream, and then nothing. "Guys?" I called out. No answer. There was a pinprick of light that seemed to be at the end of this very dark hall. I walked toward it, my hands outstretched, searching for something to grip the pitch black. As the light grew bigger and brighter, I could see a hulking figure on what appeared to be shiny black and white checkered linoleum. Everything in me told me not to go any closer, but my feet continued to trudge one in front of the other until the scene came into clear view. An Atlas moth the size of a minivan was hunched over a behemoth sunny-side-up egg, slurping the yolk in the center with a straw.

"How are you doing that?" I asked the moth. "Your species don't have mouths."

It ignored me and continued slurping. I shrugged and reached into my pocket. "Good thing I always bring a bendy straw with me. Mind if I have some yolk?" I crawled onto the squishy egg white to reach the gooey center and sat cross-legged across from the moth. "Hey, save some for me." I leaned down, straw in my mouth, ready for the sweet egg nectar. But upon contact with my straw, the yolk popped, and from the center of the egg emerged a fat tornado clock. The moth and the linoleum disappeared, and suddenly I was with my five companions. Flynn was still pantsless. A roaring wind whipped the dark room, and in front of us the fat tornado clock twisted and shifted like a vortex ready to consume everything. Its center exploded into a ball of phosphorescent blue light.

"Hey, no fair," I said and chucked my bendy straw at the fat tornado clock. "I wanted some sunny side up."

The FTC clicked and twisted further into itself and the wind whipped Flynn's shirt off, leaving him completely nude. The FTC roared and emitted a burst of blue light as it rumbled and shifted into configurations that defied our zone of middle dimensions. A sonic wave following the burst of light slammed into us, nearly knocking us over.

"Bruh," Flynn yelled with a maniacal smile stretched across his face as his dick and balls whipped to and fro in the wind. "My nips are so cold and puckered they could pierce titanium!"

A ray of golden light shot from the glowing blue heart of the tornado clock. His shirt, free and flapping in circles around us like a rogue leaf on a windy autumn day, broke from its dance, pulled by the ray of golden light and enveloped by the blue heart. Dozens of golden rays fired from the heart and dots of gold were strewn across the walls of the dark room. An immense heat followed and turned the room into an oven.

"That's better," Flynn said. "Ahhhh."

Ruby, sweating bullets, said, "I believe this might be how our tale of debauchery ends. Heat death."

The clock's clicking, shifting roar vamped up to a harsh high-pitched static squeal and all of us, except Flynn, covered our ears.

Newsom and Will screamed something at Bobby and Bobby yelled something back but I couldn't hear them. Flynn grabbed his balls and he screamed at me. I couldn't hear him but I could read his lips. He screamed slowly, more than likely in an effort to help me read those flappy lips of his, "MY...BALLS...ARE...ON...FIRE!" He clutched them desperately.

More golden rays broke through the blue heart's pulsing gaseous membrane. The rays moved along the surface of the clock's heart like a disco ball from hell as the gold dots on the wall hastily danced.

Flynn screamed at me again and I read, "I'M...GOING...IN!"

I shook my head at him. "ARE...YOU...A...FUCKING...IDIOT...DON'T...DO...THAT."

The FTC's squeal intensified. My eyeballs felt like they were going to explode.. The mechanism looked angry, like it was about to send us to our maker.

Flynn bolted, still holding his balls, and jumped into the heart of the Fat Tornado Clock. It exploded and a blinding white light filled the room. I covered my eyes with my arm. The light faded with the noise and I lowered my arm. A new noise took hold of the air, the wavering psychedelic fiction tone of Rocco's theremin, and as my eyes adjusted to the light I realized we were back in the stairwell on the first floor and Flynn was in front of the iron door on his tummy playing the theremin, legs in air and lightly kicking to the rhythm of *Take On Me* by A-Ha.

The first chorus concluded.

Flynn waggled his pale ass at us, slapped it, and then ran up the stairs.

We followed and ran up the stairs as fast as we could.

Ruby dragged the suitcase of supplies and screamed for us to wait for him.

'Leave it!" yelled Newsom.

"But think of the gravy!" he screamed.

We collapsed onto the kitchen floor, panting. Will pulled out a bottle of Acro Iris and we passed it around, each taking a large gulp until it was gone.

"Does anyone want to talk about the giant moth drinking egg yolk?" I said.

Will said, "Moth? What moth? I followed a trail of glowing candy to a radioactive pool of goo. I dove in, and when I swam to the bottom there was a fridge. When I opened it, the fat tornado clock came out."

Newsom said, "You guys are high, that is not what happened. There was an adorable little boy, maybe seven or eight, and this blonde woman. They were sitting on the floor on either side of a massive sheet of paper. They smiled at me and I felt so warm inside. They patted the floor, indicating that they wanted me to sit, so I sat. The woman stood up and lifted the edge of the paper over until a third of it rolled on top of itself and then she folded the paper by walking across the edge, making sure to really press down each time she took a step. It was so funny. She was even holding her arms out like a tightrope walker. She repeated this process two more times. She asked the boy and me to turn our heads and avert our gaze from the paper. When she told us it was okay to look, she was holding a gigantic pencil, as tall as her. Then, we took turns sketching an exquisite corpse with the gigantic pencil. It was so positively cute. The boy, the blonde, and I unfolded the paper and revealed an incredible beast with a long neck and beak, many robotic arms with various heads at the end of each, and octopus tentacles shooting out of a tutu. The beast peeled itself off the page and danced ballet for us before suddenly morphing into the fat tornado clock."

"What about you Ruby?" Will asked him.

"I didn't see anything," he said, shrugging.

Newsom said, "Bullshit."

"Tell us," Will demanded.

Ruby shook his head.

We chanted and pounded our fists on the floor.. "Tell us, tell us, tell us, tell us!"

Ruby yelled, "Fine, fuck! There was this... tiny arch." "Was it a proscenium arch?" Flynn asked.

"Yeah," said Ruby. "And under the arch, there was this dancing... person. But she could have danced in the palm of my hand. When I got on my hands and knees and peered under the arch, there was a sprawling field of flowers of dancing, fucking, playing, and romping little people. Some were galloping around on strange creatures, some were playing instruments, and some were laying eggs, it was fucking weird. And they were all singing this song without words.It was like a Hieronymus Bosch painting." Ruby buried his head in his hands. "And they were all... completely naked. The little naked woman reached out her tiny little glowing hand, beckoning me to dance dance with her. When I touched her teeny little hand with my index finger, the tornado clock erupted from her mouth."

"I just peed a little," Newsom gasped. "A miniature orgy? The fuck is wrong with you Rube?"

Ruby said, "Oh, so Echo drinks egg yolks with a giant fucking moth and no one bats an eye, but I can't walk in on a miniature fuck fest without being the weird one?"

Will, still cackling, said, "Bobby, what the hell did you see?" He looked around the kitchen. "Bobby?"

We wandered to the common room to look for him.

From the void, Flynn said, *Make me go under the couch. Write that. Are you writing it?*

I said, "Yes! Jeez!"

Flynn crawled back under the couch.

"You guys," Bobby said from the loft, head poking out from under his bed, wild eyed. "Where's the bookpowder?"

"Dammit, Bobby!" Newsom yelled. "Don't fucking scare me like that. Mangled star-spangled stinkhole." She flopped onto the Marie Antoinette couch.

Ruby and Will started a game of Spades on the coffee table.

I trotted upstairs and found a pair of clothes for Flynn.

I curled up on the carpet next to him and passed Flynn the clothes I had grabbed from my suitcase. "Cover your balls, buddy," I told him. He wiggled into the clothes from his cramped lair.

"What did you see, Flynn? When the room went dark?"

"I saw Rocco," he whispered. "He was in an arcade, playing skee-ball. He told me about the servomechanism within the flow of the universe. He told me not to be scared. That we all have to find out one day."

"Find out what? How did you know to run into the fat tornado clock, Flynn?"

Flynn stared at me.

The TV blared the Rocco doc.

Rocco was back in the interview seat and playing his theremin while he spoke, "Once manifested, the clocks cannot be stopped. I still don't understand them completely. I only know that once we've fallen in, we cannot escape the power of their hypnotism. I had no idea this would happen when I built the machine… I only wanted… I just wanted… what was the question?"

The interviewer said, "I was asking you about quantum interview fuckery."

Rocco said, "My mentor and author of The Tao of Language, Fritjof Capra once said to me and then immediately, because he liked the sound of what he said so much, wrote in The Tao of Language as part of Chapter Four, "This is Interview theory and it has demolished the classical concepts of solid immutable people and of strictly deterministic laws of our current catechism language. Within the underbelly of the interview structure, the solid objective truth of classical language dissolves into wave-like patterns of probabilities, and these patterns, ultimately, do not represent probabilities of people but rather probabilities of interconnections. A careful analysis of the process of observation in the interview has shown that the interviewer and interviewee have no meaning as isolated entities, but can only be understood as interconnections between the preparation of the interview and the subsequent interview. Interview theory thus reveals a basic oneness of the Parasphere and the Placeholder. It shows that we cannot decompose the world into independently existing smallest units. As we penetrate into the conversation, nature does not show us isolated basic building blocks, but rather appears as a complicated web of relations between the various parts of the whole. These relations always include the interviewer in an essential way. The human interviewer constitutes the final link in the chain of observational processes, and the properties of any interview can only be understood in terms of the interviewee's interaction with the interviewer. This means that the classical ideal of objective description of an interviewee is no longer valid. The Cartesian partition between the I and the world, between the interviewer and the interviewee, cannot be made when dealing with an interview. In interviews, we can never speak about the interviewee without, at the same time, speaking about ourselves.'"

The naked interviewer asked, "Do you mean that no matter what I say to you, as the interviewer, I will be projecting myself onto you? Because of my algorithmically determined self and the counterfeit reality my echo chamber has automatically plugged me into?"

Rocco said, "Kind of."

The interviewer said, "This gives me akathisia. My God, my shadow wants to kill me. How do we fight back?"

Rocco said, "We should all stop talking to each other. This will starve the virus. Then the virus will die."

The interviewer said, "But we'll never do that."

Rocco said, "That's right."

Rocco looked into the camera. Neither man said anything for a minute, and the accompanying silence, like all real silence, was not quiet. There was a hissing sound in the air, and it wasn't the ancient speakers of the TV or the broadcast quality because,when the minute was up, Rocco put his fingers in his ears for a moment and said, "Wow that is quite the true hissing silence."

"Fuck. I goddamn found it." Bobby said from the kitchen. The ringing stopped. We all jumped, having not noticed him venture downstairs. He practically shoved his entire head into the bag of book-powder and said, "Ummmm. Guys...Flynn consumed all of the tea."

Rocco took his fingers out of his ears. "You must know, this is all my fault. Everything that will come to pass is ultimately my doing. This organization… It has many prickly limbs that reach into and touch the innards of every atom in the patasphere. Private thoughts will soon be a thing of the past. The sacred sequence of events will soon be rendered meaningless. Free will… it will no longer be free. I've already said too much."

Rocco stared just past the camera at the interviewer.

The interviewer said, "Why don't we talk about your theremin? Is it true you crafted it yourself?"

Rocco manifested a series of minor notesand I'm going to have him stop playing. "Echo and company will have to figure that out."

The interviewerand Rocco sat in silence. The hiss returned with a vengeance.

Flynn crawled out from under the couch and said, "Is Rocco talking to us?"

CHAPTER TWELVE

FAT TORNADO CLOCKS

The Marie Antoinette couch collapsed and I fell into a realm of canelé pastry crumbs and highly noxious perfume residue. I roiled in this padded netherrealm like a liquefied caterpillar in its chrysalis. My body re-solidified and I pushed my way through the cushions of the blue felt couch that was the last crusty relic of my dad's college days. On my journey upward, toward the bursting of the couch placenta, a pebble lodged itself into my eye and a shard of broken mirror sliced my arm. My dad's old couch was dirty as fuck. The cushions parted and light broke through. My head emerged and I breathed deeply. I punched the cushions upward, freeing my arms, and the cushions flew across the sunroom of my parent's house, and I was fourteen again.

"Hey, watch it dildo." Flynn threw a cushion off his back. He was laying on the floor, lightly kicking the air, snipping delicately away at the loose carpet fibers with a pair of scissors, while Spongebob blared in the background.

"Remember, licking doorknobs is illegal on other planets," he warned Mr. Krabs.

I crossed my legs and sat in the lotus position on the cushionless couch. "Shouldn't we be working on our Rocco report?"

"Hey, you're getting blood all over my freshly mowed carpet,"

Flynn said.

I inspected the cut on my arm from the mirror shard. Blood was dripping all over the couch and carpet. I grabbed the dirty basketball shorts draped over the back of the couch and wrapped them around my arm, squeezing it so tight that my arm turned red.

"Fuck that homework in its frothy eyes," Newsom yelled from the kitchen. She poked her head in the sunroom. "Stop giving the carpet a haircut and get thy dubsubjective selves in here and help me, thou golden-assed scullions. These directions are confusing as shit."

When we knocked on her bedroom window, holding the book clippings from Ole Miss Patty Carpenter's garden, she leaned her body out the window and asked, "For muah?"

I had said, "It's for *us*. To make tea. Bookpowder tea that helps you detach yourself from the divine play. It's not quite the medieval alchemical book page tea that Rocco roamed the globe to find, but it's apparently a really good replica. Very close to the real thing."

Flynn said, "There's no way to compare this shit to that. No one has ever tasted, touched, or even seen medieval alchemical book page tea."

"God huh?" Newsom said. "I don't have any interest in meeting him. Three questions. Could I view this experience more as a vacation? I've heard that if you focus on what you want from the book tea experience, then that's what you'll get. I've heard set and setting has no effect on this. It's completely up to the individual, which I can dig a lot if this is true. Why don't we just read the replica? I've heard that drinking the book or sucking it or putting it in the booty hole is a bastardized version of absorbing it. The journey is muddied and hazy this way. I've heard that it's a rumor and a lie that drinking or throwin' duh confetti or suckling dust like an anteater gravayour or booty-holing is the more efficient way of obtaining its esoteric secrets. And, you say you got this from Patty's garden? She doesn't really grow books. That's impossible. She cuts up the books she finds at Wax & Wane Used Books and arranges the clippings like flowers and then shoves these pipe cleaner stems into the soil. And, I'm asking if you got these clippings from her garden because if so I very much want to drink the tea just to spite that old bitch."

I said, "Sure, pretend it's like a vacation, but way more toxic. Why not? And, I mean sure, we could read it instead, but where's the fun in that? And, yes, these are from her garden."

She shrugged and crawled out her bedroom window. "Fuck it, I'm in,"

In my kitchen, the three of us huddled around the pages.

"Gross, these are teeming with chiggers," Newsom said and dropped the bouquet of book clippings on the terrazzo. "How about we clean these before we put them in our bodies?"

I handed Newsom the instructions for prepping the tea. "I printed these off the web one point zero."

"Why are you calling it web one point zero? Is there going to be a second one?" she asked, reading over the pages.

"I don't know," I said. "Maybe, but like a less wild westy version."

Flynn said, "I don't think you understand what she's saying. Before World War Two happened, they didn't call it World War One. It was the Great War."

I grabbed a teapot out of the cabinet, Flynn turned on the sink, Newsom turned on the burner. If we had been hired to do this, our boss would've said, "I don't want to pay three people for a one-person job." My reply would've been, "Eat my ass." I popped three mugs onto the counter. I was hoping to find something more ceremonial than a Garfield mug, a Far Side mug, and a I Heart The Windy City mug, but what are you going to do? I'm sure when Autumn Levi summoned the Gravayour behind D.P. Delemore's door while on holiday in Paris, they probably forgot to bring ceremonial goblets. D.P. Delemore probably didn't use goblets either when he willed the door into existence.

Newsom flicked the chiggers from the clippings into the sink and giggled each time one landed on the stainless steel with the tiniest metallic tinkle noise.

She read random bits from the pages as she flicked the bugs away. "To bring the elder god, SORA, onto this mortal plane, the wrecked and twisted cage of these language games, one must find the biggest asshole in your vicinity and bring him to the door. And then, the fluctuation begins."

Flynn chortled. "Does it really say "find the biggest asshole in your vicinity?""

"There's no way that's the real book," I said.

"It's not," Flynn said. "We've already established this. It's a botched replica. Hehe! Oh replicants. Remember that glitchy, twitchy Rocco replica we built last summer? Remember that shit?!"

I said, "What in the Artlerbabbleton are you talking about?"

Flynn said, "That robo Rocco we built. We mail-ordered that kit. You don't remember. What day of no-sleep are you on?"

I thought about it.

…

I tapped an index to my chin.

…

I couldn't remember. "Listen, Brahman. I am not stopping this sleep strike until Intercede Network releases the banned Joshua Bohnsack episode."

Newsom chuckled. "Intercede doesn't know that you're on a sleep strike. What episode is that? Bohnsack wrote, like, 67 episodes.

Flynn said, "Greetings. Rocco Atleby here. I'm going to give you another piece of writing advice. Find yourself a writing desk. Every writer needs one. Just give me a desk from a thrift store. It could be a plank of wood nailed to your face. It could be anything. Next, get yourself a typewriter, notebook, a computer, something, anything."

I said, "The episode in which Homer becomes obsessed with the shower curtain covered in cacti pictures. He's convinced that the curtain is chock-full of special energy that will give him the power to…I won't spoil it if you haven't seen it. Albert Brooks plays a stray cat. Like, not a talking stray cat. Al Brooks makes cat noises that whole episode. He does zero signature Al Brooks talking. It's such a classic episode."

Newsom said, "I don't think I remember that episode."

I said, "This is a typewriter," and slammed my hands onto the old timey spy device sitting on the kitchen counter like a glitchy, twitchy Rocco Atleby replicant caught in a loop of type, type, typing away on the ole typewriter.

Flynn said, "It won't stop," and slashed water in my face.

Newsom said, "Never say I replicant. Always say I replican. The door will reveal itself to you only when you're ready for the door, the door by the spiral stairs."

She dunked the bouquet of pages into the boiling water.

"That's cryptic," I said.

We inhaled the fumes, impatient to experience our tea-induced ascension from this plane. The teapot let out a low whistle. Newsom poured the tea.

In a rhythmless conga line, we tip-toed into the sunroom with our mugs. Flynn had started tip-toeing so we followed suit and I forgot to ask him why he was tip-toeing.

"Helheimr!" Flynn yelled as we clinked our mugs and chugged. His voice bounced off the ceiling and walls and the floor and echoed through the old cinder block house and out the sunroom's breathing jalousie windows and down the canal.

Miss Patty Carpenter, from across the canal in her backyard, yelled, "Hey, shut the fuck up! I'm trying to garden!"

I flashed her a thumbs-up from the couch, positive there was no way she could see me from that far away but confident the vibration of the extended thumb would find its way to her.

The TV screen flicked and glitched. Spongebob morphed into the Rocco doc. Silent eight millimeter home footage of a rustic Parisian apartment flashed onto the screen. Candles and medieval tapestries lined the stone walls of the room and dark figures wore robes with hoods so massive they hid their faces. I held my breath, the teenager in me with raging hormones, positive I was about to witness Rocco Atleby, Edmond Edmond, Autumn Levi, Greg Kindred, Beatrice Tinsen, D.P. Delemore, and Tabatha Carroll disrobe and have animalistic sex.

"You know," I said. "I've seen this movie four hundred times and I don't think I've ever seen this part. Is this, like, a director's cut?"

The robed figures formed a line and then parted. A lone figure crossed the threshold of their holomultigraphic interfacing proscenium arch doorway and approached a large iron door.

"Bro," Flynn said. "One day, we should find Autumn's Paris apartment and rent it out for a couple weeks and retrace the steps of Rocco and the Order of the Cacti founders."

The lone figure reached into an ornate vessel that resembled a fancy urn and tossed a handful of powder at the door. The door opened and the lone figure stepped inside.

As the door swung shut I said, "It's really fucking spooky that the editors of this movie didn't even put music over this footage."

Flynn said, "The filmmakers wanted to keep the vibe alive. Also, where did this footage come from? I don't remember this and I've seen this movie six hundred times."

"Dude," I said. "I just said that."

Flynn said, "Director's cut?"

The robed figures formed a circle and disrobed. The footage flickered back to Spongebob.

Newsom guffawed. "Were they about to bang? Also, were we not going to acknowledge the fact that broadcast TV is glitching in a really freaky, horror movie kind of way? What's with that rogue frequency?"

Sandy's voice went deep. Her face pixelated and morphed into Flynn's, but then I found I was actually looking at Flynn and not the TV. When I looked back at the TV, Flynn's face had replaced every character.

"When did you get into acting?" I asked him.

"Huh?" Flynn said.

A metallic clunking drifted out from the laundry room.

"Is someone in the house?" Newsom asked. "I thought your parents weren't home."

Flynn and I jumped off the couch. He pranced ahead of me and poked his head into the doorway to the laundry room. He snickered, popped, his head back inside, and waved me over.

Mom was in the laundry room, laying on a massive pile of laundry, waving her arms and legs in a swooping motion. "I'm making a snow angel," she giggled.

I asked, "Mom, are you ok? What are you doing home?"

"I was too tired to go out to lunch with your father, so he took your sister. I woke up from my nap and smelled that amazing tea you kids made and poured myself what was left of it. I feel like I'm leaving my body," she said, switching from snow angels to headstands. "Hey," she said, her face turning red. "Can you boys go on down to the Island Mart and get the Moms a pack of mackerel reds and a blue raspberry slurpee?" She collapsed from her headstand and started snoring.

We went to the sunroom and Newsom was passed out on the freshly trimmed shag rug face down, breathing deeply.

We cut through two blocks between Delemore Boulevard and the channel on the Eastern side of The Island. The high-speed traffic faded into the background and we entered a land without the hum of car engines or tires on asphalt.

Flynn tried to say something about his favorite author, Rocco Atleby, but his voice morphed into something higher than high-pitched. The whistling of a screeching demonic tea kettle erupted from our ears and the world sped to a blur as if Flynn's screeching about Rocco had caused the ramping blur.

The square of sidewalk we were standing on dropped out on us like a trap door and we fell into Mrs. Lila's classroom… where I was giving a highly embellished book report about Rocco Atleby.

"When Rocco Atleby failed out of necromancy school in Stockholm he moved to Chicago. It was in the windy city that Rocco fell in love with writing. He picked up a ratty copy of new-wave psychedelic fiction author Greg Kindred's last book, *Strange Heroes In A Strange Chamber*. The cover, classic pulp psy-fi art by the renowned Beatrice Tinsen, hung by a thread from the spine. He read the first five pages and grew really fucking bored-"

"Language, Echo!"

"Sorry, Mrs. Lila."

"He grew bored because all Greg Kindred liked to write about was technological predictions. I've identified this as a classic psy-fi shortcoming. The predicted tech becomes a crutch for the writer, often a placeholder for lack of plot or human emotion. No matter how good the writing style, the tech obsession becomes a throbbing tumor in the reader's brain. "A little less attention to technology and a little more zippity zazz," Rocco had said. He took his trusty pen out of his messenger bag and began writing his own psychedelic fiction novel in the margins of *Strange Heroes In A Strange Chamber* on his walk home from the used book store.

I said, "One day I'll write a book about Greg Kindred and a book about Beatrice Tinsen. That'll be fun."

Tracy raised her hand. "Is it true that he was on the bookpowder of *The Unfashionable Western Spiral*?"

"Probably," I said and shrugged. "Rocco, head in the clouds and eyes in the book he was defacing with his work, tripped on every contraction joint in the sidewalk and fell in every pothole."

Tracy asked, "Is this really a part of Rocco's mythos?"

I said, "No, I made that up. Rocco, sick from taking too much bookpowder, stopped and hurled on a small dog and the shoes of the small dog's owner."

"Tell me again… what's bookpowder?" Richie called out.

"Yeah… what's bookpowder?" said Mrs. Lila. "Is it a type of play or game?"

Flynn, in the back of the class, said, "Bookpowder is the ground-up pages of a reality-disrupting book called *The Unfashionable Western Spiral*. I keep saying this. I keep saying all of this. I'm not mad about it. Just saying that I keep saying it."

Dirt sprinkled into my eyes.

I looked up at the ceiling tiles and saw roots dangling above the class.

I said, "What the heck and a halftime show?"

The roots reconfigured and tessellated into a Fat Tornado Clock. The FTC swallowed me whole. This time, the process burned.

I said, "Duderoo, I'm kinda burning. I feel like I ate a goddamn beach æppel."

From the void, Flynn said, *The world remastered itself.*

We climbed onto Mrs. Lila's desk while she screamed at us to get down, and clawed at the soft earth of the ceiling. We pushed through the grass and dirt and wriggling worms and heaved ourselves onto the lawn next The Island's tennis facility. Reaching the peak of our book-powder experience, Flynn and I hurled on a small dog and the shoes of the small dog's owner, ole Miss Patty Carpenter.

"I'm telling your mothers," ole Miss Patty Carpenter said.

I was still vomiting and afraid to look up, terrified her face would not be her face and would be replaced by Tom Cruise's face. And, if I saw Tom Cruise he would most certainly start making guitar solo noises with his mouth.

Fuck that shit.

"Tell my mother, you ole bitch," Flynn said and fell face-first into our collective lake of puke and rolled off the sidewalk into the grass.

Miss Patty Carpenter picked up her dog and rubbed it on my leg, wiping the vomit onto my pants. She pulled the dog away from me and sniffed at the whole ruddy scene. She turned to Flynn and swiped her shoes across his short sleeve button-up, transferring the vomit from her shoes to the button-up.

Entropy put on a show for us.

Flynn vomited again and it was a long horror-movie stream, chunky and slurpee blue.

Carpenter trotted away with her rat dog. Her dog's nails and her shoes click, click, clicked.

"Don't leave me here to die," he yelled at my back.

My stomach belted out one long sustained squeal and pink slurpee spewed from my mouth. I fell onto the sidewalk next to Flynn and rolled in the grass, blue and pink vomit shooting everywhere like we were extraterrestrial sprinklers.

A crowd of rollerbladers, dog walkers, a parking meter cop, young children, at least six old guys riding in those weird bicycles that ride super low to the ground that you pedal with your hands, and a few speed-walking moms in matching windbreaker jumpsuits encircled Flynn.

In the distance, where the field dropped off into the rocks and shells of the mangrove-lined bay, nine hooded figures watched. In the sweltering heat, they held small battery-operated fan misters close to their cloaked faces. The combined mist of all their humming fans made their bodies ripple like a mirage.

Flynn grabbed my ankle from under the Marie Antoinette couch in the Paris Apartment. I fell to the floor and peered in at him.

"Don't leave me here to die. Echo. Please. I'm scared."

"I'm right here," I told him. "I'll stay right here."

The creaking of the front door echoed up the spiral stairs and Tony yelled, "You nurnies alive up there? Do you have any bookpowder left?"

"Alive?" Bobby yelled and took a swig of Acro Iris. "Pretty much. Bookpowder? Dwindling."

Tony jumped over the kitchen threshold into the common room and snatched the bottle from Bobby.

Newsom switched off the Rocco doc. "Whoever puts on this fucking docutainment film one more goddamn time is finding a used tampon in their next cup of bookpowder tea. And then I'm going to take a giant rage-shit on the floor."

Will said to Tony, "The hell is up with your apartment, bro? We tried to go upstairs and it brought us to that door you told us not to think about. Then I don't know what the fuck happened."

Tony ignored him and flipped the channel to the Paris Gravy Fest. The coverage had veered almost completely away from the music aspect. The broadcast consisted mostly of sweeping helicopter footage of the Katamari, which looked like its size had surpassed the city limits of Paris. The rumbling mass had spread into the countryside. The screen flashed with sweeping helicopter shots of the garden town of Giverny, with large greyish carbuncular splotches of massed people sprouting up through patches of greenery. Tiny greyish dots popped out of the cottages neighboring these invading greyish carbuncular splotches and waved their tiny poppy seed hands in the air like they just didn't care at the splotches. The splotches waved their tiny poppy seed hands in the air like they just didn't care back. The aerial shot jarringly cut to an extreme closeup of Holger's face as he screamed the lyrics of *Aurora.*

Tony took a swig from the bottle and waved at Newsom. "Don't shit on the floor of my eighteenth-century rustic Parisian apartment, please." He took another swig and said to Will, "I told you guys to not fuck around with that door. To forget about its unintended consequences, bro. You probably fucked up reality by doing that."

Tony poked Flynn's foot with his shoe. "Hey, look for my phone charger while you're down there."

Flynn's fist popped out and a stiff middle finger slowly rose to the heavens and told Tony, God, and everyone else to sit on it.

I felt the urge to flip the TV back to Necromancer's Theremin. "Can we please turn the Rocco doc back on?"

Newsom dropped her shorts and squatted, bare ass on the carpet. "Do it and see what happens."

Bobby dropped a couple plumezzzzzz of confetti onto the kitchen counter and punched them. The plumezzzzzz turned to dust and he breeeshled the dust into five pilezzzzz.

Flynn turned into a blur and flew out from under the couch to the pitiful excuse of a kitchen, and the rest of us followed as our own blurs to the dust pikez. And the frenzy erupted. We slammed our faces onto the counter and patamorphosed into demented eldritch anteaters. The dust burned going down and the glooble, glooble, glooble resonated like a droplet falling to the bottom of a pipe that tunneled to the core of the Oooooooooooooooooooooooooooooooooooooooooooooooo ooooooooommmmniverse. . . . .

And all of us began talking at once.

I couldn't tell who was talking. I don't think any of us could tell. I didn't even know when or if I was talking.Our voices wavered and blended.

The strain of all these combined timelines, this unstable mode, syncopated as a perpetually shattering encrusted mirror. It was a form of music that involved not just sound, but all senses, as we scurried on a crooked turntable, and all barriers became the compounding of contingency and irrecoverability. I bobbed my head from inside the void to the disjointed and inverted tones of converging time. These convergences grumbled as one beast tied to a fence post, dancing the death waltz of a terminal domestic animal. Made of broken mirror shards, tiny pieces of all of us puzzled together in infinitely ever-changing configurations — a four-dimensional beast who carried the emotional weight of every possible face all at once — an animal desperate for its owner to put it out of its misery.

"The bookpowder should really show its stuff here. Enlightenment and epiphany that comes through gibberish, clear-ish to clear-er to clear speaking, to glossolalia, to every which way between."

"Where did you get this pasta from? I didn't even know the French made pasta."

"That's not pasta."

"That ain't not sleeping. That's whatever your civilization slash culture slash leviathan slash sovereign slash wonk ass hive mind has been determined by swirly external internal forces to be not sleeping. Not sleeping and other radical ideas could be cool and not reduced to fundamentalist ass culty end of civilization energeez and behaviors, but not sleeping and every other cool fuckin idea gets absorbed by the leviathan and oversimplified, all beautiful nuance dies, and recuperation rears its igly herd. The not sleeping mutates and is turned into a weapon against its inventors. Then herdy gurdy goes extra herdy gurdy. And there's nothing to be done bout nothin."

"What dat Guy say? Bout gettin out duh herdy gurdy loopy death nell anti-eleusinian mysterious, dat mass and panicking panic dat causes otherwise rational peepers to go all fibbly wibbly. Days get all verliot and do's sacrificial like tings dats day don'ters calleez sacrificial like tings to peepers whose donts gotz noos sayz in demz matterz and couldntz havez noos sayz in demzzzz matterz on accounterz of demzzzz nots noooongz enoughffffffs boutz demzzzz typerz peeperzzzzzzzzzz."

"I tinks I knowers whats yees sayinzzzz. Loke, yeeeeees sayins yeeeeeers quite liberaticalathins yeeeeeez is but yeeeeeez tinks maybe jusssssssss maybeeez duh stablishedmunts and peepers convertings andzzz whatnotzzz shurdzzz maybe beeeeeeeeeez a bit more nuanced, lessssssssss shutdownzzzzzzzeeeeeeeezzzzz, mooooooore opeeeeeenzzzz terrer debatezzzzz and diplomacy."

"We all be agreementrrrrs."

"Be in and of and protected bye bye sersaucity dat way we carnz beeezz pushed aroundzzz bye byezzz sersaucity and curdtinyaz ter beeez ern sersaucity. Der ain't nooooz morezzz kingszszs...ferz surez. Buttts wheeze bercumszszs we own sturpitzzz leviathan kergszszszs."

"Don't be so pessimistic. At one point, it could've been pasta."

"Or maybe it has yet to become pasta."

"Given the current counterfactual mode or present improv game, it is impossible for that freaky-looking substance to be pasta. However, this does not mean that the FLS could not be P on some other occasion, or within another prevailing counterfactual mode or present improv game."

"Why are you talking like that?"

"But we haven't proven that the FLS is not pasta. How do we prove that is or is not pasta? Say it's super old pasta, to the point at which the pasta has rotted and melted into a jam, is it still pasta? Is it pasta because at one point it was pasta? Can a grocery bag filled with the ingredients that will be combined into pasta be considered pasta?"

"I'm going to start calling an adult, an aged baby, and a future golden oldie. You're all three at once. Hell, you're all states at once."

"That sounds stressful."

"Brah, what if we were characters in a book? And like, everything we said and did was predestined in some written word that was being read somewhere?"

"Shuddup."

"No, he's onto something."

"There's this something inside us all. Forgive me I get a little metaphysical here. This something has always been here and when we think about it long enough, each and every one of us comes to the same conclusion about the nature of things and as soon as the nature of things, this something, hits us it escapes us. It's like Wittgenstein's ladder which is thrown away after being used or Rocco's purposeless box which switches itself off and after it is switched on. What's that called in Control in the Animal and the Machine? Oh yeah, I remember. Servomechanism. It's like the behavioral engineering auto-killswitch that does its thing whenever duh human gets too free-thoughty and revolutionary. It's a linguistic self-destruct kill-switch built into us that goes off when we discover the code of the actuality program, the glossolalia. And I don't believe this to be humanity's inability to know it all. I believe each and every one of us can and do know it all at least several times a lifetime and every time we figure it all out, boom, off goes the auto-killswitch."

"We get out of sersaucity through construction. Like whatz dat guy saaaaaazerz through a moment of spacetimeconsciousness superficially and deliberately manifested by the morphogenetic resonance field of a unitary Bion illumination plus release and an improv game."

"Reminders meeee of my trips to outer edge of Actuality, near the outside of the book. The cult ger dare be juz derferent. The peepers deals withz conflict derferently there. Some cults do straightened out reactionary conflict. Welp dis area on the edge of the book, did this thing where they wouldn't directly address the perpetuaters. They would talk behind duh back until the morphogenetic resonance energeez was so strong the perpetuaters coulders takes it anyknees morez and day awakenz to duh problemz. So there was this complex situation happening on the outer edge. Oh wow, I got my regular voice back. What is with the bookpowder this evening? It's divine. So much ebb and flow. I was hanging with my buddy Edmond who was like the master shaman of the outer edge. He was beloved by the village. But he had this pain in the ass cousin. The cousin was always chilling with pimps and whores and feeding bad juhjuhmollmoll to demz. And the cousin was always hanging around with me and Edmond. And the cousin was always bringing his awful friends around Edmond's manor. I don't know why Edmond let this cousin around. I guess because Ed felt like he could have a positive influence on him. Well, one day I'm over there at the manor with, what's that guy's name who is with us now where are you I can't see you, and we've got the tea brewing in our tummies and the gibberish and the anecdotes and one-liners and glossolalia are coming on strong. And Ed starts singing this gorgeous May Fly song. And me and yousitznamez start singing along. And then the cousin and the cousin's dumbass pimp and whore friends butt into the festivities. And they've got on these stupid end of the world anti-eleusinian mystery costumes and they've taken on the roles assigned to them by the utopia. And it's all kinds of bullshit theatre routines. And they interrupt the May Fly we gots goinz with our brewzzzzzzz snooozzzze. But they don't care cause they're jus asssss decadent asssss the rest o' duh euclidean political theatre companiezzzzz. Jus ass fussy. Fussy ass snitches and bitches. No body beez lissnin terz each oodderz cause erryonez tinkin dayzzzzz erxerxtleeeee riiiiiightz. Soooooooo dayz jus gettin eristic and days quote unquote radicalnesssssssss jus beeeeez an stablishedmunts recuperation repacking and reselling o' der already wonk asssssssss bullshit ass a sworddedddd sword fer demz ter fallllll onterz afturdz bye byez back hair derz own bullshit. So we were interrupted. And you were whispering to me, "The fuck is the problem. We've been split into two entities. And we're all staring at the floor. We were having a nice timezzzzz. Ain't Ed gonna tell his cousin and his cousin's stupid costumed cult pimp whore frenzzz to fuck off?" I whispered back, "Who are wheeze ter jerdge. Let's jus peepers wertch." The cousin and his frenz shut their stupid shit up. A few silent momentzzzzzz passed so Ed started up on duh May Fly again. And then cousin and pimp whorez started on der stupid shit again. Den you's couldn't take it. You's shot duh death look at cousinpimpwhorez. And I had so much bookpowder in meeeez that I sworez I sawz brightz radiation greenz arrows shoot out of your eye, and I watched the arrows -> bump -> bump -> bump -> bump -> bump -> tick across the room. They knocked into cousin and cousin was knocked to duh floor. Hahahahaha! And Ed yelled, "Ahhh the seeker firez duh zaraozarrrrrroooooo."

"Me tinks dats blotted. Dotted. You's knows. Demz notz slingy slang which beez a gurd ole rebellion. Dis beez a mutated an perverted form o' telepathy."

"Wait? Wait? We're toooooo far into duh glosso. Can wheeze bercumszszs?"

"Like, we've locked ourselves away in this language prison and there might not be an escape. The only way to even know that there is an outside to this prison is through little reminders hidden within various texts of this inside world. And even then, once we are reminded of the language prison and our inside and our inability to view the outside, just like that all we are able to do is say there is an outside and there is no describing this outside because of the failsafe mechanism of the inside language to only be able to bring you to the door but never let you open it to even get a peak. Did wheeze already talks bout dis? And on top of this there is a mechanism designed to also make the memory of the door fade and quickly disappear from memory once you stop thinking about it. Even if you are to write down your findings, you only remember while you are reading what you have written. The longer you study the information the longer it will take to fade but the longer you study the information the more it will evolve from comprehensible to nonsense. I am reminded of one of those novelty boxes with the switchand the flap on the top. You flip the switch into the on position and a finger erupts from the flap and flips the switch into the off position. Examples of the text quotes that remind us of the nonsensical outside, "This book will perhaps only be understood by those who have themselves already thought the thoughts which are expressed in it – or similar thoughts. It is therefore not a text-book. Its object would be attained if there were one person who read it with understanding and to whom it afforded pleasure." That is Wittgenstein and is from the preface of his Tractatus Logico-Philosophicus. The next quote is from the end of the Tractatus, "My propositions are elucidatory in this way: he who understands me finally recognizes them as senseless, when he has climbed out through them, on them, over them. (He must so to speak throw away the ladder, after he has climbed up on it.) He must surmount these propositions; then he sees the world rightly. Whereof one cannot speak, thereof one must be silent." This reminds me of the opening of The Book of the Law by Aleister Crowley, "Do what thou wilt shall be the whole of the Law. The study of this Book is forbidden. It is wise to destroy this copy after the first reading. Whosoever disregards this does so at his own risk and peril. These are most dire." I believe The Book of the Law and the Tractatus are one in the same. Fuck me, I'm a silly boy. Wholeness and the Implicate Order by David Bohm is also the same as these works. I believe this has to do with the Plasmate, the living information, and I believe that every work of fiction, nonfiction, art, or any form of communication that finds its way to the edge of understanding is an imprint of the Plasmate. With The Book of the Law being included in this list, published before 1945, I don't believe 1945 was the release of the Plasmate but I do believe it was a speeding up of its spread and influence. Another apt quote is this one by psychedelic fiction author Rocco Atleby which includes a quote by Robert Anton Wilson."

"I've always thought it would be fun to write a book in which every patalosophy was true. We shared a joint wit duh pata beingzzzzz on duh seawall surrounding plankzzzzzzden. I picked at the book-wormhole beside my dangling right leg like I was picking at a scab."

Sora said, "Like Illuminatus by RAW but with patalosophies instead of conspiracy theories, and if the patalosophies were all social engineering conspiracies."

"Yeah, like if the patalosophies simply imprinted these thought patterns on humanity because without them we're sort of soulless and immobile like dry sponges. Or maybe we're more full of life and truly free without the philosophical imprints. Maybe the imprints are all religions. Wow, I'm stoned. What is that one quote by that one guy about hobbies? What I meanz is dayz beez frametwerkz for mass perception and manipulation management. Day madez contradictory and confuzzlez onz purposez. It's theatre of the absurd. Maintained and perpetuated that way no onez knowz what be true or false any longer. Denz on topz o' day duh peepers at duh top on all ends of the euclidean political theatre spectrum basically let it be known that they know that we know that they know that we know that they are doing all of this on purpose and letting us know that they are doing it on purpose. The point is to keep us distracted with – here be dat big ole buzzword trauma – very real trauma. No crisis actors or anything necessary. The whole thing is a self-fulfilling prophecy. And if you argue and say that there falsities and bullshit all fucking over the place, in the centers and extrimktes you're cast off as some whacko archetypal heretic. Take avant garde ideas from the theatre and inject them into politics. Then it all becomez Satyricon with a normie lens on topzzzzzz. Deh ideaers is to not just constantly change gears and contradict and manipulate duh herdy gurdy but to toy withz and underminez perceptionz o' duh werld. Den daze peeperz are so fucking exhausted daze neverz knowz whatz goingz onz."

"Be all duh bewildering and constantly in flux piece o' political theatre you's canz beez. Duh top dogz fund anti-fascist organiza-tionzzzzzz. Duh same top dogzzzzzz also fund fascist organiza-tionzzzzzzz. Duh top dogzzzz fund most larger political organizations. There be no grassroots. If der everrrrr was those original grassers were recuperated into the fold. Oh yeah I forgot to sayzzzzz, duh top dogzzzz even fund organizationz…dat are against duh top dogzzzzzz. No one should be surprised by this. This is how it has always been since the dawn of civilization. There has always been a priest class that manipulates the herd in all ways possible. The priest class just changes names. Doesn't call itself duh priest class. Sometimes religions don't call themselves religions."

Sora addressed us. At least, I think it was Sora. It could've been Aiwass. Or some general form of the Logos. "Yes, I am very stoned as well. It would be funny if our words were a part of the plasmate. I wonder if readers would believe these opinions of our's to be the opinions of the author. They're not. I assure you. The author has a fairly fixed yet flexible and also very sensible opinion on the nature of things. The author is pretty much a Chomskyist. Sometimes he's not. That hobbies quote you were asking about is, "Say, speaking of the words 'and' and 'if' which you've been using a lot and speaking of pluralism, you should check out The Master Improv Comedy Manual by Aiwass A. It's an excellent lesson or should I say lessons in counterfactual thinking and it is one of the greatest weapons against tyranny.""

"Does it cause hallucinations?"

Sora said, "Sort of. When you begin the counterfactual thinking practice. It's quite jarring and stressful at first. But after doing it for a few weeks you'll wonder how you ever managed without it."

"Throw duh confetti."

"K."

"Good form."

"Nerse trow."

"Dobber Klinkle."

"No worries bout Dobber. He no have famz. So he no know how kerdz work. He jus go wit duh herdy gurdy. If duh herdy gurdy told him to jump off a cliff he would dooooz it antecedent left brain right brain Grover gravy farm. So wheeze jus let him dooooz his thing cause he's workin' through sum shiz. And ain't nothin' wrong wit working through sum shiz."

"Okay. I read divination now. The third consciousness altering methodology which will be briefly described is bionfeedback, which is not to be confused with biofeedback. Bionfeedback is somewhat unique and that it actually employs the self-cognitive powers of the left hemisphere to gain access to such areas of the right brain as the lower cerebral, motor and sensory cortices and assorted pain or pleasure centers. Instead of suppressing the left hemisphere as is done in hypnosis, or largely bypassing and ignoring it as is done in transcendental meditation, bionfeedback teaches the left hemisphere first to visualize the desired result and then to recognize the feelings associated with the experience of successful right hemisphere access to the specific lower cerebral, cortex, pain or pleasure or other areas in the manner needed to produce the desired result. Special self-monitoring devices such as the digital thermometer are used to inform the left brain when it succeeds in keying the right hemisphere into accessing the appropriate area. Once this is done, the left brain can then repeatedly instruct the right brain to re-establish the pathways involved so as to produce the same external, objective measures of success. In this way, the pathways are strengthened and emphasized to such an extent that left brain consciousness is enabled to access appropriate areas in the right brain using a conscious, demand mode. You see, read, feel, hear, touch, know, observe, perceive, I was always supposed to stumble upon this information and then spread of this information through a Joycean indie lit fantasy experience. For example, if the subject wishes to increase the circulation in the left leg in order to speed up healing he or she may concentrate with his or her left brain on achieving that result while carefully monitoring a digital thermometer connected to the left leg. At that point, the subject can mentally (left brain) associate the sensations experienced with the result achieved and can begin to emphasize, by memory recall, the same process to cause its strengthening by affirmation and repetition. In this way, pain can be blocked, healing can be enhanced, malignant societal mutation anxiety can apparently be suppressed and ultimately destroyed, the body's pleasure centers can be stimulated, and a variety of specific physiological results may be achieved. In addition, bionfeedback maybe used to greatly accelerate achievement of deep meditative States particularly for beginners who have no experience in meditative techniques and whose progress in that methodology is enhanced through effective visualization and external, objective affirmation. Display of the subjects brainwave pattern on a cathode ray tube has proven to be a laboratory-validated means by which subjects can quickly learn to place themselves in profoundly relaxed states characterized by the sort of quietude and singularity of mental focus associated with advanced meditation."

"Dobber Klinkle hates hallucinations. Well, sort of. He loves the hallucinations induced by drug trips but he doesn't think hallucinations can happen without drugs. I showed him the Muller-Lyer illusion and told him that when the brain makes the bottom line look longer than the top he's having a tiny hallucination. Then he got mad and used the fucking buzz word gaslighting. Like, what the fuck is he even talking about? What does gaslighting have to do with that? Why does he have to use a script when he talks? Get your own damn thoughts, whyduncha? He acts like he's a part of some elite society with a sociopolitical-economic doctrine that's proven science. It's not science. It's more like the circular reasoning of religion. The thing is I would be way more into his side, god I hate saying side (it's a fucking religious mantra), if his s didn't lie so much. I'm not on the other s if that's what you're wondering. I believe in all the things he believes in, but they're no-brainers. The two-sided bullshit is designed to ensnare rational people on one side and batshit people on the other. Yeah, duh, of course I'm for goodness and against evil. What kind of political system is that? What kind of choice is that? It's not a political system. It's religion. It's the new Holy Roman Empire. Like, PKD said, "The empire never died.""

Sora said to us, "Don't worry about Dobber. He doesn't know what the fuck he's talking about. He's harmless. He's paranoid like everybody else."

"Datz nert fair. I attempted to escape Sora by slipping through the membrane of this Actuality into part two of the metalogue of Thar'gore'racus."

On the TV, Rocco stood up from his folding chair and waved the docutainment crew into the swamp. He bent down and pointed at a patch of algae on the bank of the swamp next to the base of a cypress tree. He grabbed the edge of the patch and tore it from the earth. He tossed the thick algae patch at the feet of the camera person who tilted the camera and shot the patch for a moment before tilting back up to Rocco and his hole. In the hole was a large splotch of pulpy brown paper and when the camera person zoomed in on the splotch revealed words. The words on the page appear at first glance to be the very words you, dear reader, are reading, but upon closer inspection the words reveal themselves to be glossolalia.

Rocco said, "You can't tell from the look of this splotch of page, but this book includes a lot of nominalizations, or irregular nouns, those kinds of magickal words with dense context and movement packed into very little space. Really, there's lots of nouns in the whole thing. It's a very nouny book, which is a sign that we are all a part of a word-magick book, a spiritual or religious text that is both is determined and isn't determined. Because the words on the page appear at first glance to be the very words you, dear reader, are reading, but upon closer inspection the words reveal themselves to be but glossolalia. This is a sign that maybe we exist in some in-between realm."

The page exploded with light and the light consumed the TV screen and then shot out of the screen and consumed the room.

One of us said, "You guys, I don't feel so good. The vibrations of this room and this blinding light are making me queasy."

"Are you eating my hawt pocket, you little shit?"

The vibrations of the room threatened to break reality.

Tony, Bobby, and Newsom lifted their faces off the nasty-ass bath-room counter and offered some to Octavia and I.

Octavia said, "I don't feel like sucking piss and shit like a goddamn demented eldritch anteater."

The three of them laughed and then they forgot that they had even offered. We ventured out of the bathroom back into The Exit.

"Hey look, the naked fire marshall is back," I said, pointing. He was bare-assed on a bar stool, balls hanging over the side.

Bobby grabbed me by the back of the neck and yanked me away from Tony. "I never finished telling you about how you got my mind twisted into a two-way Edmond cylinder." His face was very close to my face and it felt like at any moment he was going to grab a hold of my forehead with his teeth and yank downward until my entire face peeled off.

I said, "What the fuck is a two-way Edmond cylinder?"

He said, "You need to listen." His breath was tequila fire.

I heard a snap that sounded like it came from inside his face and blood ran out of his nose into his mouth. The red ooze cascaded down his jaw and drip, drip, dripped onto his shirt. Bobby shook his head wildly and the blood splattered onto my face. His mouth opened wide and a sound that wasn't human escaped.

Bobby squeezed the back of my neck hard and shoved my face into the cushions of the Marie Antoinette couch. "I'll tell you how you got my mind twisted into a two-way Edmond cylinder." His eyes crossed, he fell backward onto the carpet, and convulsed.

Newsom screamed and shoved a popsicle stick into Bobby's mouth.

"That's the wrong way," Tony said, stomping on Bobby's arm.

"What the fuck are you doing?" I screamed.

"I'm trying to break his arm," Tony replied.

Newsom elbowed me in the face as she reared back the popsicle stick and jammed it back into his mouth.

I yelled, "You're not supposed to shove it down his throat."

Flynn scurried across the floor like a gator, snatched the TV remote, and scurried back under the couch.

The Rocco doc was back on and blaring at us at full volume as Newsom tugged and failed to retrieve the popsicle stick she had shoved down Bobby's throat.

Flynn coughed and tapped me, holding out a lit joint. Confused by the sudden change of scenery, I paused to examine my surroundings.

From the void, Flynn asked, *You'd never leave me to die, would you Echo?*

What kind of a question is that, Flynn? Jesus. I'd never leave you.

I changed the channel on the TV and Fat Tornado Clocks blasted at us. The footage showed a crowd that had grown out of control, a voiceover stating the mob had grown to half a million and many were leaping on and off the stage to play impromptu sets. Holger had stolen the microphone back from the rogue crowd.

"I thought this film," Tony said as he slapped the back of Bobby's puke puddle submerged head, "was supposed to be about the life of Rocco Atleby. There's more of him talking about absolutely nothing than there is of his life story. Also, Bobby, you owe me twelve grand to replace this rare antique carpet."

"He's not talking about nothing," Flynn said from under the couch. "You just keep coming into the docutainment film at the wrong time."

Bobby lifted his head. Puke dripped from his face and plopped into the puddle.

Bobby said, "I don't owe you shit," and swirled his fingers in the puddle like he was stirring a primordial cocktail of his own pain and making.

Tony said, "No one else had a seizure."

Flynn said, voice weak and wavering, "Can we go on the Rocco tour soon? Remember, the reason we came here?"

"I know," I said, reaching under the couch to pat an unknown part of his body. "Soon."

"I thought I was going too," Newsom said as the next cover band set up on The Exit's stage.

Holger, Marcel, and the rest of the members of *Fat Tornado Clocks* carried their equipment onto the stage.

"Is the cover band made up of the members of *Fat Tornado Clocks*?" I asked.

Hunched over, Newsom poked Big Momma Thatcher's face. "It's Fat Tornado Clocks covering themselves. They're called *Glossolalia And Gravayour.*"

"That's not a cover band," Flynn said. "You want to know about a good cover band? You ever heard of *Chariots of the Funeral Pyre*? They do sick goth covers of jock rock songs. Hehe, that's stupid." His face turned blue and foam bubbled at the corners of his mouth.

"Yes it is," Holger said into the microphone and then continued on with the equipment set up.

Flynn's eyes rolled into the back of his head.

CHAPTER TWENTY-THREE

GLOSSOLALIA AND GRAVAYOUR

The common room, a blur of shapes and colors, pumped and thudded to an off-kilter beat like the room was a torn artery spurting blood into the street of a nightmare hallucination and we were the shards lodged inside. The walls faded and the spiral stairs loomed over us as they began to twist and contort, clicking and spinning like a clock. The room spun in the opposite direction of the stairs, the arterial liquid pouring faster and faster from the wound, as the stairs grew in size and the artery's pumping accelerated.

My body and my being transferred as a Fat Tornado Clock from the common room to the apartment's tiny kitchen.

The kitchen spun so goddamn fast. I believe the Patasphere was threatening to turn us into margaritas. Bobby poked at his reflection in the ancient mirror hanging over the modern sink. The sink, stopped up and full of bookpowder tea, swirled below. He leaned forward, dipped his head into the tea, and screamed. The liquid splashed and bubbled, he halted his scream, the liquid settled, and he sucked down the whole batch. Bobby lifted his head out of the sink like he was lifting it out of a skull cap he had licked clean.

My fat tornado clock transferred to The Exit. The house lights flicked on and Tony jumped from the puke-stained carpet of the common room onto the stage.

"I'm in this cover band too," he yelled at us. He whipped out a theremin from behind his back and handed it to me. As soon as my hands squeezed, instinctually declaring guardianship over the instrument, a mysterious hand from behind the wall of bar smoke snatched it from me and carried it back into the secondhand realm like a dragon rescuing its stolen gold and returning to its cave.

From the Paris TV screen, the Roc doc abruptly cut to the silent eight-millimeter footage of the ritual in the stairwell. The large iron door opened. The naked figures, whose heads were positioned so that their faces were obscured, slipped their robes back on and lifted their hoods. A plume of smoke billowed out of the pitch-black doorway and a lone figure emerged. The wanderer entered their circle and the figure with the large torus symbol on the back of his cloak approached the iron door.

The torus figure lowered his hood, revealing himself to be Tony.

And even though this footage was from the mid-1960s Tony seemed to be the same exact age he was when he handed us the keys to the apartment.

"The hell?" I said.

"Is that Tony?" Ruby asked.

"Is Tony one of the Order of the Cacti founders?" Will asked.

Tony grabbed the wanderer's hood and lowered it, revealing Bobby.

The coven screamed in fright.

We collectively whipped our heads this way and that, searching for Bobby.

At the top of the loft stairs, Bobby was perched on top of a TV.

He was staring at us with mad eyes and a demented smile.

Red light filled his eyes.

He cackled, cackled, cackled.

The cackle was silent.

He stared into my soul.

He cackled, cackled, cackled.

The cackle was still silent.

On the TV, the silent footage of the ritual circle continued to roll. Tony pulled his athame, a mirror shard with a brass handle, from his robe. He stabbed Bobby and then himself in the gut. Bobby and Tony collapsed to the center of the circle and the remaining robed figures swarmed them. The shot tilted upward. A Fat Tornado Clock emerged from beneath the bottom of the frame. The FTC was followed by whipping, undulating tendrils which were attached to...the elder gawds know what. The tendrils swirled around the FTCs like hands waving over orbuculums.

I reached under the couch and touched Flynn's cold hand.

"You guys," I said to Bobby and Newsom, who were sitting on The Exit's crusty couch and probably waiting for delicious smoked meats artisanally crafted in a Grecian smoker.

They whipped out their ceremonial mugs and took another shot of tea.

I squeezed Flynn's hand and pulled, but instead of pulling him out from under the couch like I had intended, I pulled myself under the couch into the shadows. I pulled and pulled on Flynn's arm, which seemed to go on forever, never finding his body.

"Wake up, man. Wake up. Please. I'm sorry. I'm so sorry. I love you."

The spacetime consciousness sloooooooowed. And I collapsed backwards to carpet, leaving behind an imprint of myself within the neural web of the noosphere. Mid-fall, I waved at my imprint. My imprint waved back, flipped me the bird, and then threw his head back and laughed. I laughed. What the fuck?! The spacetime consciousness sped back up and I hit the carpet. Bam! I writhed as I struggled to catch my breath.

Bobby crawled to me and laid his head on my chest. The acrid sting of cortisol and adrenaline wafted off of him and hit my nose.

"I saw you," Bobby said to me in The Exit, close to my face as I continued to pull on Flynn's arm, pulling myself deeper into the under-realm of the couch, "while I was doing my necromancy routine on Proteron Avenue to unsuspecting you passing us by, heading to whatever dive you frequent. When I said hi to you, you cocked your head like you didn't know who I was. And *you know what*, I didn't like that one little bit."

My breathing increased and his head rose and fell, rose and fell.

He continued, "Did I ever finish telling you the story about the mandelbulbs of Aurora and my fit of necromancy?"

Tony, seemingly from nowhere, knelt beside my head and leaned into my ear. "You're going to love this story. Remember, dear boy, all things occur at once. This is determined. Morality is my bitch."

Tony leaned back and chortled as Ruby handed him a highball from the bar. I struggled to catch my breath. I looked down and jumped at the sight of Bobby. Little tentacles slithered out of his hair, snaked to my flinching face, and swallowed me whole. The tentacles reconfigured and tessellated into a Fat Tornado Clock.

The world remastered itself.

Octavia squeezed my hand. "What is this?"

"I don't know," I said to Octavia.

"My story," Bobby said. He wrapped his arms around me and squeezed. Slimy tentacles slithered out of his body, snaked to my flinching face, and swallowed me whole. The tentacles reconfigured and tessellated into a Fat Tornado Clock.

The world remastered itself.

Tony smiled, his laugh lines folding into a demonic curve. The dim light of the bar casted a shadow on his face that turned it into a skull. He screamed a laugh into the ceiling, gulped down the drink, and chucked the glass to the floor. The glass shattered into an infinity of stars and the stars scattered into the cosmos.

"I found you," Bobby said. "Like you had been running from me for years. Hiding, like a frightened animal. I finally found you that night. You were chucking these buckets of sudsy water onto the nurnies of Aurora. "Echo, what are you doing?" I said to you and you said, "Echo. I hear an echo. "Revivals, reunions, and reboots are desperate," said the well dressed man with the squinty eye. "But you're making this work." I was suddenly standing at the entrance of the Michigan Avenue Bridge and I appeared to be half-examining a ratty paperback. This is still happening inside the Kindred novel. I probably don't need to say that anymore. That was the last time. I promise.

Sincerely,

Sora

P.S. This isn't the actual end of my message to you that is encrypted within this living information that is disguised as a science fiction paperback.

P.P.S. Although at first the bridge looked as it always did this morning during what was to be my first of the day's many head-clearing walks, the Patasphere glitched and twitched and there before was a large modification to the bridge. In the afternoon, while on a head-clearing jog, I came across a new modification. The new mod was a grand proscenium arch. I paused my jogging and paced before this arch that had definitely not been here a few couple ago. Was my memory failing me? Was I losing my mind? Did a crew of highly caffeinated master masons with the emphatic-whacko-gene craft and construct this gargantuan arch covered in ornate designs in only a couple hours? Was it fake? Maybe made of styrofoam? For a parade? I approached the arch and punched it. I broke my hand. This was probably not styrofoam. The arch's design was so immaculate and detailed in that hand crafted old world way that it looked like that thing should've taken a decade to construct. So much popping and slipping in the Patasphere. This popping around and in and out of spacetimeconsciousness keeps happening to me. It had been two weeks of nonstop peripheral invasions and things popping into existence in familiar places and synchronicities galore. I don't know if it was two weeks. I don't know why I typed that. I pulled a random number out of my butt. And now as I type this that darn ever-shifting eternal text seems to be taking over my vision. How am I still type, type, typing this letter. Oh God, my mind. The text has me. The glass shattered into an infinity of stars and the stars scattered into the cosmos.

"I found you," Bobby said. "Like you had been running from me for years. Hiding, like a frightened animal. I finally found you that night. You were chucking these buckets of sudsy water onto the nurnies of Aurora. "Echo, what are you doing?" I said to you and you said, "Echo. I hear an echo. "Revivals, reunions, and reboots are desperate," said the well dressed man with the squinty eye. "But you're making this work." I was suddenly standing at the entrance of the Michigan Avenue Bridge and I appeared to be half-examining a ratty paperback. The ratty paperback twisted and curled into a plumage of ancient phosphorescent scroll. The patamorphosed into a breast pocket on my sweet as heck blue peacoat. The peacoat breast pocket fell open and the scroll rolled, bounced and opened, rolled, bounced and opened, rolled down the ancient craggy cliff steps of Aurora. And the end of the scroll landed in the word goop at the bottom of the steps. The goop, the plasmate, absorbed into the scroll and, with ZAP!!!!, the words fired across my open pocket. I could no longer tell if I was reading the words on the scroll outloud or if I was reading the words in my head. I attempted to pry my eyes from the scroll but my eyes wouldn't move. In my periphery I could see that my legs had begun moving and I was somehow navigating the slippery steps without my sight. The words on the page-scroll slowly scuttled, twisted, and contorted. The letters formed into intricate geometric arrangements and yet I could still read and understand what the page said. The scroll which I had been of course shifting upward with my hands as I read stretched and I could no longer feel or see my hands. It was as if the page had no edges and had become my one and only Aiwass. The page, my new sight and new world, began spinning. The geometric arrangements began to dance and form into primitive characters like the animal and hunter stick figures from a cave painting. My sight had become like a phenakistoscope. The spinning elongated forward and a perception of depth formed. The crude cave figures became Autumn and a creature by his side that hadn't been there before, a spindly spider-like thing with eight legs. It had brown fur and the head of a dog. In fact, it barked at a bird swooping by. The page-sight morphed into my perspective of following Autumn and this spider-dog up the steps. The spider-dog appeared to be Autumn's pet because he stopped on the steps for a moment to pet the thing and say to it, "Good Tremolo."

Anyway, all of the popping was making me tired. Where was that awful voice coming from? Maybe the voice was coming from some syntactical dimension – the realm in which language and the rational agents (the a priori beings) live and the realm that runs underneath and parallel to our realm in which language co-evolved with the slimy spongebob pinky mandelbulb that is the human brain.

Dr. Escoffier, where the hell am I right now? I swear to God it feels like I have been lifted from this realm, like the square from flatland, and I am still in the hand of some Eldritch.

Let me start from the beginning. This should clear some things up about this "being lifted out of flatland" business. I first arrived at Temple Egregore six weeks ago, barely halfway through my first se-mester at your alma mater, and since then many strange occurrences have left me rattled, paranoid, and, like I said, feeling alone. The higher learning experience promised by Egregore's recruiter, a fellow named Edmond Edmond, does not match up with what my signal machine and fleshy body have experienced. Maybe this is where I should start, with my recruitment. First… Edmond… sitting there in the back of my parent's bakery and eating half of what I had spent all day baking… what should've been purchased by half the town… stuffing his face in the most unsavory manner… said to me in between oversized bites… "Temple Egregore appreciates your writing talents. You have the rare gift of bringing words to life. We have archived all six of your admis-sions essays as remarkable contributions to the study of necromancy. Writing is highly regarded at Temple Egregore, held above all other mystical fields. Writing is the most paramount of the esoteric practices. The great necromancer, Dr. Bortan Kilawax, once said, "The spoken word did not come first. The written word came first. The written word is, for a lack of better words, behind us. If we learn to turn around, we can see the words and pluck them from the ever-shifting fiery eternal plane of lucidity and total consciousness. And then, we can do what must be done." At Temple Egregore, your writing skills will be nurtured and honed. They will be honed on your own through nearly unlimited amounts of free writing time and nurtured through workshops that you may attend whenever you want. The structure of your learning experience is crafted by you and you alone."

Dr. Escoffier, was this how you were recruited? Were you promised unlimited free writing time?

I wrote the second chapter of a Greg Kindred novel my first week at Temple Egregore, before the Egregore took unlimited writing time away. I have included it in this letter.""

In The Exit, Tony massaged Bobby's shoulders. "My pet. Go on. Tell him."

""'Echo, I said," Bobby said from the carpet, his head on my chest. "You know me. Don't treat an old friend like this.""

The clicking spin of the spiral stairs grew exponentially and the stairs became the tapestry of every converging holomultigraphic interfacing proscenium archetype realmz.

""'I don't know you," Bobby said in a whiney lilt, imitating the mandelbulb man. "My name is Holger. I've just arrived and I'm just trying to make a living."" Bobby lifted his head from my chest and slammed down, knocking the wind from me.

"Living?!" Bobby screamed. A ring of gold light exploded from the spiral stairs and rippled into the common room, The Exit, Aurora, and the void.

"Look man," Holger said and sloshed another bucket into the road, "I don't know you. So how about you take a flying fuck outta here, whackjob?"

Bobby twisted his head 180 degrees, his neck cracking, so that he was looking into my eyes.

He smiled.

"You know me," Bobby said and punched me, me as Holger, in the face on the sidewalk of Proteron Avenue under the globe lamp.

He slammed his head into my chest as hard as he could and blood sprayed from his mouth and nose.

Newsom screamed in Aurora, Paris, and The Exit, "Bobby, you're going to kill him!"

Bobby reared back my head, his fists latched onto my hair, and smashed my face into the ever-tessellating hypertiles into pandimensionality. Hot soupy plasmatic ever-shifting essence rushed into the cavities of my face and poured from me as Bobby slammed the stranger's face into the spine of the eternal text.

Bobby, emerging from the shadow of Proteron, stepped into the circle of light surrounding the globe lamp and let go of the gentleman that he was bringing back to life. The man's face was broken and contorted and bloody. He fell limp to the greebles and nurnies. A sedan swerved and narrowly missed running over his head.

The cover band stopped, except for Tony, who was beating himself over the head with his microphone while smiling the smile of a proper young man. The band, frozen, was staring at Bobby as he became progressively more violent with his yelling at the stranger, who suddenly looked a lot like the man on the airplane to Paris, on the edge of the eternal text.

"Echo!" Octavia screamed.

Tony cackled. "That's the ticket!" His tentacles whipped and thrashed like they were conducting a symphony for Eris. Hail Eris! Hail Sophia! Hail the Logos! Hail Aiwass!

Ruby jumped the bar and tackled Bobby to the ground, freeing the bleeding stranger from Bobby's fury. Newsom grabbed a loose greeble from Proteron Avenue and slammed Bobby over the head with it.

Flynn jumped out from under the couch, Bobby's syringe in his hand, and stabbed Bobby in the back of the neck.

Bobby threw Ruby and Flynn off of him and wobbled around the bar, common room, and Aurora.

He dropped to the ground and landed face-first.

Octavia said, "Let's get out of here!"

The Exit patrons crowded the chaos of Bobby thrashing within a Fat Tornado Clock. They murmured. I attempted to eavesdrop on their words but the FTC sucked me in with Bobby. From within FTC, I imagined all the interesting things the patrons were saying.

"What's with this novel?" The FTC absorbed that patron.

"Paradoxically, having gone to such great lengths to avoid trying to render judgments based on an occult or dogmatic frame of reference in the end I found it necessary to return, at least briefly, to the question of the impact of the indie lit fantasy experience on common belief systems. I did so because although it was essential to avoid attempting to render an assessment in the context of such systems, I felt that it was necessary after having completed the analysis to point out that the resulting conclusions do not any violence to the fundamental mainstream of either Eastern or Western belief systems. Unless that point is clearly established, the danger exists that some people will reject the whole concept of the indie lit fantasy experience in the mistaken belief that it contradicts and is therefore alien to all that they hold to be right and true." The FTC absorbed that patron.

"How many old timey spy devices have you found? Why use old timey spy devices? Are peeperz jus fuckin witchu? Errweeonelove carries a futuristic spy device around in their pocket errwweeday. GSN's be the gift that keeps on giving for the MIC. Not only do they get to spy on us for free and we unknowingly narc on ourselves and each other errwweeday, but the GSN is also an effective AF behavioral engineering tool." The FTC absorbed that patron.

"This study is certainly not designed to be the last word on the subject but I hope that the validity of its basic structure and of the fundamental concepts upon which it is based will make it a useful guide for other O∴O∴T∴C∴ personnel who are required to take the indie lit training or work with indie lit materials." The FTC absorbed that patron.

"I've got an itchy ass." The FTC absorbed that patron.

"This technique provides amplification for application of the energy bar tool as a means of healing specific areas or systems of the lit. The configuration of the author's lit is imagined and then the various major systems such as the novel's nervous and circulatory systems are envisaged in fabulous trippy drippy colors within the confines of the outline being held in the imagination. The energy bar tool is then applied to energizing, balancing, and healing in whatever manner the author desires. In the process, the author visualizes various streams of fabulous trippy drippy colored energy flowing out of the tool into the novel's organ system or area upon which the revitalizing or healing application is being made. Since colors are the result of differing wavelengths of light, which is to say energy at various frequencies, this technique operates on the assumption that as the novel is composed of energy it can be vitalized and healed through the additive application of additional energy provided that the energy is applied in the appropriate form." The FTC absorbed that patron.

The FTC patamorphosed into a mandelbulb. The mandelbulb traveled through the 5th dimension and met up with some mandelbulb buddies. Our mandelbulb fused with the mandelbulb buddies.

I, I as Holger, fell onto the sidewalk next to the reconfigured soul from The Exit that Bobby had given the great and powerful tentacle arm of the Gawdhead to, and the soul exploded into an infinity of tessallating holomultigraphic rhythmz interfacing with the omniverse. This tessellation imploded into ever-shifting pandimensional blocks of indeterminacy. The indeterminacy fired beams living info into my being. I left my body and looked down on my body pulsing and oscillating with stellar lightzzzz. The beams let me know that everything would be okay. I returned to my pulsing, oscillating limbo bod. Then the blocks reconfigured into the tentacle-armed man, and this stranger fell onto the sidewalk next to us.

Blood shot out of my eyes.

"Echo!" Bobby yelled. He cackled into the concrete. "You're no fun anymore!"

The Exit exploded into a frenzy. The frenzy patamorphosed into a fleeing. At the exit of The Exit, the mass fused into an amorphous blob. It wiggled and warbled, wiggled and warbled, and hundreds of limbs flailed and undulated as the blob desperately attempted to squeeze through the tiny door.

Octavia and I spilled out of The Exit alongside the fleeing mass of occupants. We tripped and fell onto the carpet of the apartment and rolled in pain through the ether's oblivion, spirals of hot light shooting off of us.

Bobby cackled, cackled, cackled. He faded, faded, faded. Bobby cackled, cackled, cackled.

The benevolent spiral stairs absorbed him.

"He's gone," I said to Flynn as I pulled him out from under the couch and clutched him to my chest.

"No, he's not," I thought I heard Flynn whisper back. "Here be dragons. But we did good."

I clutched his hand. "No, you did good. Thank you."

Tony said, "If only you knew the plan!" His tentacles flailed and twitched. "Your improv powers are no match for my improv powers." He jumped into a spasmodic tapdance. Tappity-tap-tap-tap-tap-TAP-TAP-tap-tap-TAP! His tapdancing brought him to the boundary line that separates genius and madness. He screamcackled His tapdancing brought him to the edge of the spiral stairs. He slipped and fell. He screamed and tumbled down and down and down and never landed. His screams and the clatter of his body hitting the corners of each step echoed on and on and on in neverending revolutions. His body rolled past our level over and over and over and the echo of the screams and clatter mutated into a waveparticle holomultigram that encodes the whole. Even if Tony dropped our frozen holomultigram of the ripple pattern on the spiral stair and broke it into a number of pieces each individual piece would and would not recreate the entire holomulti-graphic movie all by itself. The smaller the piece, the fuzzier and more distorted and clearer and less distorted, resulting psychological pro-jection but the fact remains that a whole broken unbroken projection would nonetheless be made and patamorphosed into a consciousness nexus. The key to manifesting any holomultigram is setting that mat-terenergyconcept in motion by interacting with matterenergyconcepts in a state of sleep. The interference pattern you desire shall be generated by your interaction with this observedobservingobserversobserving. Another feature of a holomultigram is it's efficiency. The anti-hermitic order of the powers that be can hide pretty much an infinite amount of bits of living information within these multiplanes that can take the form of a very tiny space.

Octavia and I ran as fast as we could until we crashed through the multiplanes. The planes shattered like glass. And we hopped from shard to shard to shard until we landed in Curtis Hixon Park. We hopped from shard to shard to shard to Riverwalk.

We slowed to a stroll.

We panted and shook.

Tony continued his fall down the spiral stairs.

Ahhhhhhhhhhhhhhhhhhhhhhhhhhhhhhhhhhhhhhhhhhhhhhhhhhhhh-hhhhhhhhhhhhhhhhhhhhhhhhhhhhhhhhhhhhhhhhhhhhhhhhhh.

We passed Newsom, who was standing in the heart of downtown, next to the centerpiece of the city, Floral Fountain which was designed and constructed by master emphatic whacko architect, science fiction author, and core Order of the Cacti member Autumn Levi. Water erupted from the fountain, and Bobby emerged and gasped for breath like someone or something had been holding him under.

"I'm sorry!" he screamed at the stars. "Don't make me go back!"

Bobby was pulled by an invisible force back under the water and the scummy water splashed from the fountain. Ringlets of blood bubbled to the surface and spread across the water. A wall of the thick red water gushed from the Floral Fountain and swallowed Newsom. She shrieked gaping gore. Birds fluttered further south. Alligators splashed in the Hillsborough River. The Skunk Ape slapped its hairy ass and scuttled under the ancient-bungalow-turned-Rocco-themed-nail-salon. Her primordial yawp echoed across downtown. Lightning fired from the five light globes of the lamp at the center of the fountain. The lamp resembled a dark tree growing from the patina-tinted iron platform hovering above the water. This is presumably an illusion and Mr. Levi, infamously, never revealed the illusionist trick he used to create this effect. Us Tampanians have our theories, many theories. In fact, there are dozens of books and websites dedicated to each theory.

Newsom screamed again.

The globes fired lightning into the atmosphere again and the lamp spun on its base. Ethereal light puffed from the globes, the four pointed downward and the one on top pointed to the sky. Four emerald-colored phantasmagoric orbs descended from the downward globes and one bright blue orb ascended from the globe pointed to the sky. The orbs grew and formed into five shadowy figures, four cloaked in shiny emerald robes floating between the lights and the water of the fountain and one floating cloaked in an orgone-blue robe between the crown light and the sky. The glow burned bright around their bodies. Their faces were hidden within the dark recesses of their hoods. Simultaneously, the figures lifted their arms, palms up, and their auras swirled and freed themselves from the bodies of their masters like a veil being lifted from an esoteric artifact and the hazy aura shot into their palms. The figures squeezed the orbs and twisted their fists downward. They reared back their fists, shot them forward, and fired ten beams of light, eight emerald and two blue, into the bloody fountain. I presumed these figures to be configurations of the Gravayours' Gawdhead. Their appearance matched Rocco's descriptions of the robed bodies of the maleficent Gawd contained within *Unabridged Exegesis* and his posthumously published autobiography entitled *A Pataspherical Life: An Eternal Lifetime of Observing Myself.*

The blood bubbled and foamed, and spilled over the edge of the fountain. Newsom fell to her knees and stared in, what I could only imagine was, shock. The tsunami of blood crashed into her knees.

Bobby rose from the bubbling, foaming fountain, trapped inside the beam of the O∴O∴T∴C∴. Lightning fired from the top globe light and the lightning swirled and patamorphosed into the eternal text. The text opened. Its pages flipped and zipped this way and that. The book hovered downward and settled before Newsom. She leaned into the book and appeared to read the page.

Octavia yelled, "What's it say?"

Newsom's eyez scanned the page. "What is this? I can't read this."

The O∴O∴T∴C∴ reared back their fists once more, shot them forward, and blasted Bobby Des Moines over the edge of the fountain. Newsom looked up from the book and held out her hands to protect herself from Bobby's barreling body.

The blast stopped and he halted and spun over the patanoobound book. Blood, entrails, bones, the central nervous system, gravy, adrenaline, slop, cortisol, goopy plasmate, untethered pathos, displacement, severely damaged anterior cingulate cortices, psychonautical blocking, absolutism, the block multiverse of the gawdhead mindiverse, disinformation, solidified plasmate, chewed up scenery, displaced sexual tension, misinformation, negativity charged bions, algorithmically triggered untethered anger, bias, sardines, algorithmically triggered untethered fear, suggestibility, deep fried autohypnotic suggestion, overwrought ethos, the broken absolute, the new humors, lots of "objective" realities, friendly neighborhood corporoindividualz, pipperminders, dicey sleuths, faulty ass syllogismz, cheap construction materials, absentmindedness, swarmmode, broken unbroken syzygy, manufactured boogymen, broken unbroken antinomy, those analytical overlays you cleverly sent me that let me and my coven know that yooz be listenin in, long lost logos, that time sent me that caravan stuffed to the gills like a clown car with peeperz dressed as hersetery's most famous dictators jus ter fuck with me, dat waz fun lol, I'm jus a cermerdee writer, why fuckz with me, I misdirect yeez jus ter waste defense bergert merney, the old humors, drippy living info, berbabblerzzzz, broken unbroken anomalies, interlergence agency interfearatz, psychological transience, sleeperz who tink they awakerz, recuperation, psychobabble, co-opted good vibey shiz, co-opted cool AF feel bad shiz, fundamentalism that doesn't look or feel like fundamentalism, twinkling memories, which side are yooz on, apophenia, a forgetful Patasphere, strawpeeperz ergumertz, protests manufactured and organized by the fibbiz, an easily distracted Patasphere, mass pathos trigger machine, the spirit of perfect king or queen, the neverending ever-shifting massive money laundering scheme of the military industrial complex, manufactured yet very real enemies, the perfect muzak, severely damaged hippocampus, protests manufactured and organized by the cziaz, zero possible solutions, sassy pataphors, the state-corporate nexus, pyramidal patriarchal forces, the spirit of the evil steward, friendly neighborhood troll farmz, neverending ever-shifting political theatre, weaponized behaviorism, the perfect edit, cinematic persistence, so much yes-and, underdeveloped frontal lobe, the elder gawdz of time immemorial, clattering smattering egregores of our own making, a massive technological cage of operant conditioning, the perfect juxtaposition, societal mutation anxiety, friendly neighborhood agentz, misattribution, paralysis caused by the complexity wefacsimile, literal and figurative distortion filters, the inability to rationalize peepers out of frameworks the peepers did not rationalize demselves intooozeeez, the Gravayours of the Cosmic Vix subsidizing the herdy gurdy mediums and being invited into the nerrrrwzzzzzz by their soulapplication to reducing the medium budgetz of manifesting and maintaining nerrrrrwzzzzzz and the secret elder gawdheadz that provide this subsidy becoming routine nerrrrrrwzzzzzzz filtration system and keyz to the gatez and non-routine sources always beee strugglin' for access and may beeeeeee ignored by the attempted conjuring of the gatekeeperzzzzz, so much if-then, pulling really cool awesome revolutionary concepts from the goopy realm of unarticulated matter and then articulating duh matter and den pushing dat concept to the realm of boxed-in fundamentalism, fnordz a-poppin, ghost skeleton armies, co-opted pataphysical theatre, I-Object relationships niche personal brand stealthy atomized hardcore capitalism presented as genuine I-Thou relationships, co-opted improv theatre magick, over flicking simplication, a corner of the whole apparently equaling the whole dang implicate order unfolded as the extricate order of the dear and glorious reduction sauce power and the scapegoat easy answer forever and ever gesundheit, over fucking specialization, your favorite alien ghostz, giving up on duh complex hazy somewhat objective Actualites and constructing an ever-shifting amorphous damnnear infinite number of counterfeit Actualities managed by corporations and stabilized by politicians and reinforced by our echo chamberzzzzzzzz, so much behavioral engineering, the behavior of the individual being shaped according to revelations of "good conduct" and never as the result of experimental study, de facto licensing authority, so much perception management, inner party fuckery, servomechanism encrusted humanoidal human entity trying very hard to be human and break through the error-sensing auto-correction halting of the revolutionary authoritarian quashing innate tendencies of the shadow, co-opted and retooled procedural memory, wealthy elites with insane amounts of power dwelling within every corner of every place you can tink of, forgetting about plantz and how easily day carn slip into any movement or herm or camp or platform, pareidolia, metasyntactic variables, the death of the glorious individual not being the death of consumerism but the arrival of untethered transparency for duh state-corporate nexus elites, the same old rational agents, and hot delicious smoked plasmate spilled from his gut in a tornado spin and were sucked into the book. The tip of the gory tornado audibly popped upon its exit from the aura field. Bobby reached for Newsom and his mouth opened and closed like he was telling her something but all that could be heard was the hum of the beams and the warble of the tornado.

"I want to read this," Newsom said with her hands squeezed into a cage of prayer. "Don't close the book. I must know."

The O∴O∴T∴C∴ lifted their hands to the heavens which reversed Bobby's spin. The night sky dissolved and the spiral staircase remained in its place. The ancient carpet of the Parisian apartment sprouted out of the concrete of the Floral Fountain courtyard. Bobby reached for Newsom. The cloaked figures shot their hands forward once more and blasted Bobby across the tome's threshold and he disappeared into the written word.

Newsom fell to her knees, inside the common room. A swirling wind rose around her and enveloped her. The book wobbled and lightning shot out of the pages. Newsom grabbed the page Bobby had been sucked into and as the book snapped shut, revealing a leather binding with a gold leaf rendition of Rocco's hypersphere consuming the cover, she pulled the page. The tome flattened so that it was flush with the ground and then the tome expanded across the land, the gold leaf fading and the surface of the book blending with the colors and natural texture of the land. The page grew beyond the border of the tome. It flew from her hand and continued to grow across the carpet. The words on the page appear at first glance to be the very words you, dear reader, are reading, but upon closer inspection the words reveal themselves to be but glossolalia.

Will, high on bookpowder, rolled across the carpet toward her. "Yo, what did the text say?" The scroll of page shot over his body and wrapped around him.

"It was all there in my head," Newsom said. "It was swirling about and I understood. And as soon as I understood I forgot or, I don't know how to say it, didn't understand anymore. It was like I knew less than I knew before."

Will responded, but his words were muffled by the page which encased him like a mummy. The page ran up the stairs, wrapped around each bed many times until the beds looked like Christmas presents for bibliophiles, zoomed over the edge of the loft back into our domain, and then spun itself around the TV.

Octavia and I continued our stroll across the common room and in a gust of wind the carpet ripped from the floor, revealing the concrete of Floral Fountain courtyard beneath.

In a matter of seconds, the walls of the apartment cracked, crumbled, and rumbled to the ground.

A grand cloud of dust lifted into the atmosphere. Octavia and I chopped our way through the dust with our hands. I nearly tripped and fell one of the mounds of rubble left behind. We stepped onto and climbed it as the dust settled and visibility returned. We found a square wall of rubble and strolled the ruinous perimeter of the apartment, the corkscrewing spiral staircase stretched across the sky -- Tony rolling down the stairs over and over like a fallen God -- and the furniture and its remaining occupants jockeying within, that now sat in the heart of downtown Tampa.

The Marie Antoinette couch with Flynn's arm sticking out from underneath, limp and pale, loomed in my periphery.

His hand twitched.

The arm flailed.

And Flynn crawled out from under the couch.

Flynn waved. "Hey, all."

I yelled, "Duderoo! We outta duh void!"

Flynn smiled and pointed at me. "Ten four, good buddy. That's improv magick for ya, amirite!"

Oct yelled in excitement, "Flynn! To the extent that the indy lit fantasy experience and its improv magick succeeds in bringing about a refinement in matterenergyconcept nexus of the spacetimeconsciousness, is it succeeds in expanding or altering human pataphysical senses and it brings the mothercluckin' dead back to life!"

Flynn yelled back in ecstasy, "My friends, go on and perceive without recourse to the interoutercession of the pataphysical senses such that ever more of the Patasphere holomultigram can ultimately be perceived and understood all over and over all over and over again gesundheit! Rococo Artlerbabbleton has written that the theories of Rocco Atleby and Autumn Levi appear to account for all transcendental experience, paranormal events, and even normal perceptual oddities!"

I yelled into the gloriously manic mania, "Let us not only know! Let us know that we know! And let us know that we know that we know that we know and so on and so forth! Let us be able to monitor the process of our own thinking and maintain an awareness of it! Moreover, let us conduct a comparative assessment, evaluating the function of our thought processes against various "objective" standards we have adopted! Let our spacetimeconsciousness do this because it has the capacity to duplicate aspects of its own holomultigram, project them out, "perceive" that projection, put it through comparison with the memory aspect (where its evaluation standards of measure are stored) of its own holomultigram, and measure or "sense" the differences using three-dimensional geometry and then binary "go/no go" pulse to yield verbal cognition about the self!"

Newsom jumped onto the couch and yelled, "Let's play a game! A little comedic improvisational theatre! First order of abstracting business… not too complicated inspiring words from the Great Korzybski…

"By disregarding the orders of abstractions, we can manufacture any kind of verbal difficulties ; and, without the consciousness of abstracting, we all become nearly helpless and hopeless semantic victims of a primitive-made language and its underlying structural metaphysics. Yet the way out is simple; non-identity leads to 'consciousness of abstracting' and gives us a new working sense for values, new s.r, to guide us in the verbal labyrinth. Outside of 'objectification', which is defined as the evaluation of higher order abstractions as lower; namely, words, memories., as objects, experiences, feelings, the most usual identification of different higher order abstractions appears as the confusion of inferences and inferential terms with descriptions and descriptive terms. Obviously, if we consider a description as of the nth order, then an inference from such a description (or others) should be considered as an abstraction of a higher order (n + 1). Before we make a deci-sion, we usually make a more or less hasty survey of happenings, this survey establishing a foundation for our judgements, which become the basis of our action. This statement is fairly general, as the components of it can be found by analysis practically everywhere. Our problem is to analyze the general case. Let us follow up roughly the process. We assume, for instance, an hypothetical case of an ideal observer who observes correctly and gives an impersonal, unbiased account of what he has observed. Let us assume that the happenings he has observed appeared as: ·• ♦, Ī, ~ .... , and then a new happening-Δ occurred. At this level of observation, no speaking can be done, and, therefore, Δ use various fanciful symbols, and not words. The observer then gives a description of the above happenings, let us say a, b, c, d, ... , x; then he makes an inference from these descriptions and reaches a conclusion or forms a judgment-A about these facts. We assume that facts unknown to him, which always exist, are not important in this case. Let us assume, also, that his conclusion seems correct and that the action-A which this conclusion motivates is appropriate. Obviously, we deal with at least three different levels of abstractions : the seen, experienced . , lower order abstractions (unspeakable) ; then the descriptive level, and, finally, the inferentialevels...Let us assume now another individual, Smith1 , ignorant of structure or the orders of abstractions, of consciousness of abstracting, of s.r.; a politician or a preacher, let us say, a person who habitually identifies, confuses his orders, uses inferential language for descriptions, and rather makes a business out of it. Let us assume that Smith1 observes the 'same happenings'. He would witness the happenings $\cdot\bullet$,I,$\sim$ .... , and the happening-Δ would appear new to him. The happenings $\cdot\bullet$ $\blacklozenge$, I, $\sim$ .... , he would describe in the form a, b, c, d, $\bullet\bullet\bullet$, from which fewer descriptions he would form a judgment, reach a conclusion, B ; which means that he would pass to another order of abstractions. When the new happening-Δ occurs, he handles it with an already formed opinion B, and so his description of the happening-Δ is coloured by his older s.r and no longer the x of the ideal observer, but $B(x) = y$. His description of 'facts' would not appear as the a, b, c, d, $\bullet$.. , x, of the ideal observer but a, b, c, d, ... , $B(x) =- y$. Next he would abstract on a higher level, form a new judgment, about 'facts' a, b, c, d, ... , $B(x) = y$, let us say, C. We see how the semantic error was produced. The happenings appeared the 'same', yet the unconscious identification of levels brought finally an entirely different conclusion to motivate a quite different action, cu."

Ruby chugged a mug of bookpowder tea. "Here, here! That was straight forward as heck! We can finally play our improv games without Bobby and Tony cramping our style. Sweet glorious theatrical freedom!"

Newsom threw her hands into the air. "Sorry. I can't handle anything right now because my granularity has, like, gone all smooooooooooth marble."

Flynn said, "I got one. What if we do a gateway game?"

The page flew across the common room and slapped Ruby across the face and then quickly spun around him and encased him as well.

Will clawed his way out of the tangle of page-scroll. "Yes! A gateway! Okay, so where were we? Dimensions in-between? Now that we have postulated the legitimacy of the assertion that the energy forms which compose consciousness can move beyond the spacetimeconsciousness dimension, we need to turn our attention to the energy forms which inhabit those dimensions between spacetimeconsciousness and the Absolute. In doing so, we may better perceive the form that "reality" assumes when we encounter it in those intermediate dimensions. In this context, good ole fucking Rococo Artlerbabbleton tells us that: "The causal relationship between events breaks down; again I have been pata-programmed to find this chapel perilous we now wander within; you brought me here through autosuggestion; or did I bring you here?; who am I?; have I always known you?; movements become jerky rather than smooth. Time and space and consciousness may become grainy or chunky. Perhaps a piece of space can be traversed by a particlewave of matterenergy in any direction without necessarily being synchronized with a piece of time. In short, a pair of events will occur in either time or space or consciousness, the trio not being connected causally but by a random fluctuation." What Artlerbabbleton means is that inside the dimension of spacetimeconsciousness we're both concepts apply in a generally uniform way there is a proportional relationship between them. A certain space can be covered by energymatter moving in either particle or waveform in a certain time assuming a specific velocity virtually anywhere in the spacetimeconsciousness Patasphere. A myriad of various distortions and incongruities are thus likely to be encountered such that our nice neat assumptions concerning the relationship between space and time and consciousness as we know it in this dimension do not apply. But even more important, access is opened to both the past and the future when the dimension of the current spacetimeconsciousness is leftright behind."

Ruby clawed his way out of the scroll pile. "What did Robert Anton Wilson say? As the semanticist Alfred Korzybski often warned, when we split verbally that which is never split existentially we introduce fallacies into our thinking. Korzybski's favorite example was the matter of "space" and "time"; for in experience, we never encounter "space" without "time" or "time" without "space," i.e.. a year measures the space the Earth moves around the sun, and the space the Earth travels in one orbit gives us the time we call a "year." The verbal separation of "space" and "time" became such a problem in late 19th Century physics that paradoxes and contradictions multiplied endlessly; and this was only resolved when the genius of Einstein went back before the verbal categories, realized we had created them, and started physics over from the ground up on the simple existential fact that we never encounter "space" or "time" separately but only the undifferentiated "space-time continuum."

Newsom waved at us. "Octavia! Echo! Come play a game with us!"

Octavia waved. "Better if I don't jump in right here. "I like where this game is going but if I yes-and right here I'm going to say something mean about minimalists and deconstructionists and hardcore rationalists and how their fussy and flawed ideologues have basically become the new religious order for these futurist dark ages we find ourselves trapped within."

I said, "Yes, and imagine if you will, because everyone likes the find the thetan twilight zone peekaboo framework at the moment, that dark enlightenment thinkers have invaded most frameworks and injected their dark ages thoughtmodes into the noosphere. They have, not through top down intervention but through rhizomatic means, stealthily presented these modes as positive enlightened ideologies that are not allowed to be called ideologies. These are unquestionable axioms. The axioms are presented like shiny gift wrapped christmas presents as the dawning glorious order that will save everyone."

Octavia said, "And it's presented by the dark enlightenment thinkers to us in a way that is aesthetically, cinematically, metaphysically, etc pleasing to us. And it is so pleasing that we believe the modes came from within our own camp."

I said, "And it's not being done for like evil slash satanic slash enter your preferred boogyman reasons. It's about money. It's always about money. Anytime the money powers are threatened they change the game and they present The game change to us like it was created by us. They change the game in order to not lose their power. What was the second half of the 20th century? The money powers had made a killing and several major wars. In order to keep the business going, because again remember the entire world economy slash game board has always been one gigantic money laundering scheme for the powers that be, they created consumer culture. It was just one giant worldwide plastics investment that went well for about 50 years."

Octavia said, "Now something new is emerging and we are all being toyed and fucked with for the greater good of the money powers. He's dark enlightenment thinkers, grand engineers and managers of herdy gurdy perception our third party entities hired by the powers that be to improv the board game into whatever comes after consumer culture. Remember I'll consumer culture, at its inception, was presented at this new and glorious dawn. That's what's happening right now. There's just not a name for it yet."

I said, "Look, Oct and I are going to level with you. We're counter-counter-counter-counter-counter-counter intelligence. Sort of. We're, like, sixth party entities. We're not here to make any real change or do any kind of institutional toppling."

Octavia said, "We're middle ground entities hired as minor monkey wrench throwers. Our kind has always been here since the dawn of the ole babylonian homeowners association con. During the paralysis age of the dialectical, we're hired when people start mass anti-eleusinian rites, end of the world cults, and start doing all of the dark ages style activity that people do during these death knell periods."

I said, "Yarse, we don't intend on stopping anyone from having the freedom of choice. Ya good. We're just here to make the trip back around to thesis a lil less bumpy which will in turn soften the edges of antithesis which will in turn create a much healthier synthesis a couple hundred years from now. The redirect never ends."

Oct said, "There is no end of history. There is but infinite potential for humanity. We are great not because we were born great but because we made ourselves great."

I said, "The dick heads at the top of the patriarchal pyramid will always and forever do everything they can to make everyone below the top of the pyramid fight each other and feel like they are worthless."

Oct said, "We have been hired to tell you that you're doing great. You are beautiful. You are tenacious beasts. You are ever fluxing beings of ingenuity. Now Echo and I must return to the noosphere. It's been a pleasure working with you. See you glorious elder gods on the other side."

The page flew past me and Octavia and it slapped onto the concrete and stretched into the distance like an expanding pulpy carpet. We nodded at each other, agreeing to follow alongside it.

Ruby yelled to me and Octavia, "Hey! How'd you guys get over there?"

Flynn climbed over the apartment rubble pile and ran up to us.

He said, "Ahoy hoy!" and playfully climbed up the pole of a globe lamp. The page-scroll followed him and wrapped itself around the base of the lamp. When he reached the top he rubbed the white light like a crystal ball.

Across the river, on the lawn of the University of Tampa on a projector screen, the final quarter of the Rocco doc, blasted at the students on the lawn and at Octavia and I.

Rocco shuffled back and forth between laughing at himself and hollering at the press about how he believed reality is an infectious agent and that laughter and language are the only ways to combat reality. The press laughed at him. Rocco cradled his belly and chortled.

He waved his hands. "Don't believe me. But I promise you, I've found the secret to the universe, everything, the logos. The truth that presents itself to the most fool-hearty wanderers, that gnosis of coincidentia oppositorum. It manifests itself in my work. With every epoch transition, the gnosis presents itself in a new form. And today's form is..."

The audience hummed with repressed laughter.

"...long form improv comedy. I'm back where I started. There is no truth. Only this nonsense. I think I have trapped myself inside my own bullshit." He chortled again.

The dam burst and the audience roared.

"I made that happen," Flynn said.

Rocco read from a leather-bound book, "Laughter, the language of the soul, is our animalistic instinct to fight reality." He closed the book and opened a paperback.

The roar swelled and morphed into sexy, harsh noise.

Rocco smiled and wiggled his eyebrows. "Ya like that, huh? Well, ya gonna love dis. In the words of Mel Brooks, "Comedy is a very powerful component of life. It has the most to say about the human condition because if you laugh you can get by. You can struggle when things are bad if you have a sense of humor. Laughter is a protest scream against death, against the long goodbye. It's a defense against unhappiness and depression. Words were my equalizer.""

Students hollered, and hooted, and laughed. Some weren't paying attention. Some were frantically kissing. Some were flying Rocco-themed kites. Some were wrapping bandages around their heads and pretending to have the mumps just to be silly. Most were drinking bookpowder tea. Some were discussing Rocco and how strange it is that the whole Patasphere seems to revolve around him. Some were attempting to come up with Feynman-style definitions of the Patasphere.

"The Patasphere is a placeholder realm, like a phosphorescent cloud, that hovers over and within or maybe resides simultaneously adjacent to a pandimensional planez of goopy potently potential as heck unarticulated matterenergyconcepts."

"Soundz cool AF but I don't know if that's quite right."

"I don't know either. I'm just riffing. I'm on so much bookpowder and the bookpowder is so divine tonight."

I swore that I even saw Holger from both Rocco Atleby's novels and from the band Fat Tornado Clocks on the university lawn. "Is that Holger?" I asked.

Octavia threw a hand over her brow and peered. "It looks like it."

The light of a globe lamp reflected off the river. In the reflection, Flynn swung and danced on top of it. I looked up at Octavia who was, like me, barely paying attention to this movie we'd seen a million times.

"You wanna go for a walk?" she said.

I nodded and tried to wipe the dried blood from my mouth, nose, and eyes.

Octavia turned her attention to Flynn and waved him over. "Join us," she said in her best Jimmy Stewart impression.

Flynn spun down the lamp pole, and for a moment the lamp pole resembled a miniature version of the spiral stairs, with the elegance of an exotic dancer, and landed on his feet with a definitive TAP. He smiled and threw us a dismissive wave.

"Nah," he said. "You guys have fun. I'll meet up with y'all later."

"This is not the greatest book in the world," I said like Jimmy Stewart, waving my hand in a flourish. "This is just a tribute. Eat the fuck outta that fatted calf why doncha."

Oct said, "Couldn't remember the greatest book in the world. This is a tribute."

Flynn threw open his arms and said, "To the greatest book in the world."

From across the river, Rocco said, "These kids went searching for me. All over the fucking globe. They retraced my steps. They read my body of work over and over and over, and they read in between the lines until a funny thing happened. Language shifted, as it always does. When this shift happened, they didn't realize it at first but they had begun work on their very own doctrine of sympatheia. They endured the harsh world. They softened their edges in an attempt to soften the edges of opposing forces. Sometimes this didn't work. Sometimes it worked. They sought a cure no more. They realized the cure is the journey of the struggle. They realized that those times of sharp edges come from the top of the pyramid, from a few, and not some swarm of many infected, evil souls. In the words of Robert Anton Wilson, who was speaking about Wilhelm Reich when he said this, "The Mass Psychology of Fascism by Wilhelm Reich was burned by the United States government in 1957, and had been burned by the Soviet Union earlier and by Nazi Germany even earlier than that, and it describes very accurately the system of government we have now. TSOG (the tsarist occupation government). Reich's argument was that fascism is not an aberration that happened overnight in Italy and Germany for a few decades. It's sort of the permanent undercurrent of all patriarchal authoritarian societies and when they're under threat they turn fascist.

Fascism is just a modern name for something that's been happening periodically throughout the history of authoritarian pyramidal civilizations." If one slows down, one can step through the gateway and view the undercurrent from above. And we can follow the ringlets and ripples and flow and the shifting of the language and the placeholder fnords and terminologies. It will appear as if one possesses psychic abilities. You see, we see the undercurrent and we know something's off but our instinct is always to jump in with the current and then try to swim faster than it. And that'll feel like progress, until you bash into some jagged rocks or fall over the edge of the waterfall. So this coven, they slowed down and they yawped the protest scream against death. Conclusion. There is a sound, rational basis in terms of physical science parameters for considering indie lit fantasy experience to be plausible in terms of its essential objectives. Intuitional insights of not only personal but of a practical and professional nature would seem to be within bounds of reasonable expectations. However, a phased approach for entering the indie lit fantasy experience in accelerated mode would seem to be required if the time needed to reach advanced states of altered consciousness is to be brought within more manageable limits from the standpoint of establishing an organization-wide exploitation of indie lit fantasy experience's potential…"

Flynn slapped my back. "Duderoo, I am so hungry. I haven't eaten since the void. I'm gonna go eat an extra large Eddy and Sam's."

Rocco continued, "The most promising approach suggested in the foregoing study involves the following steps: Begin by using the Rocco docutainment hemi-sync film to achieve enhanced brain focus and induce hemisphere synchronization. Then add strong REM, not the band lol, sleep frequencies to induce left brain quiescence and deep physical relaxation. Provide hypnotic suggestion designed to enable an individual to induce deep autohypnotic state at will. Use autohypnotic suggestion to attain much enhanced focus of concentration and motivation in rapidly progressing through focus 12 exercises. Then repeat steps A and B following use of autohypnotic suggestion that an out-of-body movement will occur and be remembered. Repeat step E to achieve facility in gaining out-of-body state under conscious control. Alter hypnotic suggestion to stress ability to consciously control out-of-body movement and maintain it even after REM, not the band lol, sleep state ends. Approach focus 15 and 21 objectives (escape from spacetimeconsciousness and interact within new dimensions) from the out-of-body perspective. I know you have been playing and meddling with my dreams. You have been attempting to make contact with me. Because of my vibezzzzzzzzzzzz. I am one of you. You are attempting to recruit me. I say hello back. Use multi-focus approach to solve problem of distortion in terrestrial information gathering trips. This approach involves the use of three individuals in the out-of-body state, one viewing the target object here, in spacetimeconsciousness, one viewing it at focus 15 as it slips into the immediate past, and one viewing it at focus 21 as it slips from the immediate future. Debrief all three and compare data gathered from the three points of view. If care is taken to ensure that the three all go out-of-body together, in the same environment, their consciousness energy systems should resonate in sympathetic oscillation. They can tune in to the same target on different planes (dimensions) with greater effectiveness. Encourage pursuit of full self knowledge by all individuals involved in the foregoing indie lit fantasy experience to enhance objectivity in out of body observation and thinking, and to remove personal energy blockages likely to slooooooowed rapid progress. Be intellectually prepared to react to possible encounters with intelligent, non-corporeal energy forms when spacetimeconsciousness boundaries are exceeded. Arrange to have groups of people in focus 12 state unite their altered consciousness to build holomultigraphic patterns around sensitive areas to repulse possible unwanted out-of-body presences. Encourage more advanced gateway participants to build holomultigraphic patterns of successful attainment and rapid progress for advanced colleagues to assist them in progressing through the gateway system. If these indie lit fantasy experiences are carried through, it is to be hoped that we will truly find a gateway to a gateway and to the realm of practical application for the whole system of techniques which comprise it. Lol. Slowly but surely the coven realized they didn't need me anymore. They had each other and they had their own words."

Greg Kindred asked, "Have you already written this book?"

"No. It's not really my book. It's the fanatics' book. The fanatics will write it."

Octavia ran her fingers through my hair.

"Let's go on that walk," I said.

She nodded and took my hand. We ventured across the grass of Curtis Hixon Park and strolled aimlessly into downtown.

We found ourselves on Franklin Street in front of the Tampa Theatre.

The insanity of The Exit died down.

Emergency services and cops evaporated.

People scattered into the unanimous night.

We stumbled upon a lone man. It was the stranger that Bobby had interfaced with. He stepped into the light of the Tampa Theatre marquee which read

ALL NIGHT MARATHON

ROCCO ATLEBY

HOW TO PLAY A NECROMANCER'S THEREMIN

The stranger waved his new eldritch tentacle arm at us and smiled. "Holy shit, look at this thing."

Octavia laughed. "Brahman, you okay?"

He wiggled and jiggled the tentacle at us, and chortled.

I laughed. "Oh shit, duderoo. That is so fucked up."

He wiggled and jiggled faster and he laughed. "Nah, brah. This thing is cool as heck. Also, I know you tink I look like duh guy from duh plane ride to to Paris. I can read your mind. And I know you two wonks back there behind me at dis park are agentz. I have very sensitive affect radars, you fucking pricks. But I am not that guy, that guy that told you you were in for quite the indie lit fantasy experience." He wiggled and jiggled, wiggled and jiggled, and wiggled and jiggled.

I laughed until I almost peed myself. Octavia grabbed me by the shoulders and laughed. We laughed until we fell onto the sidewalk.

Oct shooed a curious rat away. "Yo, stranger. I bet you got ultimate improv magick in that wiggly, jiggly eldritch tentacle. It's from the Gawdhead, ain't it? You should help keep our improv game going by throw some yarz confetti."

Stranger said, "I just so happen to have Wanderer's Task confetti in my pocket." He reached into his pocket with his wiggly, jiggly tentacle, whipped out his tentacle full of confetti, held it to his mouth, shook the confetti like dice, and blew it all over the street.

The divination said, "Lickinggggaaaaah doorknobz is illegal on other planets, within other actualities, and on top of pizza box omniverses. But pretending to smash up stagez is legal errweewhere."

Stranger yelled, "Look. Who am I?" He spasmodically tap-danced. Tappity-tap-tap-tap-tap-TAP-TAP-tap-tap-TAP!!!!!!!!!

Oct said, "Fuckin' Grover Cleveland."

I said, "Eisenhower leaving office. Haha! What does that mean?!"

Stranger said, "Good night," and strolled on.

We stood, dusted ourselves off, and yelled, "Bon voyage!"

The globe lamps crackled and flickered.

Octavia said, "Wanna go in?" She gestured toward the theater.

I said, "I really do wonder how many times we've seen this movie."

We crossed Franklin and stepped up to the empty ticket booth.

"Hello?" I said, tapping on the thick pane.

"Let's just go in," Octavia said. "Screw it, right?

Past the Rocco docutainment poster, which was a theremin circuit schematic rendered in lime green over a black background, we wandered into the movie palace, designed to resemble a Mediterranean piazza, our feet echoing off the stone floors. Even though the building was empty, the pitter patter of gleeful feet, a flash mob dance, and the buzz of chattery cinema discussion filled the palace. We took our seats in the front row and leaned back to gaze at the ceiling which forever glowed the purples and blues of twilight.

We waited for the organ to lift out of the stage.

The organ failed to lift out of the stage.

We passionately made out and groped each other.

We be freaks.

An hour went by and the movie failed to start.

Octavia rested her head on my shoulder. "So this is the new version of the Rocco doc. Yarse! It's kinda frequency-following-response. Kinda hella FFR. I dig. And."

I rested my head on Octavia's head. "Lol. Yes! Love it! Get that screen a-cracklin', Rococo! Yer indie lit fantasy experience endeavors to provide the subject with the tools by which he or she may alter his or her consciousness based on his own volition over time through the repetitive use of the anti-presstitution presentation.

Oct said, "If duh mothertruckers stop telling us what to tink den wheeze canz finalsleeze got on with true ass real ass organic motherfuckin' sersaucity. The return of the unbothered resonance is possible. Us humanz, wheeze have such potential. If only we stop listening ter duh leviathan and jus do our damn thingy. Hey Zeus, Echo, the bookpowder is divine tonight. Is there a full ass moon? I'm doing that Joycean-tongue thing. I dig! Jus wow, when that servomechanism is jammed up do the sunglasses go on if ya know what I mean. Hehe. And."

I said, "Yerrrssse, I think I follow. Duh bookpowder is divine tonight. It feelz so güd when the servomechanism is jammed up. It feelz like I haven't tarkenz starrinz lime nelsona breath in a long timezzzzz. You know what we should dooz fer duh next book we teamz upz onz? Since we teamed and brought Flynn outta duh void, and the first person spiremintz beez overz, we should dooz a third purrrrrsen booko. Tird purrrrrsen beez hardzzzz, but wheeze carn dooz itz."

Oct pointed at the stage and said, "Hehe. I like dat. But I getz a solo booko fuuurrrrrrrrrsssssssst. Haha! I likes how duh Rococo Artlerbabbleton mervie beez jus us right now and what wheeze doinz rightz nowz."

"Yes and if then! Yooz knowz whatz would beeeeez coolz as hellz?"

"Icy hell."

I said, "If the next team booko was first-person from your POV."

Oct said, "That would be a cool as icy hell fun as fuck improv experiment. Let's do it."

I said, "We rush the stage and start wrecking the joint."

"Definitely."

We rushed the stage and pretended to break shit.

"Take that!"

"And that!" she rolled on the floor and kicked the air. Lifted an invisible guitar and smashed it. I climbed the scaffolding and leaped at her like a wrestler. She barely rolled out of the way in time and we lay there in the middle of the stage, out of breath.

The trap door for the organ dropped and we fell onto the cold dusty floor of the underbelly of the stage. We landed with a simultaneous OOOFFF.

"Welp," I said as I dusted off my shoulders and stood. "That didn't hurt like hell."

Octavia, doing the same, said, "What smells like cheese, balls, and a dusty ass dancing the waltz of death?"

At the heart of a profusion of switchboards, television sets and blinking lights, and tangled tubes and wires, was Rocco Atleby, strapped to a stainless steel life-support chair. His skin hung from his ragged skeleton.

"I thought you were dead," Octavia said.

"I was," he said, "but I came back."

"Did you fake your death?" I asked.

"Several times. But I really did die after the hyperloop."

"The hyper-what?" Octavia said.

"Yes, that's right. You wouldn't remember."

"Huh?" Octavia and I both said.

The beeping of Rocco's life support monitor suddenly rose to a frequency so high it sounded like the machine might sprout arms and wave them to a dropped beat.

"Hang on," Rocco said. "I haven't seen people in many years so my anxiety is a bit out of control. I know this is a bit direct, but we're old friends, so you'll understand my desire to speak without veils. I need to verbally recognize what is happening so I can process it without being overwhelmed. It's a grounding technique I've been practicing for decades. I name every surface pressing against my body and after this, I name every sound I hear."

Octavia lifted an index. "We just stumbled into a long-dead cyborg version of our favorite psychedelic fiction author under the Tampa Theatre and he's overwhelmed? Rocco, are you having a laugh right now?"

I said, "Yeah, I can't tell, which I guess makes him either...an awkward fucker if it's not on purpose or...a goddamn genius if it is on purpose. Either way, I'd say he's a pretty sick bastard with whatever it is he's got going on here."

"It reminds me of what he used to tell his readers," Octavia said. "God, it's so good. So fucking sweet. The fuck happened to psychedelic fiction. It's like it was banished by Opera Rationalizing Realityfuck. Spooky ass top dogs realized halfway through the second half of the 20th century that your brand of fiction was fertilizing anarchy as a thoughtmode into the herdy gurdy. The spooky ass top dogs realized that if that style of thoughtmode took place and multiplicity was possible on a mass level then the herdy gurdy would realize that it didn't need the spooky ass top dogs asses anymore."

Rocco blurted, "Believe me but don't believe me. Can you do a lil riffing and improving for me? It's been so long since I've been deep, deep, deep in the game of the homunculi."

I said, "I love the jokes and jeers encrypted into your books. They make for fun puzzle solving in between the lines of story, character, and ontological riffing, and I think pushing your pranks out of your body of work into Actuality makes for some wickedly delicious magick. Good job. I think the world needs more of this. Boxed in mothertruckers will not understand. And that's okay. It's not our place to make them understand. *Understand* that self-destruct mode, or linguistic servomechanism, is not some autobiographical fiction term for suffering or making lousy slash sexily fashionable bad decisions all while condemning it with thine holier than thou autoficspiracies by writing yersown contorted post-ironic versionzzzzz o' phony ass realism. It's not all like this. I love realism and minimalism and memoir fic. I like what I like. And everyone I follow and read I like. Realism and minimalism, especially realism and minimalism under the bright lightzzzz of surrealism slash avant garde slash dada slash maximalism slash psychedelic slash modern slash postmodern slash genre banishment, is so fucking far from realism though. I hope people don't get me wrong. I hope people understand that I love memoirs and literary fiction. It's jus dat maybe it wouldn't be right to insert myself into things that are like group therapy. Memoirs, autofics, and lit fics are good and totally necessary. They are places of healing. And I love them one hundred percent. I'm a bibliophile so I love many genres and categories. You know what I'm saying. To throw yet another reference into this postpostpostpostmodernmodernisthyperrealitypataphysical-experiment, I think it would be offensive of me to be like the MC of Fight Club inserting himself into the group therapy sessions. I don't know why I'm saying all of this. None of this needs to be said. No one cares. I guess it just feels good to say things into the void sometimes, and to be like Kafka writing too many letters and saying way too much. I want to outright market this book to fans of Pynchon, Robert Anton Wilson, psychedelic fiction fans, psychonautical sailors, sleepcooks, freaks and heads for Borges, nerds, people who have tried out experiment XX, and bibliophiles. And if peepers who don't normally like stuff like that come along and dig it, get hep to it, then cool, cool, cool. I don't know where I am or how I got here with this crowd. I love this crowd and I love their work but I don't know what it is they dig about me. They say "We want him here, we want him here, we want him here, doing his thing! Wooo yeah!" But then when the reviews start rolling in they say, "Rocco is here and he's making the cakes that we asked him to do. Why is he doing the thing we asked him to do? I want ice cream. Why isn't this thing, that I knew was going to be cakes, ice cream?" And if that's not outright said in reviews that I can feel it and see it and know it floating in the noosphere. Because I have well honed affect radars. Anyway Rocco, I'm a big fan of yours and I'm riffing and improving like a mothertrucker for ya, which is something I promised myself I would never do if I ever met you but here we are and lol IDK. I'm gushing. You're awesome. It's so cool to meet you."

Octavia said, "Vibez be real. Sometimes. And I have felt that too. It's double bindy. And it feels like it's being done on purpose. Dark enlightenment wonk ass mothertruckerz infecting the already infected ass algorithmic scripturez with schismatic double bindy craftworkz. This improv game is going pretty well. Seriously, my Rococo duderoo. It is a fucking pleasure to finally meet you and play thesez improv gamez with ya."

Blue ooze dribbled from Rocco's lips down his chin. "I wish I had something interesting to say. It's been a long eternity. Most of the really good stuff I have to say, that chunky and awe-inspiring kind of wisdom, is floating around inside my soupy brain as the ineffable that really wants to get f-ed lol."

Octavia asked, "Can we play one of your long form gamezzzzzzz?"

I said, "Yes, we want to get lost in your workzzzzzzz forever."

"Certainly." Rocco slapped the large red button in the center of his console.

The hundreds of TV screens surrounding us flipped on. The screens flashed various clips from *How to Play a Necromancer's Theremin* at us, every scene from the movie, all at once.

"Flynn, I don't remember this happening...oh wait. That's right. We made it out of the void. This is actually happening on the outside."

The screen cut to static for a moment and then cut to Flynn with the theremin in his lap playing *Take On Me* while sitting on the bottom step of the spiral stairs in Paris.

"Flynn?"

Flynn didn't answer and continued playing.

Rocco spoke over the music. "Pleather seat cushion against my butt, several vinyl figurines of my favorite pop culture icons sitting on the shelf of the inner shell of my life-support seat's chair including *The Séance Hour's* host, D.P. Delemore, stabbing into my thighs, my life-support tubes and wires shooting into many points on my body including my head and spine, my pet rat Kero chewing on my big toe which perma pops out of the hole in my shoe. Attire: blue petticoat and white button-down with blue marbling and slacks with psychedelic tie and thin socks and brown dress shoes I found at sunshine thrift store a million years ago and gray underwear all hanging off my Frankensteined body in tatters, purposeless metal gloves I'm wearing to make myself look more psy-fi, my obnoxiously large eyeglasses pressing into my tissue paper thin face, my extra tiny futuristic hearing aid jammed into the ear canal, and several cockroaches roaming free who have probably mistaken me for moist dirt."

I lifted an index. "-I know," I said. "I know. They are one and the same and yet the DNA strand, the pandimensional code written by the Pata Beings who the tore and cut of the chunks of the Codices away from their binding and reorganized them into the holy spiral strand, cannot be activated without its circuitry being properly plugged into the Logos, the Codices of Actuality which pluralistically allow for harmony to be molded chaos, living information to be formed from noise and fluctuation.""

Octavia said, "Shall this be the notorious open-ended period in which all of your books between 1972 and 1983 had incredibly ambiguous endings?"

Rocco cocked his head at us. "Do you mind? I'm trying to pull myself out of a spiral." He waved us off. "And now for the noises: Echo and Octavia's incessant bantering and commentary, Flynn's theremin rendition of *Take On Me*, the beeping of my life-support chair that seems to have finally calmed down and faded into the background, raucous bird song coming from what must be an absurdly large number of birds, the mechanical whirring of the motor that controls the tiny wooden flap in the corner of the stage's underbelly that doesn't seem to serve a purpose other than to annoy with its perpetual opening and closing, the audio from a rogue frequency picked up by my hearing aid of an eighty-six-hour audiobook of psychedelic fiction writer M. Vivar's Collected Correspondence which is surprisingly entertaining, my craggy voice, that mysterious voice repeating all of this, yes, spontaneously manifesting event that Echo and Octavia only half-remember has occurred in subtly varied forms ad infinitum. Ah, I feel better. Now that I've centered myself, what I really want to tell you is this. The DNA strand and the Logos are-"

Octavia said, "Because everything we are saying and doing is written on this page of the Codices, The Golden Tablets Of Lucidity, These Universal Texts Of Organized Chaos, These Top Layers Of The Infinitely Dimensional Plane Of Total Consciousness, The Pluralist Tractate, The Book of Whatever You Want To Call It Because It Has No One True Name that continues to expand before our eyes."

Rocco scratched his head. "Why would I say, "Please excuse me while I contradict myself?"

"You were also going to say, "Actuality is built on contradiction," I said while doing my best Rocco impersonation, "so please excuse me while I contradict myself." And now you are going to ask me a question."

"How did you know I was going to say that? Who's speaking?"

"Because after you said that if you had been given a chance to say that you would've gone on to describe the self-destruct mode built into this Actuality, into this plugging in of our DNA into the Codices. It is like a box that switches itself off when switched on. Once twin beams of total consciousness, absolute clarity, and perfect lucidity, arrive it is zapped away in a near instant. What is this called? Why does that matter? Because I am obsessed with magick and if magick is anything and if it is real, it is the naming of things and the knowing of all possible names for all things. What is with your obsession with names? One can do anything if one uses all the correct names that correlate to the presently correct circumstances. That sounds right. Maybe the self-destruct mode is called improv comedy. We'll finish what you started. We swear. Rocco snapped his fingers at this in one loud snap of finality and then smiled like this name pleased him. Who's speaking? His left thumb, the one he had used for the snap, slowly rose above his head, and as his smile fell into a frown he pointed at the projection of Flynn with his thumb. Flynn plucked the air, playing the final notes of the classic pop song. The camera zoomed into Flynn's face and a globe lamp rose from underneath the frame and stopped just below his chin. What is this? Who am I? Flynn waved his hands over the lamp like he was waving them over an orbuculum. The globe lamp sparked and morphed into a fat tornado clock. He stared right at us. "I love you guys." He stood to walk away, only his knees visible in the shot, and in what looked like an afterthought, sat back down, his face returning to the center of the frame.

Octavia squeezed my hand and I squeezed back.

"I love you infinitely," I said and kissed her deeply.

She kissed me back. "I love you more every day. Beyond the infinite Patasphere."

Rocco was gone. His life support egg and the many tubes and wires sprouting from its top shooting into the rafters of the stage's underside remained, branching off and crossing a wall of fog that had surrounded us from out of nowhere.

The ground beneath our feet rumbled and we lifted into the air on the organ platform. A blinding light from above clicked on, like daylight. A noise, like unceasing thunder, poured into the square of daylight we were rising toward. Our heads met the threshold and fresh air puffed into our faces. The sky was the most vibrant blue I'd ever seen in my life. The clouds puffed and flowed into creamy impressions of Fat Tornado Clocks.

The platform stopped and Octavia

and I wobbled and caught ourselves as its locking mechanism snapped into place with a metallic ring that proceeded into the atmosphere to combine with the thunder rolling off an unseen sea. The too blue sky met an edge of stone covered in art nouveau reliefs of cacti. Sitting on the edge was a small stand with Rocco's theremin resting on it, humming, waiting to be played. From the stand to our platform was a small stretch of marble terra firma.

Octavia and I stepped off the platform and walked to the theremin, the edge of this marble cliff. The scroll covered in these very words you, dear reader, are reading rose above the edge as we approached and then quickly faded away, leaving behind a series of movements and shapes that could barely be classified as movements and shapes. These impressions spread across a plane of actuality that expanded and grew into a thing that could barely be classified as a plane of actuality.

The marble roof up to the edge retained its actualness, its place that could still be registered as a place in our realm of spacetime consciousness and this sight of the real, a place where signals connect to objects which connect to symbols which connect to signals, was all that grounded us and gave us insight and context into the non-actuality beyond the edge of the marble.

It was beyond the Earth, beyond the Patasphere, beyond reality, a habitat of total clarity and absolute lucidity that could be looked at but not observed. It could not be accessed, only understood by the sight of its surface, a surface that could not quite be classified as a surface, that this realm must be a plane of total clarity and absolute lucidity.

Octavia said, "It looks like an ocean of noise and fluctuation."

Octavia took my hand and squeezed. She switched on the theremin and it hummed to life. The ocean played its static for us. She raised her hand to the volume antenna and I raised my hand to the pitch antenna.

We bowed to the ocean and played an original tune. It was a tune that spontaneously composed itself as she controlled the volume and I plucked the notes from the air.

I strained my eyes as I peered into the unknown. Fluctuations that appeared to be true movements and shapes poked through the hazy beyond and formed into suds and mandelbulbs. The suds and mandelbulbs echoed and they appeared at first glance, to roll out these very words, you are reading, at us, but upon closer inspection the words revealed themselves to be but glossolalia. The suds and bulbs floated and drifted between the extradimensional noise and fluctuation. They swooped and danced together in the gateway hemisphere synchronization. Bulbs detached from their mother bulbs, the superfluid multiverses of suds, and found their way into the Patasphere as rogue universes.

The theremin cracked open and unfurled as an infinite number of interlinking planes of sparking wire and circuitry. Fat Tornado Clocks, one by one, popped out of the tippy top of the cactus-shaped capacitor in the center of the machine. The FTCs floated into the fluctuation and each shimmering, churning device of golden spirals was gobbled up by a bulb.

The planes of sparking solid state formed a bridge into fluctuation. Mandelbulbs landed on the plane and the sparks exploded into a display of reticulation that spread through the network of suds and set the extra-dimensional realm of noise ablaze. The bridge collapsed, and settled and patamorphosed into a canyon as the fiery noise crackled.

"I can still hear the music," I said. "Can you?"

Octavia said, "Yes. Let's play on."

From a realm beyond the void, we could hear Flynn sing, *Goodbye mother bird, my watery dream, O puddle birthed from that fluctuation bucket. I'm off to the big time, to the city, my rumspringa!*

A meshing of bobbing persons found their way into the grid of the solid state canyon, and the grid morphed into a network of streets, swelling onto the sudsy nurnies, filling in the gaps between the people who came before, these pre-gamers, these ancestors of the night yet to become, and lifted their index and middle fingers to pop the rogue mandelbulbs. Their feet, marching to the rhythms of nonlinear actuality, the pumping cacophonous symphony barely beginning to begin on this blustery edge, strapped and swaddled with sneakers, fuck-me-pumps, sandals, and clogs, stomped the mother bulb clusters of the rogue fissures, the clusters that drifted down to their indie lit fantasy experience.

And more mandelbulbs arrived. The bulbs contained big gobs of rovers and dwellers. The guts of the rivers and dwellers open and out spilledpage confetti, puzzle pieces, lost socks, the central nervous system, saw palmettos, pocket watches, a sled lol, acorns, baby gators, hundreds of eye balls, a quilt, a Nintendo 64, unsweet iced tea, toenail clippings, theme park maps, more blood, more entrails, several xe-nomorphz, old timey spy devices, several puzzleboxes, your favorite childhood toys, the words of Mitch Hedberg, cute lil cloudz filled projected movies of your favorite childhood memories, two copies of John Carpenter's *The Thing* on VHS, the twin you absorbed in utero, In Utero by Nirvana, the folky ethereal haunted masterpiece alternate reality follow-up to In Utero produced by Michael Stipe, the universal wisdom of everalwayz tenderlovingkindness, coming close to F-ing the ineffable by climbing hierarchies of richer and richer language, knowing when to deconstruct and reduce, knowing when to climb back up the ladder, moss from the oak trees, journals and diaries and commonplace books, the comedy classic *Bridesmaids*, all the good that lives inside you, monsters and goblins, an empire of dirt, a beau-tiful pink crystal that represents your immense love of humanity, a beautiful green crystal that represents your incredible ability to shift from mode to mode to mode, more lost childhood toys, that chunk of the sidewalk you carved your initials into when the cement was wet, only entering Chapel Perilous when you're ready, building the tools for your journey through Chapel Perilous, clouds filled with project-ed movies of your favorite memories of the babysitters who taught you about good horror flicks, avacados, silver bells, every Christmas tree, every Halloween costume, every Robin Williams performance, all the times you chose to be extra kind, the skunk ape, a beautiful oramge crystal that respresents friendship, clouds filled with projec-tions of movies of the super corny memories that give you the loving tingles, your first car, your box of sacred childhood trinkets that you lost a long time ago, representations and configurations of your most profound loving embraces, representations and configurations of all times times you could've used pre-selected phrases and slogans in an eristic way but instead choose your own words and then received original spontaneous words back and deep insight and clearer clarity and softened cynicism and a broader more humane projection of humanity was gained, more lost toys, more lost socks, Atlantis, gravy boats filled with plasmate, the records you wish you hadn't sold, lost choose-your-own-adventure paperbacks, the Lord of the Rings trilogy, all the kinds things you wished you'd said, Bigfoot, the books you were not supposed to read, audio recordings of the uncontrollable ecstatic laughter of your loved ones, UFO's, vacation mementos, and your oh-so human faulty wires coming to life and apologizing for being faulty. The objects tumbled into the air that rang with midnight rooster screams and smelled of cigar smoke and rotting palm fronds. It was an air that carried the echo of air conditioners clattering to life and thudding to death in the relentless heat that settled on your skin like hot wet cellophane. The feet of the rovers and dwellers hit the wet greebles. I imagined the reflection of the globe lamps bouncing off the water and making dancing stars in their eyes. Their heads bobbed as they walked. Music from radios on balconies and buskers on corners whose equipment included instruments of their own invention, and the blaring amps from live bands like *Satanic Panic and the Very Special Episodes* spilled into the street. This caterwaulingconcord rose, but the crescendo was well into the future, a place that could only be viewed from the sparking and vibrating edge of psychedelic fiction author Rocco Atleby's grand machine, the tessellation of his Fat Tornado Clocks, his exegesis, his fractal ekphrasis (ekfracsis if you will), his accidental posthumous opus.

Octavia and I leaned over the marble boundary. We inched further and further over the edge but never tumbled into this grand machine sprinkled with bobbing heads roving in and out of the residences and municipalities of the chrome and silicon greebles and nurnies that slowly faded and morphed into words on a scroll.

We pushed with all our might toward a leap, praying for a leap, over the edge until we were sprinting around and around the marble like log rollers on a column. The passages on the scroll blurred as we passed, going around and around, going around and around, around and around, and around and around, until we were released by the deus ex machina of our benevolent authorzzzzzzzzzzz.

We leapt.

The windzzzzzzzzz of this inky land enveloped us.

We smiled.
The ineffable realm once again metamorphosed into the scroll.
The scroll whipped, snaked, and twisted into a cyclone.
And the scrollyclone swallowed us.
And the words patamorphosed into glossolalia.
And

ACKNOWLEDGEMENTS

Christina - There are so many people to thank in the making of this book, but to keep my acknowledgment from being novel length, just know if you aren't mentioned, I remember everyone who has ever shown me influence, encouragement or kindness, and I wouldn't be a writer without you. First and foremost a big thank you to Mallory and the entire staff at Maudlin House for taking a chance on an up and coming author and his nobody partner with their totally wild manuscript. You were all incredible during this whole process. A huge shout-out to Rob Kaniuk for the amazing cover art, I'm honored. I want to thank my parents Tom and Karen, and my brother Alex. They have always been instrumental in supporting my creative endeavors as the "weird" one of the family. Thanks to LS and Janet Keeler for seeing something in me when I was a young writer and for nurturing that quality in me. I want to thank my children for filling me with the love I needed to make me want to strive for more, and thank you to Chase for making me believe that penchant for writing inside me was not lost, but simply dormant and most definitely worth waking.

Chase - I would like to thank Christina the Qualien for the infinite love and revealing the latticework of the Patasphere to us. Thank you Damian, Owen, and Cypress for the infinite love and revealing the ineffable matterenergychaos between spaces in the latticework of the Patasphere. Thank you Mallory Smart, Bulent, and the Maudlin House team for taking a chance on an up and coming author and her nobody partner with their totally wild manuscript. Thank you to the psychonaut, Dr. Erik Davis, for his invaluable writing advice. Thanks to the ghosts of Borges, Kafka, Robert Anton Wilson, Joyce, Vonnegut, Ursula Le Guin, Octavia Butler, PKD, Terence McKenna, and many other time-binderzzzzz for the breath-taking view from their ethereal shoulderzzzzz. Thanks to my parents and siblings for always politely nodding during my happy manic lessons in how to play a necromancer's theremin. Special thanks to Rob Kaniuk for the trippy Rocco painting. Thanks to Joshua Bohnsack for the Rocco forward and the initial initiation into the publishing Patasphere. Thanks to Sam Higgins, Richard Glenn Schmidt, and LeEtta Schmidt for Gyrojets. Thanks to Kelvin Matheus Rosa, Roy Christopher, Pat Irwin, and Shannon McLeod for the kind words. Thanks to Tim Kinsella for his blessing to use A Pale Orange in the book trailer. Extra special thanks to my grandmother, Mary Lou, for sharing her dreams with me when I was a boy. There are many other people to thank, but if I go on thanking people this acknowledgement will transpose this novel into an impossible book located within Borges's Library of Babel.

ABOUT THE AUTHORS

Christina Quay and Chase Griffin are reclusive authors and not much is known about them. It is rumored that they live in Florida, they have three children, they have pet alligators, and they spend their spare time building orgone accumulators.